Courageous
Dreams
PUBLISHING HOUSE
PO Box 4781 • Chicago, IL • 60680 • 773.772.2402

Book Design by Katie Nordt

"Back in 1979, when Anwar Sadat shook hands with Menachim Begin, under the watchful eyes of then U.S. President Jimmy Carter, we believed that perhaps for the first time, real peace might be at hand. How little we knew...

'Milledufleur Rose' has provided us with a realistic, in-depth look into the politics of both countries back then, along with a fast -moving scenario on events, that could have lead to the assassination of Anwar Sadat a few years later. It kept us spellbound until the very last page.

Bonne chance!"

Nicole and Gene Peretz

MONTREAL, CANADA

"From March through Christmas 2011 I spent more than 300 hours of my life editing the manuscript for this, Jay Moroney's first book in the story of Milledufleur of the Mossad. When I took on this editing project, I must admit my interest in the subject matter was not high. However, as I read and worked, because I knew the author had been in the oil business and for several years had actually lived and worked in the part of the world in which his story is set, this book took on a new meaning for me. It awakened a desire to understand much, much more about the reality and history of the peoples of the Middle East. Jay's scenes and real-life descriptions – of the surroundings, the culture, the people and their day-to-day lives – hooked me. And then, Kim David and Milledufleur Rose sealed the deal. Ironically I did not initially like Milledufleur Rose; then I looked through Kim David's eyes at who she is becoming and realized this is only the beginning of her story."

C. J. Pickelsimer

FREELANCE EDITOR

Murder, sex, betrayal and intrigue mesh together in this international thriller. Mr. Moroney having "walked the walked" has captured the essence of evil in what really happens in the Middle East. You can smell the sweat and grit the sand between your teeth as real evil unveils itself.

James L. Whitmer

AUTHOR OF *TATTOOED MAN* (SPECIAL AGENT (RETIRED) FBI)

MILLEDUFLEUR

Jay Moroney

MILLEDUFLEUR IS A work of fiction however there are references to events in the book which actually occurred and are part of history. Anwar Sadat was assassinated on 6 October, 1981. Israel did invade Lebanon in 1982. I moved to Cairo in 1983 two years after the assassination. At the time of the assassination I was living and working in Kuwait. About the period of his murder most of the American expatriates were apprehensive or even fearful about what might happen in that volatile part of the world. Despite our fears the transfer of power to Hosni Mubarak was smooth, without any incident. This condition existed for decades until the recent 'Arab Spring' which is hardly without incident today.

All of the characters in the book are fictional except for Khaleed Islambouli whose behavior is totally a work of fiction except that he did shoot Sadat to death. I did have exposure to Egyptian bureaucrats, lawyers and oil executives who largely confided that the assassination was not an accidental work of a madman but a coordinated re-ordering of the bureaucracy.

This is a story of what could have happened not what happened. Milledufleur Rose and Drew Cahill are pure fictional characters that I created. The same holds true for the other characters in the book. I have done readings from the book at meetings of the Union League Club Writers' Group and the Chicago Literary Club. The response from attending members encouraged me to complete the book and have it published. The only person other than my wife Kathleen who has read the entire manuscript is my editor Carole Picklesimer. I have been encouraged by Hazel Espinar, Doug Cannon, Bill Barnhardt and Gil Clapper and other members of the ULCC and Chicago Literary Club. In addition I've been encouraged by friends and relatives, especially my Montreal friends Gene and Nicole Peretz.

Even though the story occurred 30 years ago the situation in the Middle East makes the narrative topical today.

JAY MORONEY
6 February 2012

CHAPTER 1

Adieu Kuwait

THE INTERMITTENT CLANG, clang of the telephone on her bedside table startled Milledufleur. It was 6 a.m. and she had been sleeping fitfully, dreaming about Grandmère Rose who, as was her wont, was lecturing her on decorum. During her teen years her Grandmother had regularly hectored her about her duties as a young woman. Many times Milledufleur had wanted to run, but she couldn't and now this repeating dream haunted her.

Trying to decide if the jarring noise was reality or still a dream, Milledufleur sat bolt upright and reached for the sleep disruption instrument. When she lifted the receiver the awful ringing stopped and she robotically slurred a hello. She shook her head as she heard his voice somewhere on the other end.

"Milly, sorry; it seems I've woken you."

"Kim, my God, it's you! Are you in London?" She wasn't sure why she'd asked that; she wasn't yet totally conscious. Maybe she was wishing aloud.

Milly could feel his smile over the line. "Unfortunately not, my dear; wish I were, but not as yet. I do apologize for rousting you from your slumber, but I wanted to touch base with you before you meet Mr. Cahill. How are you feeling about this? Any last minute jitters?"

She wheeled around so that her legs hung over the side of the bed, and her black, low-cut negligee rode up her legs. Milly smoothed the gown to cover her thighs as if Kim was in the room with her, then rubbed her eyes with her free hand and shook her head again to clear the cobwebs. She longed for a hot, black coffee and a trip to the loo.

"Kim, could you excuse me for a bit; I shan't be long."

Kim chuckled, "Of course. Nature calls. I have

some time, especially for my favorite agent."

She slid to the carpeted floor and scurried to her bathroom. *God that's better!* she sighed a minute later, then washed her hands as she stared in the mirror at her bleary eyes and tousled hair. She ran her wet fingers through her black hair and restored a semblance of style, then cupped her hands under the cold water faucet and splashed the rejuvenating liquid liberally on her face. That did it. She was now coherent.

"Sorry, Kim, but that was necessary, and now I can give you my undivided attention. So, how am I feeling before I meet our target? Well, as I've never done anything like this before, I sense this could be quite a challenge: I don't mean the getting him into bed part, but the keeping him on track until he has complied fully with my request. Kim, I am aware that recent events are complicating Israel's ever-troubling times, so tell me, does this project have something to do with an invasion of Lebanon?"

"Milly, all I can tell you is that it is bloody important. You will know more in due course; right now, however, just concentrate on your part of the mission." She heard the voice of another man in the background at his end. "My breakfast meeting is arrived. Telephone me when you have made your assessment. Oh, and good luck. Cheerio!" With that he rang off leaving Milly still wondering. She was sure that getting Cahill to hire two Israeli geologists had something to do with an Israeli invasion of Lebanon. *But what?* She had a puzzle to solve, and she relished a challenge. She was excited to begin. Milly headed into the kitchen to fix the needed cup of strong black coffee.

***

Hassan Salam sped toward Kuwait Airport on the recently completed motorway, the finest that free spending oil money could buy for that desert sheikdom. He glanced in the rearview mirror at the white American absorbed in digesting the contents of The Arab News, the only English language newspaper published in Kuwait. His passenger smiled, acknowledging to himself that the gossip Hassan provided him from his friends in that special circle in Kuwait City was, in conjunction with the short wave broadcasts of the BBC, the only real "news" he had when he was in country.

Hassan smiled, content in the knowledge that he had been able to complete his duties to his soon to be ex-boss. He recalled his first encounter with Mr. Cahill nearly four years earlier. He and Kareem Awami, Getty Oil's Saudi PR man in Kuwait City, met Andrew Cahill on his first arrival into Kuwait on a searing night in June 1976. The summer heat shimmered off the desert sands, nearly asphyxiating anyone who had the poor judgment to inhale the super-heated air deeply. Fortunately, the air conditioning was the best that money could buy and provided a sharp contrast to the hellish outside temperature.

Hassan and Kareem watched the stream of arrivals deplaning the BOAC flight from London. At the front of the incoming horde was a tall, good-looking, clean-shaven, white man dressed in khakis, button down blue shirt, and a navy blue blazer. Kareem nudged Hassan. "There he is." They smiled at each other as if they had made a significant discovery. Cahill stood out like a sore thumb, obviously the only American in the arriving bunch. "He looks strong. He'll be good for our operation." Hassan smiled widely, his blue eyes shining as he gripped Kareem's arm. "Oh, and he is so handsome, too!" Kareem winced slightly at Hassan's assertion, but nodded in affirmation. Kareem, a non-practicing but faithful Shi'a, was painfully aware of Hassan's sexual tendencies. Not that he was worried about Hassan ever overtly being an aggressor toward anyone, least of all someone of Cahill's reputation and bearing.

***

Hassan had frequently driven his boss to the Kuwait Airport during the nearly four years Cahill had been in Kuwait, but this drive was different. This was not the annual long leave, or a business trip from which Cahill always returned. Suddenly, and for the first time, Hassan realized that this time his beloved Mr. Cahill would not be coming back. His Mr. Cahill was being transferred to London. Once they left Kuwait, they never returned. For a fleeting moment Hassan thought, *Mr. George Padgett returned,* but this hope was immediately dashed as he realized Mr. George's circumstances so long ago in the life of the Getty Concession were so completely different. A pain shot through his stomach. Hassan had been with the Getty operation since nearly the beginning, and he knew: Mr. Cahill was not coming back.

Hassan turned and looked at his passenger; he'd made this trip so many times that he could put the big American Cadillac on autopilot while addressing Cahill. "Mr. Cahill, they say that after London you will be going to Cairo. Please send for me. I have been to Cairo many times and could help you in so many ways. My French is as good as my Arabic and I know oh, so many people in Cairo, almost as many as I do in Kuwait. As a Sunni Lebanese, the Egyptians just adore me, not like a Palestinian they can't trust. Please tell me you'll send for me."

"Hassan, you've been invaluable to the operation while I've been in Kuwait. However, it will be some time before I'll start staffing up in Egypt; that is, if I even get to Egypt. I will think about it and if there is a possibility, I'll let you know." Cahill knew there was none, but he knew enough about the Arab mind to provide a dream of the future. *Dreams are all most of these people have, and they can ride them forever,* he thought. He liked Hassan and couldn't bring himself to shatter this gentle soul's hopes, not for Abu Ali. Cahill added for emphasis, "*Merci pour touts de votre effort, Hassan.* I consider you a friend and, at the least, will see you at some time in Cairo. That is, if I get there." He chuckled to himself at that remark, but not because it was amusing.

Hassan pulled into the airport parking lot very early for the KLM flight to Amsterdam with a connector into Heathrow. Cahill and Hassan unloaded the luggage and wheeled it bumping along the pavement, as they headed for the airport entrance. As soon as they broke through the entrance door they were met by a motley crew holding an oversized sign reading "Goodbye Drew. Good Luck in London. We will miss you!"

Cahill was surprised. Last night there had been a "going away party" for him at the Getty Kuwait

House attended by all of the senior staff of Getty Oil in the Zone and their spouses, and he thought he had made it clear then that last night was for goodbyes. He now realized that the largely Arab contingent of Getty employees consisting of Saudis, Palestinians, and Egyptians led by Kareem Alawi apparently needed another few minutes of emotional confrontation before the moment ceased entirely, so they could then talk about this until their collective memories fossilized. There were also a number of the Saudi contractors in attendance, several PETMIN representatives, and Zahir Mohammed, Kuwait's Minister of Oil, and his aides.

Cahill wasn't entirely surprised. He did know he was well-liked by the employees and the Kuwaiti and Saudi functionaries, so he smiled and endured the teary embraces, the kisses on both cheeks, and the jostling that always accompanied these kinds of ceremonies. However, he couldn't wait to get on the jet and leave this hellhole far, far behind. Wearing his best game-day face he went through the ritual, as he had on numerous other occasions during his stay in Kuwait. At least this was the last picture show here.

As he said his goodbyes one more time, he noticed that she was there; she who was the cause of so much of his turmoil in the Zone. She quietly proffered her cheek moist with tears of parting, and squeezed his hand. He pulled away quickly and headed for Kuwaiti customs for the final time.

As the uniformed official took his Kuwaiti work permit, Cahill's spirit soared: *Never more! Never more!* This had to be what a prisoner released from prison felt as he left the bars of his confinement behind: utter relief. He quickly transited to the passenger counter and showed his passport and ticket for a boarding pass, then boarded KLM Flight 7 to Amsterdam. When the tall, shapely, blonde Dutch stewardess welcomed him warmly Cahill nearly broke into song; he couldn't remember ever being so happy or relieved in his life! *I did my time,* he thought, *and now I'm out!* He found his seat, aft side window, and nearly melted into it before looking around to see what other escapees might be on this flight.

From time to time during his three-plus years in the Partitioned Neutral Zone, Cahill had thought he might write a book about his experiences there, but each time he had put aside that notion: Who would believe it? Who would be able to relate to it? Not many, he'd concluded, and for those souls who had a lifetime sentence the reading would be too painful. He felt emotionally drained. Cahill closed his eyes, and he was soon dreaming of Elysian Fields where he wandered arm-in-arm with olive-skinned, dark-eyed beauties, and savored the smooth red wine of the Tuscany region.

As he slumbered the 747 continued to climb, rising high over the desert of Kuwait and then into Iraqi airspace, angling northward to Amsterdam. He was surfacing from his dreams when the plane shuddered its way through an air pocket, which bought him into full consciousness. He blinked into the blue eyes of the stewardess peering down at him. In a delightful slightly-Dutch accented English, she said, "Welcome back from your dreams, Mr. Cahill. We are now safely out of Kuwaiti airspace so I may legally offer you a drink, if you would like?"

He smiled at this Nordic beauty, "I'd like. Very much! Make it two bloodies, heavy on the Tabasco, please and thank you." She returned in a heartbeat carrying two crystal glasses replete with celery stalks and lime wedges. As she put the drinks on his tray, Cahill lifted one to his mouth and sipped without breaking eye contact with her. "Fabulous!" he uttered. Giving him a view of her perfect white teeth with a smile that needed no words to confuse its meaning, the stewardess then turned and swayed up the aisle back to her galley with Cahill's eyes fixed on her performance as he again sipped the dynamite bloody. This leg of the flight would be a pleasure.

Now perfectly relaxed, Cahill thought back to his phone conversation with George Morris four weeks earlier. They knew each other from the California Getty Oil operations where Morris had hired Drew, recruited from Atlantic Richfield seven years ago. Cahill was Morris' kind of guy and Morris was a perfect boss for Cahill. When Morris had recruited Drew four years ago for the assignment in the Zone he had promised Drew that the limit would be four years, and George had been true to his word.

Hours away at the Butler Place headquarters for Getty's European and African operations, George Morris, who now ran the London Office, was huddled with his Chief Geologist, James Tottenham. Morris' mood was upbeat. The Egyptian concession had been in the bag for nearly a month now, and yesterday he'd received a letter from Togo's Minister of Energy informing him that Getty had been awarded the concession for offshore drilling rights. The timetable was favorable. It provided time to get the Egyptian operation up and running before they would have to get the Togo operation ready to drill the four wells required by that concession agreement. With a little luck and a lot of pushing, within four years the drilling program for Egypt and, then, Togo would be largely completed. If Tottenham and his group were close to guessing right, they could be sitting on new additional proven reserves of 1.5 billion barrels of crude. Morris was no neophyte when it came to exploration and he understood the risks involved, but all his instincts screamed that this was his elephant and his sure ticket to be the next CEO of Getty Oil. He'd had his eye on this prize since he had joined Getty's Pacific Western Oil Company fresh out of school with an M.S. in geological engineering from Cal Tech. Morris had been recruited by Paul Walton. Walton was J. Paul Getty's point man for breaking into that exclusive club of concessionaires in the oil rich deserts of Saudi Arabia and Kuwait. Walton had done the deal for the Saudi concession in the Partitioned Neutral Zone of Kuwait.

The Neutral Zone was the two thousand or so square miles of barren desert that had been carved out in 1922 by the British in the course of drawing a border between Kuwait and Saudi Arabia. The Zone was created largely as an accommodation to the Bedouins who wandered back and forth between Kuwait and Saudi Arabia. The concept of nationality was at best a cloudy concept for the Arab nomadic tribes, so it was agreed that the two countries would share sovereignty over the area and would divide the mineral rights 50/50. At the time Kuwait had still been a British mandate, with their own sovereignty only happening in 1961. That

Getty had been able to secure the Saudi Concession was a direct result of the to-that-date unprecedented financial terms Getty had given the Saudis. The Kuwaiti concession went, surprisingly, to an American firm, Aminoil, due in large measure to the efforts of the U.S. State Department, as well as a lucrative bid. Aminoil and Getty were locked at the hip in their Joint Operations in the Zone's desert, a relationship that was often contentious but profitable for both of these U.S. companies.

Two men were largely responsible for Getty's success in the Zone: first, George Padgett, and then, following him as Zone General Manager, George Morris. Morris was literally Jean Paul Getty's man in Kuwait, and as a result of his relationship with Mr. Getty during this time until Getty's death in 1976, Morris was as close to a corporate living legend as one man could be.

James Tottenham was visibly irked. He fiddled with the reports he had taken from his beaten up leather briefcase after Morris had questioned him on the recommendations he had made for the priorities of seismic shootings in the Gulf of Suez. He had covered this ground no less than five times with Morris, including one three-hour slide presentation made to the entire Getty scientific, engineering, and financial staff. Tottenham was nothing if not careful.

However, he thought, *no need to piss off Morris.* Morris, at least for now, was on top of his game, and he was still the American fair-haired boy in an American-controlled company.

Since Mr. Getty's death Los Angeles had transformed Getty Oil into a more free-spending operation, adding layers of engineers and geologists to its staff worldwide including London. However, given Mr. Getty's pursuit of as many women as he could bed in the shortest period of time, or at least as many as Klaus Von Bulow could procure for Getty's legendary dalliances, the company had, ironically, become almost puritanical in its corporate ethic. Senior management looked askance at sexual flings from their married employees, and divorce could be a career breaker. The senior executives were largely California Okies or from the barren desert-like stretches of West Texas, yet most of these executives had been hand-picked by Mr. Getty himself. Tottenham couldn't solve this apparently contradictory puzzle. Still, Morris paid him generously, and BP couldn't or wouldn't come close to matching his salary and perk package. He knew; he had shopped himself several times.

Morris watched Tottenham go through his predictable ritual. *He's so fucking Brit,* he thought. Tottenham was always so fucking intense and formal in his relationships both inside and outside the company. Morris had never seen Tottenham without a suit jacket and tie. Nobody addressed James Tottenham as Jim. It was James, and if one of the visiting Americans ever said Jim, Tottenham would promptly inform the offender that his name was James, not Jim or Jimmy. James Tottenham and George Morris weren't drinking buddies, but Morris knew Tottenham was a first rate geologist. Maybe the best he had ever encountered. Morris was smart and a great judge of talent, and he made sure Tottenham was regally compensated. Morris needed James and James needed Morris, however reluctantly.

"So James, one more time give me your rationale for shooting seismic in zone HH first."

Tottenham stiffened his back and inclined his head slightly. He stared at Morris for a moment with his pale blue watery eyes before intoning his findings in that perfect British Public School accent. He began his oration as he had many times before and continued his droning for the better part of half an hour. By now Morris could parrot the presentation without referring to any notes.

"That's good enough, James. Now, even as we speak, Andrew Cahill is en route to London, and he'll be in the office at nine tomorrow morning. He will be our hammer in Egypt. I'd like you and your top guys to give Drew the full-blown presentation, say about 10:30, and you should be able to wrap up by five. I'll drop by the conference room from time to time just to see how things are going. However," Morris laughed, "I've been through this so many times, I believe I can skip most of the presentation."

"Cahill?" Tottenham questioned. "I've never met him, but of course I'm familiar with his results in Kuwait." *And all of his exploits, he thought, including the rumors about his sexual adventures in the Zone!* He knew the senior Exploration executives in Los Angeles well, so Morris' choice of Cahill surprised him. Cahill was divorced, a casualty, he had heard, of that wretched existence in the Zone. He had also heard that Cahill had been involved in some inappropriate relationships, or at least one inappropriate relationship. That was the scuttlebutt, anyway. Tottenham knew Morris was no fool; but, still, Cahill?

"George, I had heard rumors that Cahill would be your man for Egypt. I mean his drilling record in the Zone was brilliant. No doubt he's a proven pusher, not just in Kuwait but before that in Peru and the valley in California, but I am a bit taken aback! I assume that Los Angeles has put their imprimatur on your recommendation?"

Morris fixed him with a laser-like stare, "Los Angeles doesn't know, yet. I told them I'd get back to them on my choice by tomorrow. And, James, the operative words here are 'my choice.' Drew is the perfect weapon, and, never forget, Egypt and Togo are my deals, not Los Angeles'."

Tottenham returned the stare and said simply, "I see." He turned and exited Morris' office wondering to himself, *Could this be Morris' Trojan horse?*

The KLM connection from Amsterdam rolled to a controlled stop and taxied to the gate at Heathrow. Cahill breezed through luggage collection and customs, where he saw Morris' driver Archie holding the regulation sign emblazoned with his name: "Andrew Cahill."

Drew had made this trip several times over the past months, but it had always been a clandestine meeting with Morris and the Getty London solicitor, John Springer. Morris had told Drew he wanted this played close to the vest; he didn't want any input to feed the nefarious Getty grapevine. He did not want any perturbations emanating from Los Angeles. Besides, as he had shared his logic with Drew, even though the Egyptian deal was looking good, really good, even, it could go south. Morris had the Los Angeles recommendations for the GM job in Cairo and he would deal with it when he felt the time was right. *I guess it's 'right' now*, Drew thought as he waved to Archie. Archie returned his greeting with a big smile revealing a mouthful of yellowed and broken teeth.

Archie was a likeable Cockney who owned his own limo and contracted his services out to several companies including Getty. As Archie maneuvered his Jaguar toward Buckingham Gate Road and the Getty flat, he dispensed his Cockney humor along with the latest rumors from Butler Place. Dusk was falling as Archie drove past sights comfortably familiar to Drew. *All those damn chimneys,* he thought. The marvel of central heating had escaped the Brits for a long time, and to some extent still did today. As they turned off Victoria Street and headed up Buckingham Gate Road, Drew could see Buckingham Palace in the not too far distance. Archie passed the St. James Court Hotel and pulled in front of the apartment building which housed the Getty flat. The building was owned by a Kuwaiti and housed mainly Gulf Arabs visiting London.

Drew took his suitcase and bid Archie a fond farewell. Archie teased him about pulling too many birds, especially on his first night in town, and Drew dismissed Archie's chatter with a smile and wave of his hand as he entered the building. Drew took the elevator up to the 6th floor and headed to unit 6C. He entered the flat and closed the door quickly to block the odor of lamb cooking with cumin and coriander and the smell of cardamom-flavored Arabic coffee. Including the stop over in Amsterdam he had been en route for more than ten hours, and he was tired and thankful Morris didn't want to see him tonight. He hung up the few suits he had. Suits were not standard issue in the Zone; when temperatures soar to more than 100 degrees Fahrenheit, suits and ties are dispensable.

Drew checked the Kitchen cabinets to see what housekeeping had provided him, and spied a bottle of single malt. With silent thanks to that kindly soul, he poured himself two fingers of whiskey, neat, and gazed out the window onto Buckingham Gate Road as he downed the drink. The street was quiet, but he couldn't get the odors of the Arab cooking out of his brain. These aromas took him back to Kuwait, but the Kuwait of a year and a half ago.

***

Drew drove straight from Wafra, thirty miles due west of the Gulf in the Kuwaiti desert, to his flat in Fahaheel, some thirty miles north of the Getty Camp at Mina Saud. His sixth floor flat gave him a great view of the Persian Gulf, and at night he could sit out on his balcony and see the lights of Basra, Iraq. The Kuwait water towers were a twenty-minute drive north of Fahaheel, and the fashionable shopping district of Salameih was just a ten-minute drive from his flat. All things considered, his place was better, much better, than living in the camp. Only Kareem Awami and Cahill had managed to not live in the Mina Saud camp. The camp was surrounded by the Gulf on two sides, and what the expats called Gettysburg but technically was the Village of Mina Saud. In truth, the Village of Mina Saud was a slum inhabited by the Saudi non-senior staff workers. Some 5,000 people were believed to live in the village. "Village" usually conjures up scenes of a pastoral, rustic place with paved streets, neat lawns, flower boxes, artistic storefronts, commons, and healthy, cheerful people ambling aimlessly or purposefully. That image is the antithesis of the Village of Mina Saud. In truth, the "Village" of Mina Saud was a ghetto of tin shacks and adobe-like hovels, and was populated by wild dogs, dirty naked children, and women in *burqas,* heads covered complete with masks so the only visible part of each face was two black eyes. The streets were paved with shifting dirty-brown sand and dirt, and red pickup trucks adorned many of the driveways. Visitors to the Mina Saud Camp had to pass through this "Village" to get to the guarded gate, and it presented them with a sharp visual contrast to the concept that Saudi Arabia was, per capita, one of the wealthiest countries in the world. The denizens of the Mina Saud Camp – expatriate Americans, Brits, Lebanese, Egyptians, Palestinians, and some Saudis – were all senior staff employees of Getty Oil. Mina Saud was a far cry from the well-laid-out, manicured camps the American oil people had in Saudi Arabia. It was even a far cry from the old Aminoil Camp some forty miles away. It was in this atmosphere that the non-Arab employees existed: surrounded by water, barbed wire, and five thousand Saudis; a tense environment for these oil people. The majority of the camp dwellers were Arab, but the operation was managed by a handful of Americans.

It was three o'clock when Cahill entered his spacious flat. It was Wednesday, the end of the work week in this Islamic part of the world; Thursday and Friday was their weekend. Cahill's week had been busy. They had completed drilling Well 3W and they had hit pay. Two more wells to drill and, so far, only one dry hole. These were step-out wells, not wildcats, but, still, two of three wasn't bad. He suspected the next two would hit oil; the geology was excellent and the seismic supported that suspicion. He guessed the Getty share from this drilling program would be about 30,000 barrels/day and reserves of 273 million. A nice addition to the balance sheet, but Cahill knew these wells would be shut in; they simply didn't need that production right now. However, it was like money in the bank. Today was the 10th of December, 1978. If things went well, he should be able to finish the drilling program before the end of 1979, wrap up loose ends, and then pray that Morris wins the concession in Egypt. Morris had promised him he would do whatever it takes to win the concession in the Gulf of Suez. He was also going after the offshore drilling rights in Togo, but Egypt was the key. Morris had left Kuwait four months earlier to take over the European and African operations. Still, in that period of time he had also jump-started the work begun a year ago by the Getty geologists and seismologists in London. Morris had assured him that Los Angeles was fully behind the program and that the bucks were there.

Drew stood for a moment enjoying the spectacular view of the Persian Gulf. If only one never had to look at the surrounding landscape. Jerry Turner, who had taken over from Morris, was hosting a bridge-cum-cocktail party at his villa in the camp. Drew hated these socials but he knew his attendance was expected, and even if his corporate fate was now totally in Morris' hands, there was no reason to piss off Turner. Although he was way down the IQ curve from Morris, Turner was a decent guy. On the other hand, Turner's wife was an unbelievable airhead; a real Valley girl, she still acted like she was in California. *Well,* Drew thought, *reality will set in, even for her.* Morris' wife, while also a Valley girl, had kept herself busy at the Kuwait House hanging with Kareem Awami's wife, Nancy, as well as taking long, long vacations back to Ventura. But she had also been really losing it at the end, and Drew figured they'd escaped just in time.

Showtime was 5 p.m., and Drew had time for a long, refreshing shower to get the grit of the desert out of his pores before the drive down to the camp. Social functions at the camp were always early; the denizens needed to start drinking. Drew found it amazing that in this Moslem country where alcohol was illegal, there were more drunks per capita than anywhere in Europe or America. He made book with himself as to who would be the first one to hit the wall tonight.

Drew arrived at the Mina Saud Camp gate at 4:55 p.m. exactly. Perfect timing; he would pull into Turner's villa just a little after five. Still, he knew he would be the last to arrive. The camp people were always early. Drew pulled to a stop at the guard shack and greeted the wizened old Saudi with a wave and a smile. The guard smiled back revealing a mouth devoid of most of the full complement of teeth. Drew had been told no one, not even the old man himself, knew how old this Saudi actually was; they didn't keep records back then, but some of the camp Docs figured the old man was at least 85.

Drew drove the asphalt paved roads of the camp past several of the trailers Mr. Getty had shipped from his Tulsa plant in the late 50's. These trailers housed the senior staff members who were not yet fortunate enough to have real houses, not even of the prefabricated variety. At least the climate this time of the year was favorable, very favorable. For four months of the year temperatures were resort perfect; except for a few days in November, no rain and hardly ever a cloud in the sky. Still, it was always eerie driving through the camp. If he didn't know better it could be a ghost town; no one on the so called streets. Drew turned left at the first intersection and headed due east toward the Gulf.

Turner's brown adobe villa sat perched just yards from the sky blue of the Persian Gulf, and the property was well-landscaped and in good trim. The Zone Manager kept five Indian gardeners, and his inside staff included an Indian cook, an assistant cook, and two maids, also Indian. *Or, were they Pakistani?* Drew wondered. Plenty of help to keep Mary Turner occupied directing their household.

Drew saw the compilation of company cars strewn haphazardly at the side of the road, and by counting cars he figured there would be four tables of bridge.

This meant there would be two British couples and probably two Palestinian couples. Jim Walters was in Dubai meeting with a sub-contractor, so Drew was needed in order to have an even number of men and women. He had frequently served as a crowd balancer since his wife, Peg, declared she'd had enough of camp life in Kuwait and had returned to Saint Louis for what she called "a resumption of real life." Truth was, Drew was wholly sympathetic, and their divorce was a civilized parting of the ways. His career was more important to him than his relationship with Peg Cahill, nee Riley. Drew had his eye on a bigger prize, and he hoped the divorce would not prove to be a lasting impediment.

T. K. warmly welcomed Drew to the Turner villa. T. K. was Turner's number one servant and manager of the household, as he had been for the last twenty-five years of Getty Zone Managers. T. K. gently bobbled his head while greeting Drew and ushering him into the great room. Bridge tables had been set out for the evening's play. Buffet tables, laden with hot and cold plates holding the offerings of the evening that had been prepared under the careful supervision of T. K and his Indian crew, sat against the east wall. The invitees hovered around the bar on the southeast end of the room, which provided its own view of the Gulf. The preponderance of the bar arrangement were clear glass bottles displaying the best of the camp's Flash production. Flash was the staple of the camp's booze supply, a distillation of pure grain alcohol cut with water to produce an almost drinkable alcohol. If the distiller was, however, too hasty in producing this spirit, the result would be a potable which smelled and tasted like turpentine. Most of the imbibers, however, were immune. Turner had also procured several bottles of Johnny Walker Red and Gordon's dry gin, but these were displayed much less prominently at the back of the makeshift bar. This real stuff was available only to those at the top of the pecking order, and all were aware of their relative status. Most of the glasses held by tonight's crowd were full of Flash, and from the noise level of the crowd and the over-the-top laughs, Drew surmised the partying this evening had begun earlier than usual.

Turner approached as soon as T. K. led Drew into the room. He greeted Drew warmly, pumping his hand while patting him on the back. "Glad you could make it, glad you could make it! We would have been one man short without you. I know you aren't so keen on these bridge get-togethers, but we must do what we can to keep the morale up. What can I get you to drink?" Drew smiled at his host, "Good to be with you tonight, Jerry; and I'll take a Johnny Walker, lots of ice."

As Turner left to fetch the drink he was immediately replaced by Turner's wife with Jim Walters' wife, Ann, in tow. Both women were California blondes but Ann was younger and better-looking, much better. Each woman took an arm with an exuberance of manner largely alcohol-induced, and even though Ann's eyes were clear and her speech not slurred her smile seemed a bit too friendly as Mary Turner handed her over to Drew. "Now Drew, you'll be Ann's partner tonight. Jim is away in Dubai or some Arab place, poor dear, he's just working too hard for a man of his...ah...maturity," bubbled Turner's wife. Drew smiled politely. He had no clue as to what Jim Walters did, and neither did Morris. Walters had been in the Zone off and on for the last twenty-five years. Six years ago he had arrived back in the Zone with new wife, Ann, in tow. Ann was a good-looking forty-something woman and her attraction was not lost on Drew.

After the obligatory four tables of bridge Drew was, happily, relieved of his responsibility for the night. Ann was pleased with the score they had produced for second place. She was pleasant and a vocally-coherent partner for the night, which to Drew's surprise had passed quickly; however, he was relieved the night was now history and he was the first to begin the goodnights. The last in the ring was Ann, and she kissed him on the cheek and whispered that tomorrow she would see him in Fahaheel.

Drew woke early the next day and did his five laps around the Gulf/BP mini park across from his flat; he figured five times around was about five miles. He walked back across the road and took the elevator to his flat. Once inside he drank a quart of the finest Kuwaiti water, then poured himself a cup of coffee before planting himself on his balcony to enjoy the view and the coffee. The doorbell rang. Drew reluctantly left his chaise lounge and went to the door. He opened it, and there she stood. Ann Walters. *Now what the fuck?*

CHAPTER 2

Gamal

IT WAS DIFFERENT, but not unpleasant, being back in Cairo and living in the Zamalek apartment where I grew up. Zamalek, that once beautiful isle sited in the Nile and connected to the rest of Cairo through five bridges; Zamalek, home of ornate rococo embassies, mansions of the wealthy and influential, and home of the world famous El-Gezira Club. The apartment was a gift from my parents, now long dead. I suppose my long absence from Egypt has changed my views on many subjects, but there is no way to replay life; one segment ends, another begins, and there is no overlap. I am now fifty-seven, and these days I wonder often: *Is this old?* Sometimes I think it is the beginning of being old, sometimes I believe it is somewhere along the spectrum of being mature and sage.

I suppose I never considered retiring from the Egyptian diplomatic corps, at least not until the offer that allowed me to retire came out of the blue. I had been on the Foreign Service of the Egyptian government, a lawyer in the Foreign Ministry, since shortly after Nasser gained power. I never saw eye to eye with Nasser, but I had the diplomatic sense to keep those opinions well-concealed. However, Nasser suspected; that had to be the reason he offered me the prestigious post of Ambassador to Togo, possibly not an important posting but, for Africa, probably the most agreeable. Lomé, the capitol city of Togo, was small and geared to provide tourist accommodations to the cult of French who had become aware of the pleasures of Togo when it was still a colony of France.

Togo, in addition to allowing me to live in reasonable style, gave me ample opportunity to read the law and French and English literature, and to mingle with the rather small group of other diplomats who were either just beginning their careers or who, through some political offense, were exiled to this out-of-the-way African post. While I was reasonably content to not be living in the turmoil that Cairo had become, my wife was not content, and as the social life of Togo became increasingly deficient, my young wife grew more and more restless. Waffa was fifteen years my junior, and she had a different set of expectations from life. However, I was out of Nasser's sight, an opportune situation for me. I was and am a fervent Egyptian nationalist, but not a Nasserite. His dalliance and alliance with the Soviets was, in my view, a dangerous liaison with a merciless, godless state that would use Egypt's important geographical and cultural position in the Middle East to advance the Communist leverage in the region – and not to Egypt's benefit, I was convinced.

In January 1968 my wife and I were on leave in Cairo. I was making the rounds of the ministry while she was being entertained by her family and by the wives of the government functionaries, including Jihan Sadat, wife of the Vice President of Egypt, Anwar Sadat. Waffa was exultant whenever she was in Jihan's company. I had known Sadat for a number of years, but we had never been close. We had a polite relationship. I respected his political positions more than those of Nasser, but disagreed with his preferences in alcohol; he was partial to vodka and Arak, while I enjoyed the peaty taste of a good single malt whiskey. Perhaps this was the British influence on me. We were both cultural Muslims, but secularist in philosophy.

Some people have said that Sadat and I resembled each other physically. We were of the same stature and close in age. Our hairlines were similar, but Sadat was very dark in complexion, almost black, while I was much lighter. Emotionally we were completely different: Sadat was vain, compulsive, and prone to exaggeration; I was a studious, calm, tactful lawyer. Though comfortable in Sadat's presence, I was never so in Nasser's presence. Nasser was pure megalomaniac; Sadat wasn't quite in that league.

A week before we were scheduled to return to Togo I was summoned to the Foreign Minister's office where, in the presence of both Nasser and Sadat, I was informed that I would be the new Ambassador to Denmark, and taking up residence in Copenhagen. I was thrilled, but my wife was ecstatic. Imagine me, Gamal Hashem, and my wife, Waffa, living in Denmark in the city of Copenhagen.

Waffa was happy like she never before had been. In addition to speaking Arabic, of course, we were both fluent in French and competent in English. She now also learned the Danish language and German, improved her English, and became a licensed physical therapist. We settled into life in Denmark. Waffa had her school and work. She quickly established her own circle of friends, mostly curious Danes but also some from the expatriate community. I had my post and I made friends in the business and diplomatic community. I learned quite a bit about the international oil business, especially from the Norwegians but also from the Brits and the Americans. The Americans were my favorite, not as stuffy and condescending as the Brits and not as guilt-ridden as the Scandinavians – especially after imbibing that awful local favorite, Aquavite. The social scene was constant and pleasurable, and we both learned a lot about the Western way of life. Certainly they had their peculiar mores and customs, but not the rigidity that we had found even in Egyptian life, and compared to the Gulf Arabs we had an open society. The years seemed to blend into each other like a continuous flow. Then one afternoon I received a cable from Cairo.

I had to see Waffa. This was a life-changing event. After the years in Denmark it felt like we would never leave. I called her office and asked her to come to our residence immediately. She arrived just after five, opened the massive oak door, and softly glided over the hardwood floor through the living rooms to my study.

"So, there you are Gamal." She spoke in fluent Danish. "A little early for the whiskey, isn't it my dear?"

Waffa was tall and had an exquisite frame coupled with a noble face, searing eyes, and, when she deigned to do so, she had a warming smile. Glass in hand I rose to greet her. "Waffa," I said, brandishing the cable, "This is important. It's from the Minister. They are asking me to retire."

She put her hand to her head and collapsed into the nearest chair. "Gamal, this is awful! I love it here. I can't go back to Egypt; it is so, so bad! That man, that pig, Nasser, has ruined my city, my Cairo; I can't live there now!"

"But Nasser is dead. Sadat is the President."

"Yes, and he has been President for four years and what has he done? I'll tell you: He started a war with the Jews – and he lost! Nothing! He has done nothing!" she cried through the vale of tears cascading down her cheeks.

"Waffa, I must go back. I have been planning for this. I will open a law office in Cairo; a venture with an American law firm. Egypt's relationship with America is building. The Americans are awaking to the fact that we too have exploitable oil reserves; and they are starting to go after the Egyptian concessions in earnest. My firm will be their advocate. I have made many friends in the American and British circles. My friends in Egypt believe Sadat will make a dramatic overture to Israel next year. Now is the time to build for the future. Our future is now, and it is in Cairo!"

That had been nearly two years ago. I knew she wouldn't come, but I had to go. Not that it's been perfect, but I have built that law firm, and now have six American lawyers from Sidley Austin in the U.S. and four from their correspondent firm, Jacoby, Smith, Tomes from the U.K., as well as ten Egyptian lawyers, two paralegals, and an administrative staff of seven. More importantly, we are making money! Tonight, in less than two hours, I'll meet with John Springer and his boss, George Morris, from Getty Oil U.K. My work with Springer and the American ambassador to Egypt will pay off, of that I'm confident.

***

George Morris had been in London for six months now following his five-year stint as Getty Oil's GM in the Neutral Zone of Kuwait. He knew that gaining the concession to drill in Egypt's Gulf of Suez was critical to Getty's future and, more importantly, to his own. He thought of the years spent in that desert prison called the Neutral Zone as payment for the opportunity he could now taste, the chance to find an "elephant" in those waters called the Gulf of Suez. Being in charge of the European and African operations of Getty sounded better on paper than it was in reality. There were no operations in Africa, only the farm-ins in the North Sea put together by old man Getty, alone, just like he had built the empire named after him.

John Springer nudged his companion as their taxi approached Nombre Dix, Rue du Paix, the Zamalek residence of Gamal Hashem.

"Hashem is our man. I'm not concerned about the legal side, we all know what these concessions are about; it's the interface with all of the Egyptian bureaucrats, and Gamal knows the system. He'll be of immense help to whoever we send here to run the operation."

George smiled at his chief counsel. "You can quit selling John. You've convinced me that we should use his firm, but I think it's important that I meet him before we give him the official nod. What do you say?"

"So right, couldn't agree more. You'll like him. He is smooth."

Springer and Morris exited the cab and stood in

front of Gamal's Zamalek residence for a moment to gaze in awe at the splendor of the structure. It was a pleasant March evening in Cairo; the oppressive desert heat was yet to come, and the moist evening air wafted the fragrance of jasmine and the ever abundant lilies. The two men approached the entrance.

"Must have been quite magnificent in its day, what!" said Springer, to himself as well as to Morris.

Morris nodded assent as he activated the over-sized clapper on the massive door. Instantly the ponderous frame creaked open, and before them in the dusk was an enormous black man outfitted with a fez and a colorful tunic and red vest. Morris thought this was one of the blackest men he had ever seen. His broad rough features would have complimented the meanest gladiator Africa could have ever produced. In contrast to his imposing physical appearance, however, this "gladiator" flashed a broad and warm smile and uttered what may have been his only English word, "Welcome!"

The welcoming giant beckoned the two men to follow him. He led them past an elaborate dining room on the left and what had to be a large formal lounge replete with over-sized chairs, sofas, and a mural depicting a scene of the famous El Gezira Club. They followed him up a spiral staircase to a large room with a fifteen-foot ceiling and elaborately-carved wainscoting bordering the area. A huge crystal chandelier emitting a yellowish light was suspended from the middle of the ceiling, and the room opened onto a balcony overlooking the Rue de Paix and its elaborate mansions. Most of the mansions here housed foreign embassies. The black giant motioned for them to be seated in two oversized chairs facing this open balcony; then with a smile and a bow, and one more "welcome," he left the room. Gamal Hashem entered the room and greeted them in Arabic, French, and English.

Gamal Hashem cut an impressive figure. He was of medium height, trim, and had a preference for double-breasted dark blue pinstripe suits. He also favored either red or dark blue silk ties; tonight blue had won out. His mustache was always trimmed just so, and as he walked toward the two Getty men with an athletic bounce to his stride, his ever-present pipe was cupped in his left hand. The two men rose to greet him. Gamal had never met George Morris, and he maintained constant eye contact as he fixed Morris with an infectious smile. Morris responded with an engaging smile of his own. Morris' sandy hair framed a handsome, almost boyish face. He had a winning personality and he loved to talk. When he talked he loved to smile, and the crow's feet surrounding his pale blue eyes testified to that fact. Gamal stopped in front of John Springer and vigorously shook his hand, greeting him as an old, old friend. He then turned to Morris and fixed a dark-brown-eyed stare on him as he also shook the American's hand with enthusiasm.

Gamal maintained eye contact with Morris. "I am Gamal Hashem. Welcome to Cairo, Mr. Morris, and enjoy your stay, you are my guest. You have spent many years in Arab countries so you know the special meaning of being the guest of an Arab. It is even more so being an Egyptian." Gamal motioned, "Please sit."

As Morris and Springer took their chairs, Gamal remained standing and clapped his hands thrice. Through the doorway the black giant re-appeared. Gamal turned to his guests, "Whiskey?" Both men smiled and nodded together. Gamal softly addressed his servant in Arabic and requested single malt Scotch neat, with a bucket of ice and a pitcher of water. Bottled, of course; after all, this was Egypt and the water from the Nile was lethal.

The drinks came quickly and Gamal toasted the two oilmen. "To you and to your wonderful company; you will have a great future in Egypt. Egypt needs your talent and skills, and for that reason you will be justly rewarded. In fact, I am told you have good news about your efforts to acquire the concession for Area B and D in the Gulf of Suez."

Morris smiled, "You are connected, Gamal! I may call you Gamal?" Gamal nodded, and Morris continued. "Please call me George; we Americans are pretty relaxed about forms of address," he slapped Springer's leg, "not as stiff as our British friends." They all laughed with the camaraderie that old friends share. "John has spoken highly of you, and all the reports I've received confirm that you are an outstanding talent. Of course, your long career and association with the British and American law firms speaks for itself. We are told by the Oil Ministry that we have the winning bid, with just a few details to clean up."

Gamal smiled broadly and shook his head, "Welcome to Egypt. There will always be a few details to clean up!" They all laughed, and then began the discussion about the deal structure and the timing. Morris' enthusiasm was apparent, and he did most of the talking. He was a very happy man; Gamal could read that in his eyes. Gamal liked this American.

"So, Gamal, we want to tell you formally of our corporate decision to retain your firm to represent Getty as its counsel in Egypt. You have studied the bid proposal; it's pretty straightforward boilerplate just fill-in-the-blanks stuff: $33 million to be spent over a three-year period; provide significant Egyptian employment; have the Egyptian National Petroleum Corporation approve our expenditure for cost recovery when we bring in the elephants. But, Gamal, we want you personally involved with this deal. We'll be bringing an American General Manager to Egypt as soon as the deal is signed, and we want you to be his advisor in all matters Egyptian – especially the politics."

Gamal nodded in agreement. "But, of course. Your success is paramount; I will do all I can to help your man. Have you selected your General Manager, and when do I meet him?"

Morris sat back in his chair and took a sip of the neat whiskey. He shot a glance at Springer, then answered Gamal's question. "Yes; our man is an American oilman with experience in the Middle East: more than three years in Kuwait, where he worked directly for me; before that he worked in our California operations, also for me. He's thirty-nine years old, and he can get more out of a drilling program than anyone I've ever come across – and I've come across a lot of them. Gamal, you'll like him; he's a lot like me, only younger." Morris laughed at his own humor. Springer shot a look at Morris that seemed to say, "What?" It was clear from the expression on his face that this was new to him.

Morris pulled a folder from his leather case and

pushed it across to Gamal. "This is the resume of Andrew Cahill. He will be leading our team. It looks like you'll meet him in about six weeks; that's when the three-year clock will start. John will bring him down to introduce him and you fellows can begin the work. We will need to hump it; there's a lot of ground to cover. With the level of activity in the oil world, especially now in Egypt, oil field services contractors are getting booked up, and we need to make our way to the front of the line."

The three men continued their discussion for several more hours, with Gamal including a lot of background on the more important Egyptian bureaucrats and politicians. He even threw in some juicy tidbits about the Sadats. Finally Morris looked at his watch.

"We forgot about dinner!"

Springer and Morris left Gamal's apartment at 10:30. They said their goodbyes and ended the night as close business associates and as good friends. The oilmen got into the taxi summoned by the giant, and headed straight back to their hotel. The Marriott Zamalek was originally built by the Khedive Ismail, supposedly for Empress Eugenia. Marriott had more recently bought the property, and had renovated it with great attention to detail.

During their ride back to the hotel Springer asked,

"Well, what do you think about Gamal?"

"You were right, John. He's perfect. You were surprised about Cahill, though, weren't you," Morris said with a twinkle in his eye.

"You are full of surprises, George! I know I'm just a lawyer – this exploration business is your bailiwick – and I don't know Cahill very well, but based upon what I've heard about him from our London technical people, and some of the rumors coming out of the Getty Kuwait Operations camp, I'd say the Getty Headquarters people in Los Angeles will be more surprised than I am. Difference is, I report to you – but you report to them, and they guard their privileges. If you haven't cleared the deck with HQ, I expect you'll have some tender moments over this choice."

"I've had many tender moments, John. I'll handle them. Drew is the best man for the job, and, John, this is my deal!"

CHAPTER 3

The Egyptian Deal

MORRIS STARED AT Tottenham's back as he strode out of the office. It was still too early to call Los Angeles; he would wait until 5 p.m. GMT. Morris wanted to get this out of the way. Cahill would be here tomorrow morning. He rang for his secretary.

"Mary, would you bring me the Egyptian candidate file, the one from Los Angeles? Oh, and a cup of black coffee, please?"

Less than a minute passed before Mary Brown entered Morris' lair. She wore a crisp white blouse with a plain brown business suit, and carried the file as if it were a parcel containing precious jewels. Morris nodded as she handed him the file and placed his coffee on the desk. "Thank you Mary. And please place a call for me to Los Angeles before you leave tonight, say 5."

"To Mr. Burdick's office, sir?"

"Yes. He'll have the HR VP there, the VP of exploration, and probably also the engineering VP."

Mary turned and exited the office. Morris thought Mary had the personality of a doorknob and resembled Agatha Christie. And that was the way Morris liked his secretaries: loyal, efficient, tight-lipped, and ugly. Mary Brown filled the bill perfectly. Morris had a big mission, he needed no distractions.

He had promised Mike Burdick, the Senior Vice President of International Exploration and Production, that he would get back to him today. Burdick, Mort Bistrisky, Head of Human Resources, the Head of Exploration, and the Head of Engineering had collaborated to send him their list of recommended personnel to head up the "African show," as they liked to call the deals in Egypt and Togo. There were six men on the list. Morris knew them all. Andrew Cahill was not on the list. None of the recommended people had the international exploration experience that Cahill had, unless you called one year in Calgary, Canada, international experience. Morris did not. One thing for sure, Morris was not about to put his future into the hands of any of the suggested candidates. Cahill was the perfect instrument. He was the best pusher. He had actually found oil and had survived in Arab Kuwait surrounded by Saudis, Kuwaitis, Palestinians, Lebanese, Iraqis, and Egyptians. Probably no Western mind could fathom the Arab mind, but at least Cahill had figured out how to survive in that environment. Egypt would be easier, Morris was sure, and Gamal Hashem would no doubt be an immense asset for Drew.

Mike Burdick had been with the Getty organization forever. At one time, Morris thought, he was an effective geologist, and he did play a big part in the exploration of Kuwait. That is what gave him his current job, but Burdick hadn't run anything in years. *Now he just wants to keep his nose clean so he can retire in two years!* Burdick would put up a fight for show, Morris was certain, but then he'd come around as soon as Morris assured him he would take the heat himself about Cahill. *Bistrisky, however, could be a prick.* HR was a powerful force within Getty, too powerful for Morris; but in this case Bistrisky would be an ally. Bistrisky and Cahill were fairly tight. Cahill knew how to take care of Bistrisky, and that was another vote for him. Finally, the exploration and engineering guys were weak and would go with whatever Burdick said; their necks wouldn't be in the noose. They would both write their CYA memos to file, so when the shit hit the fan they could proclaim they were clean.

The intercom rang. "Mr. Morris, Mr. Burdick is on the line."

Morris picked up the phone. With a yellow ruled pad on the desk in front of him, Morris twirled a ballpoint with the fingers of his right hand ready to record the essential elements of the call.

"Mike," he bellowed into the phone, smiling broadly as if Burdick was in the room. "How is your lovely bride?"

Morris went through the prescribed protocol, inquiring as to the state of health of each of the conferees' spouses then moving to the state of their respective golf games. Morris was a low-handicap golfer, and he promised that on his next trip back to California they would play a couple of rounds. Morris talked about the last time they had played in Palm Springs, and the banter went on for several minutes. Once Morris felt the atmosphere was relaxed, he switched gears to address the issue at hand: the GM of Egypt.

"Gentlemen, thank you for your recommendations for Egypt. I know all these guys, and they are certainly assets to the company. They are all hard workers and are doing a good job where they are now. But – and I know we all agree – we really need this play. Kuwait could be nationalized at any time. Not that we wouldn't have an ongoing relationship with the Saudis and access to the crude, but the reserves would come off the balance sheet. We all think we can delay this, but one of these days...I mean, we have to find reserves fast! The North Sea production will be declining in the next decade–"

In a rare show of impatience, Mike Burdick interrupted Morris. "George, we all know the implications here, no need to rehash the capital expenditure justification. Hell, the Board approved this a light year ago! Let's get the position filled and get going. Mort, why don't you tell George about the timetable for relocating one of these candidates."

"Sure Mike. George, I've interviewed each of the candidates, and in the best case we can have Mr. Egypt in your office for orientation in six weeks, worst case, ten weeks. How's that sound?"

Morris thought it sounded like shit, especially since he didn't want any of them. He wanted Cahill, and he would be there tomorrow. "Mort, it sounds like you've done your usual excellent due diligence, but six weeks is just too long and ten is out of the question."

"But George, it's impossible to move any faster; you know the details that we have to clear. Each of these guys is closed. Whoever you want will go, no indecision. You can't act any faster than that!"

"Look, fellows, my candidate can be here tomorrow. I want Drew Cahill."

The silence was deafening. Morris leaned back and smiled. He would wait until somebody from L.A. said something. After a moment, he could hear muffled whispering, and even though Morris couldn't make out what was being said he had a fair idea what the conversation centered on – and Morris was ready. He had not gotten to where he was in the organization by being a compliant follower. Morris was an intimidator.

"George, are you still there?" said Burdick.

"Yes Mike." Morris smiled to an empty room.

"Sorry about the delay, we just needed to have some discussion about Cahill. You did recommend Cahill to me some time ago; however, we didn't put him on the list for a number of reasons, some you may be aware of and some, maybe not. First of all, we all agree he's done a bag up job in Kuwait and no one doubts his talent, but–"

Now Morris interrupted. "But, what? He's clearly

the best man for the job. He's had Kuwait and Peru, he's able to get the most out of his crews, and he's proven himself with outstanding results. He's also still young enough to withstand the physical rigors of Egypt. This will be punishing, gentlemen, and he's not encumbered with a wife and kids to worry about."

Now it was Mort Bistrisky's turn to take the stage. "George, what you say is obviously true, but the company also has other opportunities. We agree that Drew should come out; – his job in Kuwait is over, and a job well done – but Gene Peretz needs a good number two in Australia, and Gene is comfortable with Drew and wants him as soon as he can shake loose."

Morris had his fill of the bureaucratic mumble jumble, but he also knew that he had to keep it civil. He could blow later, and when he blew it would be to Burdick alone. He knew they were avoiding the elephant in the room, the real reason they didn't want Cahill in Egypt. Seen through their myopic prism, the Middle East was one monolithic block. *Christ!* he thought. *These jokers don't know the difference between Sunni, Shia, Druze, Copt, or other Christian Arabs!* Egypt was different. Egypt wasn't Kuwait. It wasn't Lebanon before the PLO presence started the Civil War between the Christians and the Moslem population of Lebanon, but it still wasn't Kuwait or Saudi. Also, Getty Oil now wasn't the Getty of Mr. Getty's day. Jean Paul Getty was one of the world's most prolific lechers. After he died, top management turned the corporate ethic 180 degrees. The top management were largely conservative Christians who frowned on extramarital sex, and even on divorce; there was no written policy to that effect, but it their position on divorce was well understood. The company liked marriages that looked solid, with children. They had moved rapidly and completely away from the era of Jean Paul Getty's womanizing.

Drew Cahill was divorced and there were rumors of adultery in Kuwait. Morris knew he had to eventually take this on head-on – but not just yet.

"Mort, I'm sure that Drew would be impressed with an offer to move to Australia, but we know that the play in Australia is second-rate compared to the potential in Egypt. Besides, recruiting for Australia is a snap: damn good food, great beaches, and the beautiful Aussie women! Also, they speak the same language. Well, almost," Morris laughed. He was joined in knowing chuckles from his company brethren nine time-zones away.

He continued, "Mort, have you talked to Drew about Australia?"

"Well, no, but I have discussed this with Peretz. I

wouldn't talk directly with Drew without informing you first."

Morris took this as a signal from Mort. Morris was no longer running Kuwait; it reported directly to Burdick, just as he did; everyone understood this. Mort had not talked to Drew because he didn't want to; he knew that Morris wanted Drew and he knew that Drew wanted the Egypt deal.

"Mort," he said. "Mort, let's be frank about this: Drew and Gene have some issues. First of all, Gene is Drew's junior in the company. They're both geological engineers; difference is, Drew has an M.S., Gene doesn't. Gene also graduated from the same school but four years later. Gene needs a geologist, not an engineer."

Mort now spoke forcefully. "Excellent points, I agree. It's just that Mike has some other issues."

Morris jumped at the opening. "So, Mike. What is the issue? Sounds to me like it's not a qualification issue?" *Well,* thought Morris, *now we can start to undress the elephant!* On the yellow pad in front of him he noted that he owed Mort a dinner, either in London or in Los Angeles. Whichever came first.

"George, I won't beat around the bush. You know how serious appearances are in the Arab world." *How the fuck would you know?* Morris thought. Burdick was in Kuwait, in the Neutral Zone, in 1953 when the

Aminoil team hit pay dirt where Getty's chief geologist, Paul Walton, told them to drill. Burdick was there in support and spent only three months in the Zone. He did return for brief periods in '54 and '55, but he was there long before Arab pride had started to re-emerge. Back then they were dirt or sand poor. He was there before the 1958, 1967, and 1973 Arab/Israeli Wars, before the petrodollars allowed the funding of terrorist organizations, before the Arabs morphed back into the Salahadin model.

Morris decided now was the time to put the cards on the table. It didn't make sense to challenge Burdick's Middle-East qualifications; he still signed Morris' expense reports.

"Mike, you're right. Appearance is all important in the Arab world, and Drew understands that as well as you and I do. He is very respected by the Arabs in Kuwait, especially the Saudis. He's had three Egyptian engineers reporting to him, and he's made close friends with their families. Additionally, he has spent a lot of time recruiting engineers and geologists for the Zone in Egypt, Jordan, Lebanon, Iraq, and the United Arab Emirates. Our payroll is loaded with Saudis, Palestinians, Lebanese, even some Iraqis. Mike, I think there is something else going on here, something that we're not talking about. Am I right?"

Burdick hemmed and hawed. "Ah...well...this is sensitive, but, yes, there is something else. There have been rumors about Cahill and some of the women at the camp, about improper relations with women at Mina Saud. Drew is a good-looking guy and does have an eye for the ladies, as they say, and his wife left him over a year ago. There's a lot of talk."

Morris was ready. He didn't hesitate. "So, Mike, you're concerned that Drew is going to go to Egypt and start indiscriminately fooling around with the Egyptian women, or with Americans, or Brits, or the French, and embarrass the company? This is bullshit, Mike! I've heard those rumors; the Zone has its snitches, like Jim Walters, who go back to L.A. and plug into the rumor mill. Christ, Mike! I ran the Zone for years; I know what goes on, and it's 99 percent pure bullshit! The rumors about Drew are nuts!"

"How do you know, George? Have you talked to him about it?"

"You better believe it! I probably heard the rumors before you ever did, you know our communication with the Zone is intensive. Hell, Turner hasn't been there that long, yet he calls me at least two and three times a week. And you know we send our people down there to help out and our London people are frequently in Los Angeles. They bring back tales from all over the company. Sure I've talked to Drew about this, and, Mike, it is bull! This is all about Ann Walters. God bless her, but she's spent too much time in the sun. She drinks way too much, and she has too much time on her hands. She gets drunk and tells everyone around her that Drew has been banging her. Let me tell you what really happened. I think that will put you at ease."

Morris then suggested that he and Burdick continue the conversation in private, and, to the relief of the rest of the group, Burdick agreed. He picked up the receiver and turned off the speaker phone as he dismissed the Los Angeles people. Morris began to recount the events that had spawned the rumor controversy now alive and breathing in the office of the Senior Vice President of International Exploration and Production.

Morris was pretty sure that none other than Jim Walters was the source of the furor surrounding Drew Cahill, even though Walters would have identified himself as the victim, a cuckold. For some reason Walters hated Cahill and it had nothing to do with the alleged sexual encounter between Ann Walters and Drew Cahill. In the normal course of events Morris would have dismissed the rumors out of hand, but these were not the normal course of events. Drew Cahill had been his choice to run the Egypt deal if they won the bidding contest for the concession that covered some three hundred square miles in the Gulf of Suez.

Morris was an astute politician in the turbulent waters of corporate bureaucratic reputation-assassination mongering. Even though he knew that this rumor-mongering was not unique to Getty, Morris suspected that the Getty environment was perhaps more virulent than others. Often he thought the sole purpose was to bring down as many potentials as possible, and indirectly this was a shot at him. Morris had no doubt he was a likely candidate to become the President and CEO of Getty within six years, and lines were already being drawn and sides taken. He needed success in Egypt. He needed Cahill in Egypt.

Morris knew that the ranks of management were occupied by two basic types: the doers, and the spear-chuckers. The doers did what they did because they had to, but the fatality rate was high. The spear-chuckers did what they did because they couldn't do; they did little to avoid mistakes and, instead, sought to thin the ranks of competition, hoping they would be the last man standing. Morris knew the spear-chuckers could be effective – but not always.

Right now, Morris had one objective: to secure

Burdick's assent to Drew Cahill becoming General Manager-Egypt and President of Getty Oil's African subsidiary, Getty Ras Gharib Ltd. Burdick wasn't the enemy; he just wanted to hang until he could retire. Morris needed to convince Burdick that approval of Cahill would be politically safe. He began by recounting in picaresque detail the testimony Drew Cahill had provided him after he had confronted Cahill about the rumors he had been hearing in Kuwait.

"Mike, let me put this sordid business in perspective. You know how the rumor mill in Kuwait runs. The life there is particularly hard, and not many can survive in that environment without diversions. For some, gossip is that diversion. For others, work and exercise is the diversion. You and I both know that Ann is married to an older guy who can't get it up. Ann's diversion is the bottle and making herself available sexually. The availability sex pool in Mina Saud is limited unless you go outside the camp. Drew would be a coup for her. Once I'd heard the rumors about Drew and camp hanky-panky with Ann, I called Drew and had him get his butt up to London. I wanted him for Egypt, and I knew this rumor would spread like wildfire to Los Angeles and to you, so I needed to get at this fast."

"That comes as no surprise, George," said Burdick.

"Are you going to tell me that this is all a bunch of bull?"

"In a word, Mike, yes. It's a bunch of crap. One night several months ago Turner had one of those bridge social gatherings in the camp. Jim Walters was in Dubai, so they needed a player and Drew was the sub. Hell, he's done this dozens of times. You know how this drill works, Mike. It gives the Americans a chance to let their hair down and commiserate with each other; the Flash flows, and so does the nattering. So Drew was assigned to be Ann's partner, and they played for about two and a half hours. Ann was drinking, and the more she drank the more she flirted with Drew. When they all finished and Drew was saying his good nights, Ann grabbed him and thanked him for playing so well. She then gave him a full-bodied hug in front of everybody, kissed him on the cheek, and said she would see him at his apartment in Fahaheel the next day. Drew wasn't surprised about the flirting or the kiss, he figured she was just tipsy and she wouldn't remember what she'd done or said."

"I've been to a number of those camp socials, and the script is always the same. What you're telling me sounds real. But are you telling me she didn't show up at Drew's apartment the next day?"

Morris hesitated; he was encouraged that Burdick

had referred to Cahill as "Drew". He sensed Burdick was coming around. Morris was pretty sure who was the camel putting his nose under his tent. He was also pretty sure the story was much exaggerated; Drew Cahill would not be attracted to this woman, in his mind Morris was certain of this. He tottered on the brink for a moment, then decided to give it to Burdick straight. "No Mike, she did show up. Drew was flabbergasted! He said he didn't know what to do about her, but he couldn't keep her standing in the hall; this is Kuwait, after all. So he asks her in and offers her a coffee. Ann says no thanks to the coffee and pulls a bottle of Flash out of her bag. Now, says Drew, it's getting hairy. She fixes herself a drink and starts gabbing, camp gossip, that kind of stuff, until he finally convinces her to leave. She leaves, but guess who she runs into in the parking lot?"

"Not Jerry Turner's wife!"

"You nailed it." Morris inhaled deeply as he awaited Burdick's reaction. He didn't have to wait long.

"Damn it, George, this is starting to smell!"

"It does smell," Morris agreed. "Let me tell you, Mike; Cahill is the best man for the job. Don't you agree?"

"He can get more out of his men than anyone, I'll give you that. But now Pandora's Box has been opened, if there is any hint of scandal coming out of Egypt because Drew gets it off with some Egyptian women, I'll be looking at a really early retirement. I'm told that the Egyptian women are really good-looking and can be...ah, well, let's say available. Problem is, they are still Arabs and they look at things like that differently; not that I condone that kind of stuff, but we have to be really careful."

Morris felt his pulse surge. It was time to close Burdick. "Mike, you have the right to be concerned; however, I am not concerned. If Drew steps in it down there I will fire his ass, and I will go to Egypt myself and finish the job; and I will give that to you in writing! In fact, I'll have Springer draft up something today and I'll send it to you by pouch."

Morris could hear Burdick's wheels turning, he could almost smell them burning as he rapidly weighed his options. Burdick wanted a complete asscover, and Morris felt certain he had just given it to him. Burdick would appreciate that if Morris had to take over Egypt on the ground, Morris' career would be over – but Burdick would probably be clean. Besides, Burdick would be retiring in two years.

"When will you see Cahill, George?"

"Tomorrow morning."

Burdick laughed, then bellowed, "Morris, you are a real son of a bitch!" Burdick kept laughing.

CHAPTER 4

London in Transit

DREW WOKE AS sun blasted through the bedroom window in his Getty London flat. He felt rested and eager to get over to Butler Place and get going with George Morris and the Getty geologists, and, especially, to have James Tottenham brief him.

After Jean Paul Getty's death, Getty management decided that the sumptuous Sutton Place property should be sold and the Getty London offices moved to Butler Place just off Buckingham Gate road only several hundred yards southeast of Buckingham Palace and St. James Park. The company moved quickly to get rid of Sutton Place, and established the London office at Butler Place with room for three hundred plus professionals. This was an explosive increase in staff that wouldn't have been countenanced by Mr. Getty. Getty management had been quick to reverse the parsimonious ways of the company's founder.

London was now headquarters for the company's operations in Europe and Africa. The existing Getty operations in Europe consisted of "farm ins" that Getty had set up with oil majors in the U.K. sector of the North Sea. Getty had no operating control, just a minority financial share, but Getty London was planning to control offshore drilling off the coasts of Norway and Denmark. Morris thought operation control was important, that's why the potential of an Egyptian deal was important, in addition to the pure size of the play. However, Africa was the major thrust for adding to the much needed reserves of the company. The operation in Kuwait's Neutral Zone was assigned to the newly formed International Exploration and Production Division located in Los Angeles. Mike Burdick, a Getty veteran, was named to lead this new division. Morris had lobbied Los Angeles to take over responsibility for Kuwait;

he knew Kuwait was neither his future nor the company's.

Drew turned on the BBC more for background noise than information, and made himself an instant coffee. He had two hours before he had to be in Morris' office. When he'd visited London previously he had discovered that St. James Park was a wonderful spot for running, and the weather this morning was mild and sunny. He put on a pair of shorts, running shoes, and a light sweatshirt and exited the flat on his way to the park and a five mile run. Running had become an obsession for Drew when he was in Kuwait. He would rise before sunup to avoid the debilitating heat, and he had managed to log thirty plus miles a week despite the stifling heat of that desert state. He believed the jogging was a major factor in maintaining his mental stability, and he expected that devotion to a physical regimen would be as necessary in Egypt as it was in Kuwait. He walked up Buckingham Gate, and when he arrived at the Queen Victoria Memorial he stopped and faced the Beefeaters on guard outside Buckingham Palace. He gave them a perfunctory salute and a smile, then broke into a jog and headed away from the Palace towards Admiralty Arch. As Drew ran he knew he couldn't be the only person who believed that this park created by Henry VIII was the most beautiful and tranquil in all of London.

Drew experienced a sense of relief when he ran which usually allowed him to think through whatever issues he found pressing, but this morning was different. A number of notions floating through his consciousness were overwhelmed by one emotion, the elation of finally being out of Kuwait. He couldn't be more thankful to George for picking him to lead the Egyptian operation.

Based upon a letter from Mort Bistrisky he'd received weeks ago in Kuwait, Drew guessed that Mort had been trying to cushion the blow in case he didn't get the nod. George, however, had reassured him that he was the choice, the clear choice. That was one of the things he loved about George: absolute confidence in everything he did, always upbeat. To Drew's mind George Morris was not just a competent oilman, he was a leader. Drew increased his pace, breathing deeply but effortlessly as he neared the turn toward the path that would take him past the building complex that housed the Horse Guards. He had not encountered any fellow joggers as yet; Londoners generally weren't early risers.

The fragrance of the shrubs and flowers in St. James Park blended to provide an invigorating aroma, and the bouquet took his mind back to another essence, an essence of Kuwait. She was attractive, warm, and available. He was there and aroused. He knew that just her being there would be a source of wagging in the camp, no matter what did or did not transpire. No one would need to see her go in or out of his apartment in Fahaheel; Ann would be sure to tell anyone interested – and the American women in the camp were always interested. When George called him, not even a week after the incident, to get his butt to London, he wasn't surprised. George wanted to go over the deal with Drew, and thought he should nip this gossip bloom in the bud before it got blown out of proportion in Los Angeles.

Drew made the turn to Birdcage Walk and headed for the first lap ending at Buckingham Palace. Morris was great. He didn't see any problems, and assured Drew that everything was in the bag.

***

Drew walked into Butler Place five minutes before the time of their meet, and took the stairs up to Morris' third floor office. Drew smiled a good morning to Mary Brown, and she indicated he was to go right into the office. Morris' door was literally always open except when he was in a confidential meeting. Drew walked into the spacious, but Spartan, office. Smiling broadly George jumped up to greet him. They shook hands warmly, and George had Drew take a seat in the conference section of the office across the room from Morris' functional desk.

"Drew you look great! How was the flight? Everything suitable at the flat?"

"The flight was absolutely the best flight I've ever had! I felt like I'd been given a pardon from the Rock. When you're there you can't think of getting out or you'll go nuts, but once the doors closed and the plane's wheels were up, I realized I was out, actually out, of Kuwait. It's great to be here! Thanks, again. I definitely owe you!"

"Drew, I know how you feel! I put more time than you did in that hellhole, but you know what, it was worth it." Morris laughed. "Adversity makes men of those who can master it, and the Zone was nothing if not adverse! You know, if you could live in downtown Kuwait or Salamieh it wouldn't be so bad, but Mina Saud surrounded by all those Saudis?... Jesus, that was tough! But here we are, couldn't be better."

"George, we, ah...I mean, I lived in Fahaheel, not the camp at Mina Saud, but that didn't matter; Peg still couldn't handle it. Maybe it was me she couldn't handle, but living and working at the camp would have been hell. I don't know how you handled it, all those people, including the Saudis, pulling at you!"

George laughed, "I'm not sure how I survived. I think just taking it a day at a time. Tennis and sailing were diversions. But, you know what Drew? We're both out of there, and I know Egypt will be one hell of a lot better! The Egyptians are different. I'm not even sure they are Arabs. I just have a good feeling about them. And we've retained Gamal Hashem as our company counsel for Getty Egypt. He's a good shit and he knows his way around the bureaucracy; and being an ex-diplomat, he also knows whose chain can be pulled. I want you to get down there as soon as we take care of some housekeeping and some Los Angeles HR items here."

"Springer briefed me on Gamal when I was here for your, uh...your 'pep talk' about Ann Walters. He sounds great, and I know he'll be a big help. But, what are these HR things you're talking about?"

George smiled, "It's not a big deal, but Los Angeles insists you go through a cross- cultural training session at the BCIU offices; they will have some faculty from the SOAS School of London University do the lectures. It'll only be a week, you can get at it next week."

Drew started to protest. "George, I went through this in Washington at the BCIU at American University, and I've been living in the Middle East for more than three years! Why waste time now going over plowed ground?"

Morris held up his hand as if to say "Whoa!", and leaned forward in his chair, drawing closer to Drew. Morris wasn't smiling as he gave Drew a look that clearly said "shut the fuck up and listen to me." Drew had seen this look a number of times, and he knew it was time to shut up and listen. "Drew, this is from HR. You know their policy about international assignments. Their position is that Egyptian customs and such are different from the Gulf. I think they may have a point. Besides, this is coming from your buddy Bistrisky, who has been on our side in this."

"Our side in what?"

"Just some bureaucratic bull about who should be the GM in Egypt; you know the game. Some of Burdick's people were pulling for their guys, but with Bistrisky's help we stood our ground. Burdick is on our side and he has more votes. It's a done deal, no problem."

Cahill reddened a bit, he hadn't considered there was any problem. Morris had assured him there wasn't, but he should have known that there could be. "George, if you want me to take a course in Swahili, I'll do it," Cahill grinned. "Just get me to Egypt!"

"You're practically there. Now, let's get Tottenham and his guys in to brief you. I know you'll be impressed, they've done one hell of a job on this. Oh, just one more detail. Whatever you do when you're in Egypt, Drew, don't even think of getting it on with an Egyptian woman, not even if she's Cleopatra! I don't care if you fuck Princess Margaret, but no Egyptians." Morris stared at him for added effect.

So, this was about the Ann Walters story. Should have known that could be a problem. Drew now realized that Morris had put his nuts in the ringer for him. "George, I owe you. No way am I going to mess you up. You have my word. No Egyptian women."

Drew wasn't happy about this news. It wasn't that he cared about the ban on the local women; that wasn't something he would do. He knew enough about the Arab culture not to chance that. No, he was a little disappointed that he wasn't the unanimous choice of the Los Angeles brain trust. However, on reflection he figured it couldn't have been. Egypt was too juicy a plum not to be political. He was just happy that George, and Bistrisky to a point, were in his corner.

"Oh, before I bring in the geologists, Bistrisky will be here on some other HR business this week and he wants to see you. You two could have dinner or something. He is a friend."

Drew just smiled. This was good news. Mort was a friend, if you can ever have a friend in this high stakes game. Everyone had an agenda – even him.

CHAPTER 5

Cairo Preview

DREW FINISHED PACKING for what would be a quick trip to Cairo. His first week on the job as the newly-minted General Manager for African operations had been a whirlwind, a blur of activity that included a late night with Mort Bistrisky in from Los Angeles. It was great to relax and do some controlled partying with, if not his best buddy, at least an old acquaintance he genuinely liked., As head of HR, Mort was a good source for company news, real or imagined. Drew was as ambitious as Morris and worked hard to cultivate the relationship with Mort that had begun even before he'd joined Getty. While Drew was still married, the Cahills and the Bistriskys had seen each other socially and Mort had been involved in the recruitment of Drew into the company.

What had begun as a scheduled four–to–six-hour presentation by James Tottenham and his geologists and geophysicists had turned into a two-day event. Drew was fascinated by the work of the London exploration team; it was the most thorough and detailed analysis he had ever seen. Drew was on an excitement roll; he could smell success. Tottenham's group had identified seven probable drill sites where the data indicated the permeability and porosity were favorable for the presence of sizeable hydrocarbon deposits. The first thing Drew would do was to get a seismic boat to shoot the area thoroughly to help further determine the probability of finding the Egyptian elephant deposit. Drilling was the only certain way; it transformed a probability to a zero or one result. Morris didn't need to be infected with enthusiasm for this play, but after Drew finished debriefing him about his feel following the presentation, Morris' oil fever climbed several additional degrees. He had to figure out a way to drill two more wells within the budget. $30 million was a lot of money, but offshore drilling was expensive and tricky and every additional well increased the probabilities proportionally. So Morris had wisely padded the capital expenditure proposal, and instead of the budgeted three wells Drew was sure he could get two more down.

Drew and Morris huddled for a couple of hours after the Tottenham presentation. Morris thought it would be a good idea for Cahill to fly to Cairo on Friday, meet with Gamal Hashem to get the lay of the land, then return Sunday night and make the Egyptian orientation program on Monday. Drew still thought the orientation was a waste, but George wasn't coming off this ball. Drew would also meet Mort for dinner before he left, and Morris had a couple of issues he wanted Drew to run by Mort. Morris knew that he would need to send a number of geologists and geophysicists to work for Drew in Egypt and he would need to replace them in London with local hires, so he wanted HR to increase the salary grades in the UK and to transfer earth scientists from Los Angeles until the new hires were on board. Drew also had a bone to pick with Mort: he wanted Frank Frick and Joe Clark, two top drilling engineers who had both worked for Drew in Kuwait, transferred to Egypt as soon as possible.

***

Archie rang Drew's company flat and announced his arrival in the lobby ready to drive Drew to Heathrow. Drew grabbed his carry-on bag and briefcase and took the elevator down, where Archie greeted him warmly with his cockney-accented banter. "So Mr. Cahill, it's off to Heathrow. It's Swiss Air isn't it? They say it's the best way to Cairo, better than BOAC, bloody 'ell." Archie continued nattering the entire way to Heathrow. He had bits of gossip about his corporate clients; none of interest to Drew except the bit about the managing director of Canadian Pacific Ships, Joe Harvey. Drew had met Harvey years earlier, when Canadian Pacific was trying to promote a deepwater port at St. John, New Brunswick. The CP group was interested in buying crude from Kuwait and Saudi Arabia for shipment through St. John and transshipment by pipeline to New England for local refining. The CP group had put together an interesting proposal and Getty was interested. However, the deal was abandoned in 1973 after that Arab-Israeli war and the ensuing Arab oil embargo. Drew had been in Los Angeles at the time and he'd gotten to know Harvey during the process, and liked him; but he'd lost track of Harvey, and he wondered now why and when he had been moved to London. Drew made a mental note to call Harvey when he returned. One never knew who could be helpful, and if Archie's gossip was close, Harvey knew his way around London.

The Swiss Air 747 began its approach to the Cairo Airport. *Morris was right,* Drew thought, *this is the best way to fly.* Swiss Air knew how to operate an airline, and he was impressed with the service of the flight crew: neat, friendly but professional. Drew had enough undivided time to review his agenda for his meeting with Gamal. Based on Springer's and Morris' input, Gamal sounded like a very interesting character. He would meet Gamal at his place in Zamalek, and then dinner. Gamal had set up appointments with the Egyptian state petroleum company that would be the watchdog over Getty's operations. Because the weekend in Egypt, as in the rest of the Arab world, was Thursday and Friday, he could have meetings on Saturday and Sunday then fly back to London in time for the dreaded Egyptian orientation course.

***

Gamal sat in his den going over Drew Cahill's résumé one more time. Morris and Springer were right,

Cahill had an impressive background. Gamal mused to himself while he noted on his yellow lined legal pad what he considered to be the more significant points: he then jotted down a summary. Born 13 August 1941 in Wilmette, Illinois, a suburb of Chicago. Gamal knew Chicago well – that was where his American joint venture partner in the Egyptian firm of Hashem/Sidley Austin was headquartered. Attended Mt. Carmel High School in Chicago, graduated in 1958. *So he must be a Catholic,* Gamal thought. *That is good; not a Jew. Of course, after the Camp David accord between Egypt and Israel, not critical; but why push it.* Graduated from St. Louis University's Institute of Technology in 1962 with a B.S. in Geological Engineering and a M.S. in 1964; 3.1 GPA undergraduate and 3.5 graduate. Joined Getty in 1971 in Los Angeles as a senior petroleum engineer; spent two years in Peru leading and running the drilling program; returned to Los Angeles in the exploration department until he went to Kuwait in November 1976; left Kuwait April 1980. *Last week,* he smiled.

Let's see. Gamal added up the number of wells drilled, capital expended, and results: twelve wells, $40 million, and more than 150,000 B/D discovered. He was with Atlantic Richfield from 1964 until he joined Getty in 1971, and he was part of the North Slope exploration and drilling team. *Very qualified,* he thought. *Morris wasn't exaggerating.* Gamal was anxious to size him up personally; if he was, as Morris said, a younger version of himself, he would be perfect. Gamal checked his watch. Cahill's plane should be in, so he would be there within an hour. Gamal couldn't wait to size up this young American oilman.

In London earlier that day, Cahill's background was undergoing a different kind of review. The file she had contained more, much more, than his résumé. It included, among other things, the details of his marriage to Peg Riley in June of 1970, and their divorce in June 1977. She was a native of St. Louis; they had met when he was in graduate school and she was enrolled in Nursing School of St. Louis U. The details of the divorce proceeding were not scandalous; it seemed like a matter of her wanting to return to her hometown and him being committed to his career with Getty. The move to Kuwait had been the kiss of death. He had been reasonably faithful during the marriage, but there were indications that on occasion he had been indiscreet. Those lapses, however, paled in comparison to his *escapes sans spouse*; apparently, in addition to being a committed company man, the single-again Mr. Cahill was a bit of a Casanova. That should make this as interesting as shooting fish in a barrel. Still, he could gag on her demands; easy to hook but maybe complicated to land, especially if it could pose a threat to his mentor, George Morris. She thought she could finesse this, but there might be conditions that could lead to complications that weren't immediately clear to her. If that was the case, she would have to bring that fact out quickly.

During his time in Kuwait he visibly had gotten along with all of the Arabs he had encountered; he wasn't political and hadn't taken sides between the Palestinians and the Israelis. He did what he had to in order to produce for his company. It was highlighted, though, that he was anxious to quit Kuwait, he'd had his voyage there. *Well,* she thought, *not a surprise.* As with any young executive on the rise he did have some enemies within Getty, but was shrewd enough to have courted the right people – including the VP of Getty's Human Resources Department – in addition to George Morris. *So,* she thought, *a hungry young man clawing his way to the top of the corporate ladder. Clever, smart, but willing to cut his losses if needed. Peg Riley was one of those cut.* This could be a bigger challenge than she'd initially thought, and she was warming to the game. This would be exciting. This was why she'd joined.

***

Gamal's black giant entered his den and announced that Mr. Cahill had arrived and was waiting in the foyer. Gamal instructed his servant to usher Mr. Cahill upstairs to the room with a balcony overlooking the Rue du Paix, the room where Gamal had met and entertained Springer and Morris not so very long ago, but to do so only after Gamal had preceded them to that room.

Seated in a wingback chair with his back to the balcony, Gamal awaited Cahill. Gamal believed this to be the most impressive view he could provide his American visitor. Cahill was ushered into the room by the black giant, who then bowed and uttered "Welcome" as he smiled broadly and revealed some of the most impressive ivory in all of Africa, then backed away and stationed himself in the doorway ready to receive his master's instructions. Cahill walked smartly toward Gamal, who had risen from his chair when his guest had entered the room. As Cahill approached, Gamal looked him over as a general might give his soldiers an on-parade inspection, and he was impressed. Gamal returned Cahill's smile with one of his own as he said *"Salaam Alaikum"*, to which Cahill responded *"Alaikum a Salaam"*. Still smiling, Gamal grasped Cahill's hand in a vigorous handshake while maintaining eye contact and staring into his guest's dark-blue eyes. *Irish no doubt,* Gamal thought to himself. *This is no ugly America; au contraire, he is a handsome American. The Egyptians will love him, if his demeanor matches his appearance.* A fact to be confirmed, certainly, but Cahill's response to his greeting in Arabic portended a sensitivity that bode him well as a guest in Egypt.

Gamal motioned for Cahill to take a seat facing him and the balcony. "I have heard so much about you Mr. Cahill. Now we meet. Your flight must have been on time; I hope it was pleasant. But I am rude after your long journey; you might be in the mood for a drink. What would be your pleasure?"

"John and George tell me that you are a connoisseur of single malt scotch, but I'll have whatever you are recommending. And please call me Drew, short for my given name, Andrew."

Gamal turned to the black giant waiting in the doorway and requested two Oban whiskies, neat, in a short glass with a glass of water on the side. "Now that we have the important business taken care of, allow me to give you a brief on what I've arranged for your initial visit to Egypt as General Manager. I've taken the liberty of preparing an agenda I hope meets with your approval."

Cahill took the folder as Gamal motioned with a wave of his ever-present pipe for him to open it. He leafed through the agenda. Saturday was to begin and end with meetings at the Egyptian General Petroleum Corporation (EGPC) offices, starting with the General Manager, Hosni Radwan. As Cahill read it seemed to him that he would be meeting with every department within EGPC, maybe, even, with all of their employees. On Sunday he was scheduled to meet with several people Gamal had identified as candidates for the job of Administration Manager, then finish off the day meeting with Gamal and his top American lawyer, John Burke. Gamal noted that the purpose of this meeting was to agree on the request for proposal for shooting seismic in the Gulf of Suez.

As the black giant arrived with their whiskies Cahill finished reviewing the agenda and closed the folder. He looked up quizzically at Gamal, and Gamal returned the question with a smile. "You are wondering why I want you to meet with candidates for the Administration Manager's job. I will explain over dinner. I have booked a table for us at my favorite local restaurant, the Don Quixote, a fortunate holdover from the days of the British. It's just down the street." Gamal picked up his drink as he continued. "Other than the Admin Manager interviews, I gather all else is to your liking?"

Cahill picked up his drink before responding. "I

understand the EGPC meetings and the need to get bids out for the seismic, and you've said you'll cover the admin job at dinner. However, we need to find an office, apartments for staff, a place for me to live, cars, and get visas for the ex-pats; the whole support staff situation. I'll need to get moving on that right away."

Gamal smiled broadly. "But, of course. That is why you'll need an admin man right away. He will take care of all of that. I will elaborate at dinner. I will explain how the mundane but necessary things are handled in Egypt – as well as the more important matters."

Cahill smiled and hoisted his glass in a toast to his lawyer. He liked this man; Morris had chosen well. They finished their drinks while Gamal gave his client a more elaborate review of his own background, and by the time the scotch was drained these two men from totally different cultures had formed a bond.

Gamal stood up. "You must be famished by now, shall we go? I think you'll like the Don Quixote. It's a residue of the British, but, ironically, a French menu. The Brits did many things well but *haut cuisine* was not one of their accomplishments; however, their diplomats knew fine food and French chefs went together. I would wager that during your prior visits to Cairo you did not dine at the Quixote; it's not a tourist spot. We residents of Zamalek like to keep some of the finer places on our once gracious island for our own pleasure. Am I right, you are new to the Quixote?"

Smiling as he rose, Drew replied, "Right as rain, Counselor."

Gamal warmed to the title bestowed on him by this young American. *Counselor indeed,* he thought. *Counselor in all aspects.* Gamal felt certain that with his help, Drew, and as a consequence, Getty, would be very successful in Egypt. Gamal was first and foremost an Egyptian; his country needed this oil, and he was convinced this oilman would give it to them. Gamal smiled warmly as he ushered Drew out of the room.

The restaurant was just a few meters from Gamal's building, and as they walked Drew took in the edifices of old Edwardian mansions. Many of the buildings were in disrepair, with large untended lawns shaded by cypress and eucalyptus trees. The better-maintained mansions were now embassies for some of the countries that had diplomatic relations with Egypt. Notably missing, however, were the embassies of Russia and the United States. The Soviets had been made *persona non grata* by Sadat, while the American embassy was located on the other side of the Nile. Drew and Gamal ambled leisurely as they drank in the pleasant smells of the varied plants, trees, and flowers, along with the not so pleasant smells of Cairo's omnipresent soot, dirt, and smog. This contrast was, in fact, the contrast that was Cairo. The stifling heat of Cairo's summers had not yet arrived. *But arrive it will,* thought Drew.

The two men presented quite a contrast strolling down the streets of Zamalek. The older man was some six inches shorter than the younger and had a dark complexion, a deep brown. The younger man, although tanned, had a light complexion and close-cropped brown hair. The older man was balding, and his remaining hair was black with a tendency to curl. He also sported a neatly-trimmed mustache. Drew was clean shaven. While Gamal could be described as dapper, Drew was the all-American boy at nearly forty.

They turned the corner, and there nestled between two neatly-maintained mansions was the Don Quixote Restaurant. The restaurant was a perfect replica of an English country house, complete with thatch roof, leaded bay windows, and a white plaster front bordered with dark-brown-stained wooden slats. The entry door was massive, with a stained glass depiction of Don Quixote on a rearing steed and letters forming the words Don Quixote in old

English characters. Gamal led the way inside where he was immediately greeted warmly by the *maitre d'*, a handsome forty-something Egyptian who could easily have been taken for an English country gentleman; he was attired in a tan cashmere sport coat with dark brown slacks and tasseled loafers, and his complexion was closer to Drew's than to that of his fellow countryman.

Gamal and the *maitre d'* embraced and kissed on both cheeks, and it was apparent to Drew that Gamal was a frequent and valued customer. Gamal introduced Drew to the *maitre d'*, Sami Garber, and with a twinkle in his eye, as if this was all Sami needed to know about Drew Cahill, Gamal told Sami, "Drew is the newly-appointed General Manager of Getty Oil. This American oilman will find the Egyptian elephant oil fields in the Gulf of Suez."

Sami seated Gamal and Drew at a four-seat table in front of a bay window, giving them a good view of both the street and the interior of the Don Quixote. The restaurant was mainly lit by table candles highlighting the dark paneling, which provided a warm ambiance. The restaurant was sparsely populated and no one was within earshot of the table.

Their waiter brought the menus, and deferentially greeted Gamal before welcoming Drew to the Don Quixote. He then bowed his way into a retreat from his customers, giving them time to review their options. Drew went through the menu quickly. "Gamal, this is a fabulous place; I feel like I'm somewhere in the English countryside! The architect should be proud of his work. How old is this place?"

"The Don Quixote is pre-World War II, actually 1936, and, incidentally, the architect was Welsh. He was a friend of my father; I got to know him through my father. Unfortunately, he was killed at Dunkirk."

"Sorry to hear that, but he did do a wonderful job." Drew hesitated then continued, "I should know this, Gamal, but when did the Brits quit Egypt?"

Gamal smiled and motioned to the waiter. "I thought we might first order a pre-dinner drink. Do you agree?"

Drew nodded as the waiter approached. Gamal ordered two Scotch and waters with ice, and when the waiter left to get their drinks Gamal quietly explained his choice. "You know I am a single malt whiskey man, but it's impossible to find here, or in any restaurant I know of in Cairo. As you will discover, if you don't already know, we have many limitations in Egypt. The whiskey here is not good enough to drink neat."

Gamal continued, "The British, or Brits as you call them, left Egypt in 1954. Did you know that this ended some 2,300 years of foreign rule? The

Persians broke the Pharaonic line, then there came the Greeks, Romans, Arabs, Mamaluks, Napoleon, Turks, and, finally, the British. True we speak Arabic, but we also speak other languages – at least the better-educated class does. These foreign rulers left their impact on Egypt. We are different. We are what we are in part because of each of them, but in my heart I believe we are still, first and foremost, Egyptians. But, I understand that you are scheduled to take a cross-cultural seminar at London University next week, so I can dispense with my Egyptian history lesson, *n'est pas?*"

Drew looked at the smiling Gamal, and responded with a grin and slight shake of the head. "Counselor, you are on the ball. So, you've been talking to George Morris."

Gamal nodded. "I value my relationship with your boss; how else would I get to know so much about you? But rest assured, I am here to work for Getty's interest, and since you are the Getty man in Egypt I will do all in my power to help you. I won't do any runs around the end."

Drew laughed. "Gamal, you mean end-runs."

"*Je m'excuse mon ami*, but of course you know what I mean. George told me that the course will be conducted for the BCIU by the professors of the SOAS School of the University of London. An impressive group they are, real scholars of the Middle East including Egypt. While I was Egyptian ambassador to Denmark I had the opportunity to meet Bernard Lewis, a distinguished professor at the School. He has visited Egypt many times. I was in Cairo on leave and attended a dinner for him given by Anwar and Jihan Sadat. Lewis was accompanied by a young protégé, Milledufleur Rose, I believe. If you are lucky she will be one of your instructors."

"Why do you say that?"

Gamal smiled conspiratorially, "Because she is so beautiful. A modern day Cleopatra."

Drew beamed, suddenly warming to his unwanted assignment. *Maybe it won't be so bad after all,* he thought. When they'd had dinner in London, Mort had given him a syllabus of the course. "Professor Rose" was listed as one of the instructors; however, Mort hadn't mentioned that Professor Rose was a woman, and a beautiful woman at that. Maybe Mort didn't know; if he did, Mort would have told him. *Hell,* he thought, *Mort probably would have audited the course!*

"You seem to be amused, Mr. Cahill," said Gamal.

"Gamal, amused isn't quite the word. Relieved maybe; possibly excited."

Gamal's eyes twinkled. *Excited you will be my young friend,* he thought.

***

About the time that Drew Cahill and Gamal Hashem began their dinner, Milledufleur Rose sat at her desk putting the finishing touches on the outline she would use for her lectures next week to one Andrew Cahill. She had a scheduled engagement to meet with Joe Harvey at the Ménage a Trois at 8 p.m., and she was anxious; she needed to hurry if she was to arrive close to the meet time.

She had done this lecture four times previously, but she wanted to tailor this one to Cahill. *What in the bloody hell is a strat trap play?* she wondered. *Maybe Harvey would know? His company is in the oil business; sure he will know.* She was looking forward to her play for the night. *I've never done a Canadian before, but they are probably as horny as the Americans. At least I hope,* she laughed to herself. She had met Harvey at the Ménage a Trois the Friday before, during one of her outings looking for new game. The pickings had been slim, and Milly was about ready to take herself to another club or to just call it a night and return to her flat, when this good-looking forty-something man walked in. It was Joe Harvey, and he was obviously a man on the hunt. Harvey surveyed the near-empty bar, then ordered a whiskey and selected a perch a respectful distance from Milly. When his drink arrived, he caught her eye and lifted his glass as in a toast. She demurely smiled and returned the gesture, and that was all it took to activate Harvey. He donned a wide smile accentuating his perfect set of pearly whites, and began the ritualistic pre-mating march to the bar stool that was supporting what he thought looked like a truly gorgeous ass.

Harvey was an attractive man, well-dressed in a dark blue pinstripe. He introduced himself and settled into a routine which he had undoubtedly used on more than one occasion. At first she thought he was American, a notion he quickly decried. He proudly announced he was a Canadian and an anglophile. He downed his whiskey and promptly ordered a replacement. The Canadians had a reputation for being large drinkers, and Harvey, she was now sure, would not detract from this legend. Harvey then chronicled his background as if Milly was interviewing him for a position at the University. He amused her, but she decided that in this case delayed gratification would be the better choice. She feigned weariness tonight, and Harvey quickly took the bait and asked her to have dinner with him any time of her choosing. "Why, next Friday would be delightful; say 8 o'clock, and say here?" Harvey looked as if he had won the lottery. Next Friday would work wonderfully for him.

***

After dinner Gamal walked Drew back to the Zama-lek Marriott, located just blocks from Gamal's residence, and as they walked the two men exchanged bits and pieces of their pasts. Drew was impressed with Gamal's intimate knowledge of the Egyptian power players, and he was interested in Gamal's gossip about Sadat and his predecessor, Nasser.

From his days in Kuwait Drew knew Sadat was held in low esteem by the Saudis, Kuwaitis, Iraqis, Lebanese, and, of course, by the Palestinians. The Palestinians he knew were, for the most part, well-educated, and basically ran the oil ministries of Kuwait and Saudi Arabia. He had usually avoided conversations with the Palestinians about what they called "the occupation" of their homeland by the Jews; making peace with Israel was anathema to the Islamic world. Most of the Palestinians Drew knew were citizens of Jordan, which he thought was the homeland of the Palestinians. He had been made aware by his Palestinian acquaintances of what they called the dire circumstances in which most Palestinians lived throughout the Arab world. Except for the most unusual cases, Palestinians could not become citizens of any Arab state except Jordan.

From what Gamal told him Drew deduced that Sadat was more popular with Americans than he was with his fellow Egyptians, and that surprised Drew. Like many Americans, he had always thought Sadat was as popular with his countrymen as he was with the Americans. In any case, Getty was comfortable with Egypt; the company analysis concluded that Egypt posed little political risk. Getty was making a big investment in Egypt, and that was good enough for Drew. Drew was comfortable with their position in Egypt.

As they neared the hotel both men lapsed into silence, deep in thought, each man thinking of questions for the other but being sensitive to how far they could go with each other. Gamal broke the silence as they approached the hotel entrance. "Drew, I am curious about your experience with Atlantic Richfield. Actually, what I am curious about is why that has not been given more emphasis in your résumé? After all, that was a discovery of billions of barrels of oil, and you worked on the Prudhoe Bay project."

Drew smiled, "Good question. Getty PR put the résumé together, and my take is that they wanted to highlight my Middle-East experience; not exactly downplaying the Richfield experience, but everyone in the oil patch knows the significance of the discovery of that elephant field. Besides, I was just one of many on that project; it was my first job out of school. I started out as a Petroleum Engineer, and by the time we hit Prudhoe Bay State Number 1, in December 1967, I was a senior engineer. It certainly didn't hurt my career, but I wasn't a big part of the decision-making process at that time; I was just one of the many who put forth technical information. I did have a big part in the drilling program, though, and I learned how to push people and get the most out of them. One thing for sure, Robert Anderson, the top Richfield man, put his neck on the line by approving the eighth well. ARCO had already drilled seven dry holes, but Anderson believed in the geology and he approved the well that blew the lid off everything. We later drilled a step out well which confirmed that we had a true elephant. However, we had giant environmental problems in getting other wells down, and we were all frustrated. I was ready to leave, so when Getty headhunters called I was ready to go!"

Gamal took Drew's arm, "I can guarantee you won't have any environmental problems in Egypt."

Drew smiled. "I know."

"Drew, how big do you think our program in the Gulf of Suez could be?"

"Big! Not Prudhoe Bay big, but maybe two to three hundred thousand barrels per day. Let me tell you something, Gamal. I learned from the ARCO experience that if the geology looks really good, do not stop until you hit. I guarantee you, I won't quit!"

Gamal grinned like a Cheshire cat. "I know."

***

Drew relaxed as his driver, Ahmed, sped towards Heliopolis and the Cairo International Airport. Ahmed and the car were a result of Wafik Tewfik, Drew's brand new Manager-Administration, Getty Oil East Gharib Ltd. Following Saturday's all day meeting with EGPC, Sunday's meetings with Gamal Hashem's American lawyer, John Burke, and then with Wafik Tewfik, were productive and, indeed, relaxing.

Burke was a young lawyer from Chicago, and he had done his homework. With the aid of Hashem and Sidley Austin's word processor, Burke finished the Request for Proposal (RFP) which would be sent to the only two companies that had seismic boats in the area. Drew's seismic shooting in the Gulf of Suez could proceed on schedule. Gamal and Burke would also run the RFP by EGPC for their approval, which was necessary under the terms of the concession for "Cost Recovery." Cost Recovery was critical if all of the company's expenditures were to be recoverable from sales of oil when they began production. Any costs not approved by the Egyptian bureaucracy Getty would have to eat. Of course if they did not find oil, Getty would eat it all. This was clear-cut, a real no-brainer, and just a formality. EGPC also had to approve all of the Egyptian hires, and this was a real gravy train for the bureaucrats. They would only approve their "favored" candidates, those who would give the EGPC section heads a kickback of 15% of their annual salaries. Drew was familiar with the *baksheesh* of the Middle East; you had to grease the system or you came to a screeching halt. He learned from Gamal that Egypt's bureaucracy was second to none. It was the oldest in the world, and it had spun red tape for at least three thousand years before the Arabs arrived in conquest. From what he had observed on Saturday, Drew was sure Gamal was right. Dealing with the Saudis and Kuwaitis was no trip to Hollywood, but he had a feeling that the Egyptian system would trump anything. He had heard about this when he was in Kuwait, and after the meeting with Wafik on Sunday he was a believer. In addition to their thousands of years of practice, Drew felt that the Egyptians were more intelligent and craftier than the desert Arabs. However, the desert Arabs were sneakier, and they could be ruthless if they had an advantage.

Following his meeting with Wafik, Drew and Gamal had dinner with Wafik and his wife, Bridgette. Several times during dinner Gamal caught Drew's eye and gave him what Drew now recognized was Gamal's "I told you so" look, always accompanied by Gamal's already-familiar grin. Gamal was right about Wafik. Drew had made up his mind about him after the first half hour, and the rest of the day had just confirmed his impression. When he'd met with the EGPC people, they had recommended Wafik to Drew; even the EGPC General Manager had suggested that he talk to Wafik about the Administration job. After spending the day and dinner with Gamal, Wafik, and Bridgette, Drew felt he understood why the bureaucrats were so high on Wafik.

The interview with Wafik had been conducted at Wafik's residence in Zamalek. When Drew and Gamal had first reviewed Sunday's schedule, Drew had expressed some reservations about interviewing Wafik at his residence, but Gamal had assured him there was no problem. "This is Egypt," he'd said. Prior to the meeting Gamal had also explained that Wafik and his wife were of Circassian origin, so when he met Wafik, Drew wasn't surprised at his white complexion, straight dark hair, and dark blue eyes. What did surprise him was Wafik's size. He towered over Drew. *He must be over six foot five and weigh at least two hundred and fifty pounds,* Drew thought. Wafik had an infectious smile with perfect-looking white teeth, and he moved smoothly with the grace of a large cat. Drew thought he could have played linebacker for his beloved Bears. He looked a little older than Drew but, as was revealed in his résumé, he was actually a year younger. Drew's observation was that most people in the Middle East looked older than their Western counterparts; the worst, he thought, were the Jordanians.

Wafik was a fine-looking man and his wife was simply an elegant beauty, tall, slender, and well-proportioned; Drew thought she had the body of a Grace Kelly. Her hair was not blonde but a dark ash, worn touching her shoulders. She had light blue eyes that radiated warmth and an engaging smile, and she spoke English with a slight French accent. While Wafik's English was less accented, he did speak with a slight English accent that was probably a carryover from his schooling in Britain.

The Tewfik residence was just down the street from the famous old Gezira Club, and just around the corner from the apartment building in which Drew would later take a unit to live when he finally settled more or less permanently in Egypt. Their house was an older Georgian mansion undoubtedly from the early British era. It was typical of Zamalek, beautiful style reminiscent of a wealthier time. They had arrived early; Drew had a plane to catch later that afternoon that he didn't want to miss. Wafik welcomed them with all the grace of a diplomat greeting a newly-arrived Ambassador to his country, which in a sense Drew was. They had tea in a parlor off the foyer. Bridgette poured and began a light banter, inquiring as to Drew's home in the states and his impressions of Cairo. After a few minutes, Gamal suggested that Drew and Wafik withdraw to another room for the more serious interview.

They withdrew to what Drew surmised was one of seven or eight spacious rooms on the first floor of the aging mansion. As in Gamal's apartment, the ceilings were at least thirteen feet high and bordered by elaborately decorated cornices. Wafik beckoned Drew to take a seat in an overstuffed wingback chair facing him, which Drew guessed was as old as the structure itself. *Comfortable, but a bit dated,* he thought. Drew wanted to ask Wafik about his house but thought better of it. He could do that later, after they'd gotten to know each other better; that is, if there was to be a later.

Drew began the interview as he began all of his interviews. "Tell me about yourself; tell me why you want this job and why you are the most qualified." Wafik smiled and launched into an uninterrupted twenty minute answer to his questions. Drew was very impressed. Wafik gave as good a performance as he had ever encountered. He was obviously qualified. He was very qualified. Drew was satisfied, but he became completely convinced he had to go no further when he asked Wafik the question, "Do you have any questions for me?"

It was Wafik's question that had convinced Drew he need look no further.

Ahmed made it to the Cairo Airport in what Ahmed informed Drew was record time for this busy time on a Sunday. Drew would later come to understand that every drive of Ahmed's was in record time.

As Ahmed sped and cut in and out of traffic he kept up an incessant stream of chatter on a full range of topics. Ahmed gave his passenger what he called "the insider's view" of Cairo, unavailable except from such an astute observer of life and politics in Cairo. Ahmed also assured "Mr. Cahill" that he could never find a driver that came close to him in driving expertise or local knowledge. Ahmed informed Drew that he was also a law student, now in his seventh year, and Ahmed assured him that his studies would not interfere with his duties as "Mr. Cahill's personal driver." Drew was sure that Ahmed wouldn't be deterred by any non-company business, and, according to Wafik, Ahmed needed the car as at least a secondary residence.

Two of Ahmed's attributes Drew valued especially highly: first, Ahmed could drive, no mean feat in Cairo, and, secondly, Ahmed was a funny man.

The Swiss Air 747 reached its cruising altitude on its way to London via Zurich, and the first class stewardesses began the cabin service. Drew was comfortably ensconced in seat One A, window, bulkhead, in front, and, best of all, no seatmate. He could use his time reviewing what had happened in the last two days and writing his trip report. He loosened his tie, took a sip of the champagne, and mentally reviewed the last two days.

Even as he completed his review Drew was still most impressed by Wafik's question, and with his answer. Drew closed his eyes and wouldn't waken until the Swiss Air jet began its descent to land in Zurich.

***

Milledufleur lounged in her oversized Chesterfield, occasionally sipping chardonnay from the fluted glass on a coffee table adjacent to the couch. She paged through the outline she had completed on Friday. She was satisfied that she had been thorough in her preparation, and she had no doubt she would be able to deliver a comprehensive and intense course for Mr. Cahill. They would meet tomorrow morning at ten in the staff conference room adjacent to her office at SOAS. Four hours per day Monday through Thursday, with a two hour finale on Friday. She was supremely confident of her academic capabilities, but for the first time she questioned her ability to ingratiate herself solidly enough with Cahill that he would accede to her request when it came. She was unclear as to why the Mossad needed her to convince this man to hire her two geologist "cousins" as part of his Egyptian staff, and Kim David of course wouldn't talk with her about the Mossad mission, even though she was aware of the events engulfing Israel.

One month before the signing of the peace treaty with Egypt, Israel had lost its most important ally in the Middle East: the Shah of Iran was toppled by the Ayatollah Khomeini and the Iranian Revolutionary Guard. Khomeini not only was opposed to the very existence of Israel, he came very close to being the most radical of its Palestinian enemies. The handing over of the Israeli Embassy Building in Tehran to the PLO was more than a symbolic gesture. The Israelis' fear was that the PLO control of Lebanon would give them a base from which they could continue to mount attacks on Israel. She agreed with those who foresaw that the move by the PLO could lead to the eventual ultimate control of Lebanon by the Palestinians, and this would put the Israelis' head in a noose. She knew this could not stand. She believed Israel would have to counter this move. Their Phalange allies would need more than luck to prevail. The Palestinians were embolden by the recent events and were constantly shelling northern Israel from their redoubt in southern Lebanon. The constant chatter she had picked up during her Mossad training program had convinced her that the Palestinians had to be dealt with once and for all. She knew Kim David hated the PLO; she had no doubt that her assignment had something to do with an invasion of Lebanon from Israel, but what, exactly, she had not yet resolved in her mind. She could only assume that this assignment was vital to the interests of Israel.

What if she failed? Failure was a concept that was foreign to her nature, but, until now, she had performed only to satisfy her own desires, her own objectives. No one else would have been worse off if she had not achieved her goals. *Not so in this case,* she realized. The Mossad were deadly serious, always. The Mossad had gone to great lengths to set this game up; whatever it was, it was important. Milledufleur forced the big picture from her mind; she would focus on completing her immediate assignment. The puzzle would soon be solved.

She had read and re-read Drew Cahill's file and she felt she had more than a passing insight into her prey, but she wouldn't meet him until tomorrow morning. She took another sip of wine as she reflected on her plan – if it could be called a plan. She was certain she could seduce him, but this had to be more than a one-night stand; this had to be a deep enough relationship and last long enough so he would take a personal risk, even if a small one, to perpetuate the relationship. She had never had a relationship; she had never even made it to breakfast. She was a nymphomaniac who abhorred the thought of a repeat. However, she was determined. *But,* she thought, *what if he won't commit? What if he only wants a one night stand?*

***

Drew woke early, 6 a.m. By the time he'd arrived at his flat last night he was exhausted. He was so exhausted that not even Archie's constant nattering could keep him conscious, and after he'd told Archie he wanted to see Harvey, he'd passed out. He now felt refreshed, and he was anxious to get going. He still thought this Business Community for International Understanding (BCIU) course was bull, but what Gamal had told him about "Professor M. Rose" did intrigue him. Right now, however, he would stop by to see George Morris and update him on what he considered to be a couple of good days in Egypt. He had plenty of time before he had to be in the classroom of Milledufleur Rose.

Drew entered the Butler Place Getty headquarters in the U.K. and, taking the stairs two at a time, propelled himself up to the fourth floor office of George Morris. Even though it was not quite seven a.m. he knew he would find Morris in his office. Morris habitually began the working day early; he could sort out the important messages and plan the day without any interruptions from Los Angeles. Conversations with Los Angeles came at the end of the day, and were generally not initiated by him. He didn't go out of his way to piss off the brass in L.A., but he certainly didn't need to play babysitter to the corporate bureaucrats.

Drew saw Morris standing at his desk sipping coffee and reading what had to be a field report. Drew knocked lightly before entering, and Morris looked up. He broke into a big smile. "Drew, come in! I was hoping you would drop by before your cross-cultural class today. So, how did it go in Cairo?"

"The trip was great, and we covered a lot of ground in a short period. Gamal is fucking fantastic! You and John hired a real jewel. He knows everyone there is to know in the government, and also in EGPC. We never had anyone remotely like him in Kuwait! Well you know that better than anyone. You had to take the Saudis on, and that was a constant battle."

"Gamal is going to be a big help to us, no doubt. What else happened?"

"I hired a great guy to be Manager of Administration. His name is Wafik Tewfik, an Egyptian who is working for Compagnie Française des Pétroles (CFP). About six months ago they announced they were pulling out of Egypt, and Wafik is just cleaning up. He'll be ready to join us within three weeks, and his first job will be to get us office space. There are some choices available in Maadi; it's a not too bad suburb about ten miles south of Zamalek, but it's a 45 minute drive during traffic. Most of our expats will live there, except me. I'll take a flat in Zamalek."

Morris laughed. "Just like Kuwait, Drew; away from the camp! Although Maadi won't exactly be a camp; all the oil companies have their offices there. Makes sense. How were the rounds at EGPC?"

"My God, what a body swamp! Talk about bureaucracy! But the General Manager, Personnel Head, and Finance Chief were all polite and positive. My sense about the Egyptians is that, contrasted with the Saudis, they are pretty friendly to us. I felt comfortable. As long as we play by their rules I don't think we'll have any problems. The bureaucratic bullshit will be a challenge, though."

"Sure, but that's why we hire Egyptians. Fight fire with fire." Morris laughed at his attempt at humor.

Drew continued. "I'll have time to get together with Tottenham this week to get a relocation plan for his geologists and geophysicists to transfer to Cairo. EGPC agreed that for a reasonable period our London work will be cost recovered; we agreed that two months would be reasonable. Obviously they want our people down there asap for the economic benefit. They'll forward résumés for earth sciences, finance, engineering, and other admin personnel. We won't need our drilling people from the States until this fall; September would be good."

Morris nodded in agreement. "You did give Mort Bistrisky your preferred list when he was in London, yes?"

"We're covered. Mort is on base."

Morris then asked Drew about the seismic. "Listen, how about the seismic shooting, and a boat?"

"The Request for Proposal for the seismic shooting is written and will be sent to all contractors who have seismic boats in the area of the Gulf of Suez.

Gamal's American lawyer put it together. They'll get EGPC approval this week. We should be shooting by early September."

"Sounds like a good start Drew. And look, I know you don't want to attend this course, but HR in Los Angeles is big on this sort of thing. Besides, you might learn something; Egypt is different from Kuwait and Saudi."

Drew shrugged, thinking back to Gamal's comments about Milledufleur Rose. "You're right; no sense going against HR. We'll need their help, and maybe I will learn something. Gamal told me they are an impressive group of Middle East experts." He turned to leave. "I should get moving, George; I'll check back in with you later this afternoon. I want to tell you more about Wafik; in particular, the question he posed to me."

"Fine, I'll be free close to five. Oh, almost forgot. Mrs. Morris wants you to have dinner with us tonight. Any problem?"

"No, I'll be there. Haven't seen Sandra since you left the big beach."

***

Drew left the Butler Place offices and walked down to Victoria Street in front of the Prince Albert Pub.

It was a beautiful day in London, horns blaring, buses bumbling along, the smell of flowers all mixed to provide pleasant aromas. The sky was clear, and so lovely in its greenish-blue hue. *Nothing like it in the world,* thought Drew. Drew loved London. The only negative about this job was that it would be in Egypt and not in London. Today was unusually warm for London, but in comparison to Kuwait and Cairo it was a mild spring day. Drew had wanted to walk to the SOAS campus, but because of the heat and the time he decided to take a cab. He didn't want to arrive late and sweaty.

Drew was always amazed at the efficiency of the London cabbies. They knew, it seemed to him, every street, lane, path, and building that existed in the huge metropolis. His cabbie that morning was typical: courteous, cheerful, but direct. He asked Drew what part of the States he came from. Drew told him he was a Chicago native but had gone to school in St. Louis. He had lived in a number of places after school, most recently Kuwait, and he would be moving to Cairo soon. The cabbie whistled at that, commenting that he must be in the oil business; they seemed to be the people who usually lived in such awful places. Drew laughed and agreed with him.

"You have to go where the oil is, and usually the oil is found in hell holes all over the world!"

In what seemed a matter of minutes the cab pulled over in front of the main entrance on Thornhaugh Street, close to Russell Square. "Here you are governor, the main entrance to the school. If you don't mind me asking, gov, what would an oilman be doing at the School of Oriental and African Studies?"

Drew laughed, "I'm not exactly sure myself, but my company thinks I should learn something about Egypt since I'm going to live there for a long time."

"Well gov, my advice to you is to keep your hands in your pockets. My brother was there during the war and he says that the Gippos have got sticky fingers; you know what I mean?"

Drew laughed. He thanked the driver for his advice and handed him a five-pound note. "Keep the change mate." *Thank God for the Yanks,* the cabbie thought. *Big tippers they are. Well, they are all rich, aren't they?*

Drew thought the school looked like a University of London school should look: beautiful stonework and some gracious age to it. *Very impressive,* he thought. He went into the lobby and told the receptionist that he was to meet with Miss Rose in room 204. The receptionist looked like she had been there from the beginning, whenever that was. Her graying black hair was tied up in a bun that, combined with the wrinkles and the thick spectacles, gave her the aura of an old spinster. She didn't smile, and when she talked she forced the words out through clenched lips. She acknowledged that she would call Professor Rose to let her know that a Mr. Cahill was on his way up. She pointed to a mahogany staircase and told Drew that Room 204 was up those stairs and to the left. Drew thanked her. He took the stairs two at a time.

The door to room 204 was ajar. Drew looked in and saw a tall, slim woman standing in front of a flip chart, with her back to him. He knocked on the door, and she turned.

"Mr. Cahill, I presume. I am Milledufleur Rose. Welcome to my school."

CHAPTER 6

The Arrangement

SHE SAT AT her desk reading the papers her students had turned in for an assignment she had given them three weeks earlier: to argue whether or not Stanley Lane-Poole's 1898 publication "Saladin" (el-Melik en Nasir Salah-ed-din Yusif ibn Ayyub) was relevant to the current situation in the Middle East. She was now through more than half of the papers and smiled as she determined there was a pattern to the essays.

Her class of twenty-four was composed of six Jews, five Arabs, three Americans, and the balance Britons. To a person all of the Jews dealt harshly with Saladin's embrace of Jihad, and suggested a relationship between that act and the Arab world's violent opposition to the existence of an Israeli state in what the Arabs considered Arab land, Palestine. Most of these students alluded to the rise of the Islamic Brotherhood in Egypt as a direct result of the belief in Jihad. The position of the Arab students was generally that Saladin was a magnificent warrior who was munificent in victory, as was exhibited by his treatment of the citizens of Jerusalem in his conquest of that Christian Kingdom. *This all in the fine tradition of Arab behavior,* Milly noted wryly to herself. Although he was a devout Muslim, Saladin was not an Arab but a Kurd. On the other hand, the Britons in the class were united in their opinion that Saladin was a military genius, and they saw no relationship between the glory and ability of Saladin and the inept performance of the Arab nations' military in modern times. These varied positions did not surprise Milly. Philosophically she was closer to the position of the Britons than to either the Jewish or Arab position. She had some, but not much, sympathy with the Jewish perspective. Though she was technically a Jewess, she felt no emotional bond with Israel or Jews either as a race or religion. She considered herself English and a British subject. Period.

Milly did not care what her students' leanings were; she was only interested in the logic of their analysis and ability to elucidate their arguments in the English language. She was Milledufleur Rose, English, hedonistic, and a superb academic. She was fluent in the languages of the Middle East and could read Aramaic. She was an expert in her field. No less a personage than Bernard Lewis assured her that she was one of the most qualified experts in the history of the Middle East, past and present. She had only two passions in her life: her work, and her pursuit of gratification. She was a confirmed atheist and worshipped only at the altar of pleasure, her pleasure, and she was a devoted Anglophile; nothing else in her mind. She wanted to finish the papers before five o'clock. It was Friday and she was eagerly anticipating an evening at her favorite club, the Ménage a Trois.

Involuntary visions of the evening's pursuits brought her tingles of pleasure, which she quickly forced out of her mind. Her task at hand had to be completed. There would be time enough later to plot out her approach for the night. She was anticipating a fresh quarry of visiting businessmen at the

Ménage tonight.

Just as she finished evaluating and grading her last paper, the phone rang. She allowed it to ring several times while she put the papers aside before picking up the receiver. "Allo," she said harshly, annoyed at the interruption.

"Miss Rose?" asked the caller.

"Yes. And who might you be?" she uttered flatly.

"Oh, pardon my lapse of decorum. This is Kim David calling. Given your profession I believe you may know of me," he intoned in a proper British public school accent.

"If you are the Kim David who is the purported Number Two at the Mossad, then I have heard of you. Are you that Kim David?"

After pausing a moment for effect, he responded in a dramatic tone, "I am that Kim David."

"If you are that Kim David then you could tell me who is the Mossad Director General and your direct superior."

"Miss Rose, as you and countless others also know, Yitzhak Hofi is the head of the Mossad. I'm also certain that if you are trying to determine my veracity, I have a better way."

"And what might that be?"

"Meet me tonight, say, at the Ménage a Trois, about eight. You most likely have seen photos of me, and, if not, I am prepared to offer proof when we meet tonight. I have some serious matters I would like to discuss with you, so shall we say we have a date?"

Milly was anxious. *Why does he want to meet me?* she wondered. *And how would he know that the Ménage is one of my places. Of course! It's evident. He is a spy. They are very thorough,* she thought. "Mr. David, I plan to be at the Ménage about eight. I assume you will recognize me."

"Then it's a date. I'll be there early and save a table. It will be at the back, away from the bandstand." The phone went dead.

Well, she thought, *he gets right to the point. He's efficient.* She checked the time. *I'll have to hurry and finish here, then get back to my flat so I can change into something appropriate for my adventure.* She did know what David looked like, and if he was as handsome in person as in photographs then who knows, maybe... She didn't finish the thought but she felt enflamed by the possibilities. As far as she knew she had never had sex with a spy, and the more she thought about this unlikely encounter the more excited she became. She made short work of clearing her desk, bounced out of her office, and hailed a taxi. She had some work to do.

As soon as he cradled the phone David picked up the file he had been reviewing. The file was labeled

"Milledufleur Rose." It was only a short walk from the Connaught Hotel to their meeting place, so he went through her file one more time. He wondered if she had any inkling of what they knew about her or had any idea of what he wanted from her. He felt that in the hours before their meet she would run the options, and he concluded that she would not be shocked by his proposition. She was, after all, very, very bright.

Milly was putting on the finishing touches of her makeup and preening in front of the full length mirror. She smiled at her reflection as she smoothed the black cocktail dress, running her hands over her well-shaped body. Two thin black straps supported the bodice which left little to the imagination, and her black hair was pulled up and fastened with a simple clip adorned with six diamonds. Milly knew that her olive complexion was enhanced by her black hair and the black dress. She turned from one side to the other and uttered approvingly to herself "Not bad." She was ready. She pulled on white silken gloves before opening the door to her flat. She was eagerly anticipated the evening. *Who knows where it will go,* she thought. She also thought that she did have some ideas.

David sat at the desk in his hotel room and browsed through the file on Milledufleur Rose compiled by

Mossad field agents in London. The file had been opened the summer of 1970 at Kim David's request. The Mossad had been aware of Milledufleur from even before her birth. Milledufleur's father was Michael Ronne-Lotz and her mother was Yolande Sabbaagh, and they both had been Mossad agents. They had met and had a love affair, which resulted in Yolande's pregnancy, when they were both operatives in Egypt. David remembered the concern this had caused in the Mossad. Ronne-Lotz was a top operative in Egypt, as was Yolande. The complication was that Ronne-Lotz had a wife in Tel Aviv in the then-new nation of Israel. Yolande had been thrice married, but had been widowed a year earlier. When he had learned of the pregnancy, Ronne-Lotz refused to leave his wife and had demanded Yolande have an abortion. She had refused and fled to London were her mother lived. Her mother, Rachel Gheriani, had moved to London from Cairo in 1932 after her husband, Elie Gheriani, had died. There she'd met and married John Rose, a socially prominent and wealthy dentist. Yolande had died in childbirth, leaving Milledufleur an orphan, and, technically, a bastard. Rachel Rose had persuaded John Rose to adopt Milledufleur, and he had readily assented in order to appease his much younger and sultry wife.

Kim David knew Michael Ronne-Lotz and was

aware of his refusal to take any responsibility for Yolande's condition, and, indeed, that Ronne-Lotz had confided to David and others in the Mossad that he felt he was probably not the father. It was true that Yolande had many sexual encounters in the course of her spying for Israel, but most who knew the story were of the opinion that Ronne-Lotz was indeed the father. However, the Mossad had decided not to take any action against him as he was of critical importance to their network. This was a decision which later proved fortunate; his contribution to Israel's knowledge of the Egyptian Air Force was critical to Israel's success in the 1967 Arab War.

Rachel Rose despised Ronne-Lotz. Milledufleur knew nothing of her father until she was sixteen, and from the moment she had learned the story of her birth her grandmother's venom was shared by Milledufleur. According to the report she refused to acknowledge any relationship to her father. The knowledge, however, did shape Milledufleur's life. According to the report, she had developed a cold personality as well as other characteristics, including her sexual behavior, which had resulted in, among other things, an inability to form committed close personal relationships – particularly with men. The report went into detail about her sexual escapades, as well as her significant academic success. She had become one of the foremost experts in Middle East affairs.

David knew the survival of Israel depended in large measure on the success of Israel's spies and their recruitment was one of his highest priorities, especially the recruitment of women. He knew he was the best recruiter – an opinion shared by most – and he felt confident that Milledufleur Rose could become one of their best. It would be a significant challenge but he had supreme confidence in his abilities, especially with women.

He paused to look at the many photos of Milledufleur Rose. *What a beauty!* There was no doubt in his mind she was the product of a father who was half Dane and half German Jew. Her mother was a Turkish-Circassian Jew, raised in Egypt. David lingered over the photos of Milledufleur playing tennis; they revealed a superb body toned by vigorous exercise. He smiled as he thought of the job at hand.

He was comfortable at the Connaught Hotel, particularly the attic on the top floor. He loved the spacious high-ceiling room; it gave him plenty of pacing territory to aid in his thought processes. He was now looking out over Grosvenor Square, the Eisenhower Memorial, and both the American and Canadian Embassies as he mentally went through the argument he had prepared for the recruitment of Milly.

He was confident, and he was eager to begin. *Well,* he thought, *it is time to arrange my wardrobe.*

He felt the dining room at the Connaught would provide an excellent environment for his recruiting pitch. After giving her some of his personal history as well as the mission of the Mossad, he would suggest they have dinner at the Connaught; in that environment he would advance his closing argument. He didn't anticipate he would close her with one meeting; that was why he had booked the hotel for three nights. He felt, however, he would have an excellent sense of success by the end of the evening, no matter what time that might be.

She was greeted at the door by the Maitre d', obsequious as usual. "Miss Rose, welcome back to the Ménage, you are as lovely as ever."

She gave him a condescending smile. "Why that is good to hear Arnod." *Or whatever your name might be, you goose,* she thought.

"Miss Rose, there is a gentleman waiting for you; he did not give his name, but he has taken a table at the back. Let me escort you," he finished with an exaggerated bow.

As was usual at the Ménage, the lighting was dim and the pervading odor was of oriental spices with a hint of myrrh the most prominent. As the owner of the club intended, the lighting, aroma, and strobe effect reflecting from the revolving crystal chandeliers combined to produce a clearly sensual atmosphere; as many times as she had been there each new visit pricked up her sense of arousal anew.

As they neared his table she was able to bring into focus details of Kim David's countenance, and, as he rose at her approach, she stopped about three paces in front of him. With only a nod of acknowledgment Milledufleur Rose studied Kim David thoroughly. What she observed was a trim man, at least a hand taller than she, with light brown hair neatly parted to the left, and eyes of sky blue. *So much for the typical Jewish look,* she thought. He wore a navy-blue suit, white shirt, and blood-red tie, with a neatly-trimmed mustache that added to his continental appearance. *He could be an advertisement for Savile Row.* He smiled revealing a perfect set of teeth, and nodded to welcome her. *Much better than his black and white photographs,* she thought. *He is electric!*

She closed the three paces as she concluded her examination, and proffered her hand in such a manner that only a boor could resist taking it into his and greeting it with a kiss. Kim David was not a boor. As he applied his lips to her silken glove, his eyes smiled at her as she formally introduced herself: "Milledufleur Rose, Mr. David, and I do hope it will be my pleasure." She held his eyes as if she was searching for a glimpse of his soul as he continued to hold her hand.

"Miss Rose. We meet at last."

He directed her to a place on the paisley settee, next to where he had been seated before he'd risen to greet her. She sat and very carefully smoothed her black dress so as to expose a portion of her legs above the knee.

She then smiled and fixed on his eyes. "You say that as if it was inevitable that we were to meet. Like kismet."

"Perhaps it is kismet; we shall see," he responded with a broad smile and tilt of his head. "Thank you for meeting me tonight on such short notice."

"Not a problem. As you well know, I was coming here anyway. As you also well know, my Fridays are special to me. So please get to the point. What do you want with me?"

She is spectacular, he thought. *She has animal magnetism!* What struck him especially, however, was the cold glare of her dark eyes. She could smile with her lips, but her eyes were flat. Was it hate he saw, or was it just contempt? Maybe it was both. She was beautiful, sensual, and distant, almost frightening, at the same time. *She will be perfect,* he thought. "Could I interest you in a drink? It would give us a chance to relax and get to know each other better."

"You know what I drink; I'm sure that is also covered in your brief. It is isn't it?" She took a pack of Players from her petite black bag and slowly tapped one out, put it between her lips, and lit it with a match. For an instant the smell of sulfur invaded the pleasant odor of the club. She tilted her head and exhaled the smoke upward to let it escape to the ceiling. The smoke wafted as a cloud toward the heavens. She stared at him as if to say "So, what is it?"

David smiled at her and motioned to the waiter hovering nearby. "A G&T for the lady, Bombay Sapphire, and I'll have a whiskey, Oban, neat." The waiter acknowledged and was quickly off to fetch the drinks for his customers. The noise level of the Ménage was rapidly increasing as the denizens of the club made their way. Most of the new arrivals, male and female, came in as singles; women in cocktail dresses with plunging necklines and men dressed in conservative business suits were the order of the day. An occasional couple wandered in, but they were clearly the exception.

"So, you do have a file on me. What do you know about me?"

"Everything and nothing. We know what you do, what you've done, but we're not sure about the why, your motivations. We have some ideas, but we are only guessing." He smiled as he directed the smoke away from his face. "I think I have a fair notion."

"So you know everything and nothing about me, and I know who you are and I know of the agency you are with. I don't know exactly how spies operate, but I do know of some of the gritty results. Like the tracking down and killing of the Palestinians who murdered the Israeli Olympic athletes in Munich in '72. They found them in Beirut and shot them one by one. That is what you do, isn't it? You are assassins, right?"

David paused as the waiter brought their drinks. The noise level, to his delight, was steadily increasing. He took his glass and raised it to hers. "Cheers. Here is to a long relationship."

She stared coolly into her eyes. *So, they want me to do something for them. How preposterous!* she thought. She felt Kim David was an extremely attractive and urbane man. If he didn't have an agenda and she'd met him only by chance...! Well, he was better than the majority of her conquests. She sipped her drink. "Care to dance?"

The band was playing a muted version of Cole Porter's 'Night and Day'. He smiled as he took her hand and led her to the dance floor. He pulled her close as they blended together and began to move with the music and glide across the floor. They pressed closer and closer against each other, and for a few moments they seemed oblivious to everything except the merging of their bodies.

She slightly touched his ear with her tongue as she whispered. "You are a lovely dancer Mr. David."

He shuddered involuntarily as he felt her moist tongue and trembled as she pressed him closer for a few seconds he forgot what he was here to do. She was overwhelmingly sensual.

"Miss Rose you are totally lovely!" They continued exploring the crevices of their bodies slowly, but with increasing intensity, while they danced. Only their clothing stood in the way.

The song ended and he led her back to the table. They were both aroused and oblivious to any of the eyes upon them.

As they sat he kept his hand gently squeezing her leg while gazing into her eyes as she rubbed his other hand with both of hers. Finally he edged away slowly. "Milly, I have a proposal to make. But before I do I would like to put the proposal into some perspective, and this isn't a place we can talk. I suggest we do this over dinner. The Connaught has a wonderful dining room, an exquisite chef, and an excellent wine list, and I've booked a table in a quiet nook that will allow us to converse privately. I hope you will accept."

She parted her lips and lingered for an instant before replying "You are a seducer Mr. Kim David."

***

He'd spent half of his life flying from one time zone to another, and he had largely overcome 'jet lag' by a diligent application of common sense precautions: sparse consumption of alcohol, lots of water, regular exercise. This morning Kim easily woke just before 6 a.m. GMT, but instead of opening his eyes he lay still, thinking, remembering. He knew she wasn't in the bed; he'd heard her leave shortly before one a.m. She wasn't in the bed, but her scent was; it floated in his hotel room. He couldn't identify the perfume by brand, but he did recognize the aroma she wore; a heavy, musky fragrance which complemented her appearance. As he'd known she would, she had gotten ready to leave quietly. He hadn't wanted to break the mood that had prevailed throughout the evening, so he had feigned sleep as she'd slipped out of his room. Now, even though she was no longer there, he could still feel her presence, as well as smell it.

She was excitable. She was very physical. She was very unusual. He hadn't known what to expect, but what had transpired had surprised him. He was overwhelmed by the ferocity of her lovemaking. She had become trance-like during the encounter, and had screamed her way into orgasm, which she had induced with her fingers after Kim had, reluctantly, released in a wave of spasmodic relief.

When he'd questioned her about her postcoital masturbation, she informed him it was the only way she could climax. When he'd asked the obvious follow up question, "Why go through the preliminaries then; why not just go for it?" she'd smiled as she told him that without the penetration she could not bring herself to orgasm. Watching her do this to herself had excited him to the point where he'd needed to take her once again, which he did with a passion he had never before experienced.

He rose and donned the white terrycloth robe provided by the Connaught. He rang room service for coffee then picked up the note addressed to him on the desk. He wondered when she'd written it. *She must have night vision,* he mused. He opened the note and read.

My Dear Kim,

You are a delicious man, but you already know that. The drinks, dancing and dinner were only surpassed by what topped off the evening. Your arguments as to why I should align myself with the agency you so ably represent were not without effect. Your sense of history and your logic made an impression and have me leaning towards accepting your offer. I agree that the Arab argument depicting the Palestinians as victims of a cruel West exploiting the Palestinians, especially the Muslim Palestinians, is historically specious. As we agree, the historical reality is that the Islamic world was built by war and blood as it destroyed the existing Christian civilization. After the seventh century when Mohammed and the Arabs came roaring out of the desert bent on jihad it was the Greco-Christian empire that stood in its way until it was destroyed by the Turkish Muslim empire.

The anti Israeli arguments are fallacious in their attempt to define a geographical and historical moral superiority of people called Palestinians in a geographical area named Palestine by the conquering Romans to the right to the land itself. There never was a state or government of Palestine. Palestine was the name given to that sector of the Roman Empire, following the Romans that area called Palestine was populated by various ethnic peoples who have shared the land which is now Israel. The Israeli state was created in 1948 by the U.N. and immediately recognized by President Harry Truman. Israel then constituted a good part of the area called Palestine. The Jews have no less a claim and may even have a superior claim to this land by virtue of history and actuality. History has chronicled the various ethnic bodies who have shared this land now called Israel. The Jews have no less a claim, and may even have a superior claim on this land by virtue of actuality.

Your most compelling argument, though, concerns the tenuous situation of the Jews in Israel. Since the Jewish state of Judea was destroyed by the Romans in A.D. 70, Jews have not fared well in diaspora. Without a Jewish state in Israel it is more than probable the Jew may very well disappear from this world. Israel may not survive, but it does have a chance. And being a part of this effort to survive as a part of Israel does have a sense of excitement that appeals to my competitive nature. I believe I do want to be a part of this adventure.

I look forward to meeting with you this evening; I do have some questions and issues that you may resolve. I suspect the nature of our encounter this evening will be different in tenor.

Till then,

Milly

Since he'd felt his recruiting pitch last night had gone well, he was pleased with her note. He knew tonight's meeting would only be a formality; he had landed his target. He knew the challenge and the chance to be a member of a very elite, accomplished group was the hook for Milledufleur Rose. Tonight she would insist that he be her operative, and he could handle that through a series of alternates as needed. He had no illusion that his sexual prowess had anything to do with her recruitment. According to the report she would have sex with anyone who could mount an attack, but she never had sex with the same person twice. One of her rules. He thought she might have to relent on this rule once she was working for the Mossad, but he didn't anticipate any real problem. She would do what was necessary. He was a bit surprised, however, that she hadn't raised any issue about Ronne-Lotz, her father. That might be broached tonight. If so, he was ready.

He then put in a call to let Hofi know he would be going to Morocco a day earlier than planned, as he was wrapping up this business tonight; Hofi, who had questioned his ability to recruit Rose. *Another opportunity to rub salt into Hofi's crude ego!*

CHAPTER 7

Milly's Lineage

BENJAMIN MEIR LIT another cigarette. Milledufleur Rose was two weeks away from completing the grueling mental and physical training that made the Mossad the lethal, feared, and most effective Israeli agency, dedicated solely to the survival of the Jewish state, and he was completing his final review of her performance. He inhaled deeply as he pondered what he could write that would not be just a repeat of the outstanding reviews that had filled her folders over the past 11 months. It was not in his nature to give anyone a perfect score, and he felt he had to find some negatives to tone down the final evaluation.

Meir was a former agent who had operating mainly in Europe and the U.K. before he had become the department head in charge of Mossad training. He'd lost track of the number of agents who had successfully completed the course during his ten years running the program; it had to be tens of dozens, at least, and many more than that had washed out. This one, though, stood out; she could be one of the best ever, and that opinion was shared by the entire training staff. As easily as she breathed she could decapitate a man just as he was beginning to climax on top of her. She had nerves of steel and ice water ran in her veins, of that he was sure.

This train of thought was interrupted by the buzzing of his private phone. Kim David was one of the few who had Meir's restricted number.

"Benjamin, it's Kim; I need a few minutes of your time to talk to you about Mme. Rose."

"Certainly Kim; you did recruit her and you will be her controller. Are you going to stop by, or handle this by phone?"

"I'll be there in ten minutes. This is a sensitive issue. It involves Michael Ronne-Lotz."

"Holy shit! Lotz?"

"Yes," said David, "Lotz. You knew him fairly well back then."

"I did, but I haven't seen or heard from him in nearly ten years! He and his wife were arrested for espionage in Egypt after the '67 war; we swapped four Egyptians prisoners for their release. Obviously that notoriety ended his use as an agent, and he and his wife returned to Israel. They settled in Haifa, where he operated a trading company, and I hear things have not gone very well for him since then."

Ten minutes after their telephone conversation Kim David was escorted into Meir's office, where they greeted each other eagerly as the friends they almost were. Kim apologized about the very short notice and accepted Benjamin's offer of some very strong Arabic coffee before presenting his rationale for the meeting.

"Benjamin, let me get to the point quickly. Milledufleur is an outstanding candidate for field work. I already have an important assignment waiting for her return to London, and plans for follow-on assignments in Western Europe and the U.K." Meir nodded silently as Kim continued. "As you may have heard, her mother, Yolande Sabbagh, contended her father is Michael Ronne-Lotz. Michael has always denied this, but we believe Yolande's contention."

Meir didn't show any emotion at this brick David had just dropped on his desk. He fumbled with a pen as he silently digested the information. He thought for several minutes before replying.

"As a result of their work in Egypt, both of them became heroes in Israel. However, both of them also had reputations for living on the fast side of life, so it could be possible. Yolande did have a number of affairs as she pursued her craft." He frowned and slowly shook his head. "But, with Lotz; I wouldn't know. Michael was married to Sara Marzuk and they had one child. Sami was killed in the '73 war, and Sara died shortly thereafter. Michael remains, a fading hero of the '67 war, alone, and not well off." Meir looked questioningly at David. "Kim you didn't come here just to tell me that Lotz could be Milledufleur's father. What is your point? Obviously Yolande is her mother, but Yolande died in childbirth, and I know that Milledufleur was adopted by her Grandmother and her English husband."

Kim David picked up the story. "That's a matter of record. Rachel spared no expense providing her granddaughter with an excellent education and she used her influence to make Milledufleur a member of the faculty of the SOAS of London University; at Rachel's urging, John Rose donated large sums to the SOAS. Then when Bernard Lewis was at the

SOAS, Rachel befriended Dr. Lewis and arranged for Milledufleur to spend time working with him. When Milledufleur graduated with a Doctorate, her appointment to the faculty there was a fait accompli.

"Her Grandmother literally shaped Milledufleur's life, for better and for worse. Part of the 'worse' was brainwashing about Michael. Rachel detested him. We believe there could be some negative psychological feelings about our Agency that Milledufleur may harbor as a result of this 'brainwashing' by her grandmother, and I feel a meeting between her and her father could be beneficial. I think you agree that she is outstanding, and we want to remove any emotional obstacles that might exist and could get in the way of her performance."

Meir wasn't exactly sure where Kim was going with this train of thought, but it was apparent that if Kim had a concern, it was warranted. Meir said, "So you want Michael and Milly to have a meeting? That is your call. But when?"

"In an hour if you agree."

"Certainly I agree. Where do you plan to have this meeting?"

"A neutral spot: a bar called the King David, a mile or so from the Training Headquarters."

***

Kim had met with Michael on several occasions recently to lay the groundwork to convince Michael that meeting Milly Rose was not only in his own interest, but was also – as a loyal Israeli – in the interest of their country. Michael's father was a Danish/Swedish national who became a German following his marriage to a German Jew, Marlene Behnke of Mannheim, Michael's mother. Michael's father, Casper Ronne-Lotz, immigrated to Germany before the First World War, and continued his export/import business in Germany, where he also joined the German army and served as an officer. Michael was born in Mannheim in 1921.

Casper's Danish brother had immigrated to the United States at the turn of the century and he provided an entrée for his brother to represent several growing U.S. manufacturing companies. Casper's trade with the United States was the bulk of his firm's business and his trading company was reasonably profitable.

Casper Ronne-Lotz travelled frequently to the U.S. on business, and it was on one of his trips to New York that Casper contracted pneumonia and died. Marlene Ronne-Lotz (nee Behnke) became a widow at age 33. That was in 1932. The growing concern of a number of German Jews due to the ascendancy of the National Socialist (NAZI) party and their leader Adolph Hitler was not lost on Marlene, and she soon became convinced that the Nazis would turn on the Jews and accelerate the anti-Jewish programs that were already in progress.

Her uncle and cousins had emigrated to Palestine, and they encouraged Marlene to emigrate as well. She believed that there would be a Jewish State in Israel, so she, with the help of her relatives in Palestine and International Jewish organizations, emigrated to Haifa with her 12-year-old son, Michael. Events that followed proved her decision had been a wise one.

Michael received an excellent education, and in 1948 he became a member of the newly-formed Mossad. He was fluent in German, French, Arabic, and Hebrew. He was educated in military tactics, especially aerial warfare and engineering. He stood 6'5", had a muscular frame and Nordic good looks, black close-cropped hair, and dark-blue eyes. Michael Ronne-Lotz had the ideal attributes to pose as an ex-German Luftwaffe officer when he was sent by the Mossad to Egypt in 1962.

It was largely due to Ronne-Lotz's activity in Cairo that the location of the Egyptian Air Force was acquired by the Israelis. The subsequent destruction of the Egyptian Air Force by Israel assured the Israeli victory in the Six Day War of 1967, and Ronne-Lotz became a national hero in Israel. However, this was to be his high water mark. As a result of his later arrest by the Egyptians, both his career and his life were now in decline.

Michael was not sure what benefit, if any, would come from a meeting with this modern day version of Mata Hari. Sure he'd known her mother. Yolande was an Israeli agent operating in Egypt at the same time he was beginning his assignment in Egypt. She was beautiful, intelligent, and a woman who had many lovers – as did most of the female Mossad agents. He knew that Yolande had ascribed her pregnancy to him, but in truth, it could have been any one of her many lovers.

He despised Rachel Rose. He was sure she had filled her granddaughter's head with many sordid tales about him. He knew her as Rachel Gheriani, then the wife of the Egyptian-Italian Jew Elie Gheriani. Following his death, Rachel had trapped John Rose, many years her senior, into what became a very lucrative arrangement for her. She was hardly the faithful, obeying wife of an aging British socialite. She had many lovers, the younger the better so the stories went.

Michael had a high degree of respect for Kim David, and out of this regard he had finally agreed to meet with Mme. Rose. According to Kim, Milledufleur Rose would be a first class agent for the Mossad, and certainly now, as ever, Israel's survival was dependent upon a formidable Mossad. If his meeting with her could help, how could he refuse David's entreaties.

Kim didn't have many obstacles to overcome in order to get Milledufleur to agree to meet with Michael Ronne-Lotz. He agreed with the Agency's psychologists that this meeting could have a positive effect on her. He couldn't be wrong.

***

Kim said his pleasantries and took leave of Meir. It was a beautiful clear day in the Tel Aviv environs as he picked up Milledufleur and drove the very short distance to the King David bar. He escorted Milly inside. It was early and the King David was sparsely populated. Kim greeted the bartender, Daniel, a Jewish immigrant and recent arrival from Brooklyn, who took them to a booth at the extreme rear of the bar. Michael Ronne-Lotz rose as Kim made the introduction.

"Milly, this is Michael Ronne-Lotz; Michael, Milledufleur Rose. The Agency and I appreciate you both agreeing to this meeting. You both know some things about each other, but there may be a lot more it could be useful to learn. I'll be with my friend from Brooklyn at the bar. Take whatever time you want; there is no time limit, and I'll be here to talk to you when you've finished."

Kim turned and headed for the bar and his new friend. From the new and the old Mossad agents Kim knew that, because of the distance of his perch at the bar he wouldn't hear a peep – unless, of course, they began screaming at each other. However, he was nearly certain that would not be the case.

Milly and Michael stood examining each other silently for what seemed like a very long time. Michael was completely taken aback. It had been more than 30 years since he had seen her mother, and, unless his memory was really faulty, the woman before him was a near-perfect copy of Yolande. Milly had her mother's classic beauty, with facial features that could only be called outstanding: from her lustrous black hair and prominent forehead to her aquiline nose and full red lips surrounding a perfect mouth inviting and sensuous. Her slender neck flowed gracefully into a body both athletic and fully female. The only difference he could see was that Milly was 4 or 5 inches taller than her mother had been. Aside from that single feature, she was a beautiful carbon copy. He wondered if her height difference was the result of nutrition, or genetics.

What Milly observed was an extremely attractive man. She knew he was approaching seventy but he appeared closer to sixty, with sparkling eyes and smile to match, and displaying well-formed and still-white teeth. His black hair was softened with silver highlights and graying at the temples, which did not at all diminish his good looks. *What a handsome man, even at his age!* she thought. However, she could not recognize anything of him in herself...except, maybe, her own black hair – and her height. *But that doesn't mean anything!*

"Please?" Michael motioned for her to sit, and Milly did so gracefully as she smoothed the rather plain, courtesy-of-the-Mossad, gown she wore. They sat silently reviewing each other, as if to ensure the initial impressions would hold. Michael was first to break the silence. "This is a bit awkward for me, Milledufleur...or, do you prefer Milly?"

She smiled and fastened her gaze on him as if to re-inspect his face. "People usually do call me Milly, except Grandmother Rose." Michael winced visibly as she mentioned Rachel Rose, and his reaction did not go unnoticed.

"As I said, this is awkward for me; however I couldn't refuse David's request. I've known Kim for a long time, and I have enormous respect for him as a man, a fellow Jew, and as a member of the Mossad. He has deservedly advanced in that agency that I am proud to have been a part of at one time. He tells me you possess the attributes of an outstanding field agent, and if Kim believes this, I am certain it is so. As you well know our survival as a Jewish homeland is precarious and we need people of your caliber." He hesitated very briefly before continuing, "I must say, you are a taller version of your mother."

"So you did know my mother."

"I did. She was an Israeli agent operating in Egypt. I was posing as an ex-Luftwaffe officer who had escaped from the allies after the war, and who had then managed, courtesy of other German officers, to take up residence in Cairo. Yolande had no connection with my mission; however, on occasion our paths crossed in Cairo. She was working seductions on several Egyptian bureaucrats. The social life in Egypt was wide open and very active at that time, and she was an extremely attractive woman." Michael smiled. "You, young lady, are a near carbon copy."

Milly acknowledged the compliment, then rested her arms on the table in front of her and leaned in closer.

"Michael, I never had the opportunity to know

my mother for myself; I only know her as Grandmother Rose spoke of her. Tell me how you saw her... not her physical appearance, but more: What interested her? What did she talk about? What did she like? What kinds of things did she do? How did she act? Was she cheerful, or was she morose? Was she happy?"

And then Milly stopped.

Michael was startled by the intensity he had heard in her voice and now saw in her eyes as she stared into his. He lowered his eyes to his clasped hands on the tabletop directly in front of him. He needed to think. Milly sat still and silent, watching. Michael finally took a deep breath and looked up.

"Your request...it took me by surprise, and I needed to think if I could respond. For the most part I knew your mother as a fellow agent – a colleague, so to speak – and our meetings were infrequent, their tone suited to the people in the vicinity and the roles we were playing." He hesitated, then continued, "There was only one instance in which we spent time together as just ourselves, and I don't know if that is the kind of thing you would want me to tell you about."

She spoke quietly, just two words: "Tell me."

Michael nodded and sat back. Milly got comfortable in her chair. She smiled ever so slightly.

Michael sighed and began his story.

Both Michael and Yolande traveled out of Egypt frequently, and they had both spent time in Zurich in 1945: Michael was squiring Egyptian Air Force officers around Zurich, while Yolande was enmeshed in a tryst with Khamis Hashem, the Egyptian Deputy Minister of Finance. Hashem was one of several Egyptian bureaucrats from whom she bled information. On that day Michael had met Yolande purely by accident. Zurich was, in reality, a small town, and they were both staying at the Widder Hotel. The Widder was a unique private hotel within the walls of nine historic homes in the Old Town, close to the Bahnhofstrasse. The rooms were large and well-appointed, and each had a loft where the bedrooms were located, and the large living areas were furnished with comfortable overstuffed sofas and chairs. The rooms were designed for long stays and for entertaining. Near the hotel there was a wide selection of restaurants and bars with live music.

He'd checked in and was being escorted through the lobby by the bellhop; Yolande was snuggled into an overstuffed sofa perusing a fashion magazine. She looked up as they passed in front of her, and called out to him. "Michael, this is a surprise!" His own look of surprise turned to pleasure as he recognized the ravenous dark-haired beauty. He motioned the bellhop to wait, and returned her greeting. He asked if she also was staying at the Widder. "Or are you simply meeting someone here?" Yolande closed the magazine and placed it on the table alongside the sofa. "I checked in earlier this morning. I have a meeting tomorrow, but I have little to do today," she nodded toward the abandoned magazine, "as you can see." She smiled up at him. "I've been considering having lunch, and then exploring the shops."

"That sounds like a practical idea. If you want, I could join you for lunch – we are both being paid for by the organization – and I promise I will not ask you who you are here to exploit."

"And I won't ask you." She gave him a brief mischievous grin. "Lunching together does sound inviting, but no business talk; just idle chit chat. Why don't you drop off your luggage then join me; I will wait here. I'll be thinking of an exotic restaurant where we can spend time eating, drinking, and maybe flirting a bit."

Michael was hardly flustered, but his interest in Yolande was rising to a new level. *Well,* he thought, *this could be an interesting afternoon.* He realized he was famished, and he was curious. He quickly changed and hurried back to the lobby, where Yolande lounged awaiting his return.

"You look comfortable young lady. Are you certain

you don't want to stay put and have a nap?"

"Absolutely not; I plan to put this idle time to good use! Furthermore, with the help of this wonderful hotel staff I have booked a table for us at the Burgli, and it's only a short walk from here, at Kilchbergstrasse 15. They tell me it has a gorgeous garden and a lovely view of Lake Zurich, and is especially charming in the summer months. I am also told the menu is exquisite, in particular their veal dishes."

It was a beautiful summer day, and Yolande took every opportunity to comment on the buildings, the businesses, people they were passing, as they strolled to the Burgli. When they arrived they were taken to a table for two under a gorgeous crystal chandelier at the rear of the restaurant, looking out over the garden and the picture-perfect lake. The room was small and exquisitely furnished, and at this hour the lunch crowd had departed. Only one couple, an older man with a much younger companion, remained, and it didn't seem like they were even aware there was anyone besides themselves in the dining room.

The menu for lunch was extensive, and their menu examination was still in its early stage when Michael asked her if anything struck her fancy.

She lowered her menu and smiled at him. "Actually, this is a rather extensive selection, and I could stand a glass of wine first to get me in the mood."

Michael didn't ask her what she thought the wine would get her in the mood for; he assumed lunch, but as she held his eyes he realized he wasn't all that certain. He signaled the ever-attentive Swiss waiter and asked for a wine list. After a quick review of the selections Yolande chose a 7-year-old Italian Pinot Noir, and Michael gestured that would be his choice as well. Normally he preferred a more full-bodied quaff, but he decided that could come later. As the waiter produced two crystal goblets and poured a tasting sample, Michael motioned he would defer the tasting to his female companion. Yolande nodded her head in approval and the ritual was over quickly.

"If you are not in a hurry, I will give you more time to make your selections," suggested the waiter, and when he had their agreement he bowed and was away in a blink.

"What strikes your fancy, Yolande?"

"It is an excellent menu, Michael, but unless you have some pressing agenda to follow, let's enjoy the wine and then get down to the stress of having to make a selection."

"That suits me fine. I have nothing on this afternoon, so I have only to attend to your needs for the rest of the day."

"Voila! And one never knows what needs might

develop, does one."

Her statement fairly well set the stage for the rest of the day. They opted to share a leg of lamb replete with garden roasted vegetables and sautéed potatoes, with a consumé to start. They slowly consumed the sumptuous platter of food while they talked almost continuously, and as the meal ended they both agreed that, since the wine was so superb they needed to order more – a bottle this time.

They both knew Zurich very well, as well as Switzerland, and they chatted about their favorite places and their favorite activities. It turned out they were both avid sailors and swimmers in the warmer months and addicted skiers in the winter. They were enjoying themselves, and the hours melted away. Several times when she wanted to emphasis this point or that she took his hand and squeezed it, and as the afternoon wore on the taking of his hand evolved into holding his hand. The other patrons had long since quit the premises, and the more wine they consumed the more freely the laughter and outright flirtatiousness flowed.

Finally Yolande suggested they settle their debt with the waiter and stroll a bit. Michael agreed, and they strolled and talked, and enjoyed the fabulous Swiss weather, until they realized the sun had set and they were in front of the Widder Hotel. They entered the lobby and were giving each other a farewell embrace when Yolande asked if he wanted to take her to her room. "I have some very nice wine. We could have a 'day cap.'"

Michael didn't need any more encouragement; he accompanied her to her third floor apartment. He left at 5 a.m. They both needed to prepare for their day's business.

That was the last time Michael saw or spoke with Yolande – until she called him a couple of months later to tell him she was pregnant, and he was the father. He told her he had grave doubts he was the father. He also reminded her that he was married, and implored her – for her own sake – to have an abortion.

Some months later he'd learned she had moved to London to stay with her mother, Rachel Rose, until the child was born. It was a girl. Yolande, however, had died due to complications from childbirth, and Rachel and John Rose had adopted the baby girl. Michael had denied paternity to all he knew and, in fact, had always believed his denials to be truth.

***

Michael's story was ended and they both now sat in silence. He felt inexplicably sad; his heart was beating as though he had been running. Michael closed his eyes. He concentrated on his breathing until he felt relaxed and his heartbeat returned to normal. Then he opened his eyes and looked at Milly. She was staring into the distance, to where Kim David was seated; he was still talking with the bartender from Brooklyn. Michael could not read the look on her face. Suddenly she blinked rapidly, then turned her head and looked at Michael. She sat up straight.

"Michael, I thank you for telling me your story. I'm not sure what Kim intended to be the outcome of our meeting, but I must say I am glad that we have met. You are an Israeli hero, and you are a very erudite and charming man. I never got to know my mother but I know that she was my mother. At this point it doesn't matter to me if you are or are not my father; by now it's a moot point. Under Jewish law the child always assumes the religion of the mother; one always knows who the mother is, but the father could be anyone.

"I am now committed to the agency and to the survival of Israel; nothing will change that. I understand the contribution you have made to the Israeli state by virtue of what you did in the '67 war. You have lost a son and your wife because of a later war with the fucking Arabs, and for that I feel sorrow. Now I will leave."

They both rose. She shook his hand, and he remained standing, watching as she headed back to the bar and Kim David. She nodded to Daniel and told Kim she was finished. "Let us go; there is nothing more for me here."

On the drive back to the training center he probed her about the meeting. "Kim, I don't know what you thought would be achieved by this meeting but my position has not changed. If he is my father I think this meeting will kill him. If he is not my father, I am not interested to find out. At first I was somewhat sympathetic to him, but the more I think of it, if he is – and I suspect he is -- he deserves the misery he is now wallowing in, and I never want to see or hear of him again. If he's not, then who was? Believe me I could care less! I will take care of myself and our cause; fuck everything else!

Kim was silent as they continued their short drive back to the center. Of one thing he was certain. He didn't know Drew Cahill, her first assignment, but he did not think he would be a match for – or, maybe, even survive – this lioness.

Was Kim pleased with what he had set up? On balance, he was. He never had expected this would be a melodramatic reconciliation. A fledgling recognition of who she was and what her mission on this earth was seemed a satisfactory first step.

CHAPTER 8

March 1980

SHE HAD BEEN back from her training in Israel for ten weeks now, and was once again fully immersed in her academic life. It was almost as if the twelve months she'd spent courtesy of the Mossad had never occurred. Her cover story for the sabbatical, that she would be staying and working on Kibbutzim in Israel, had been so well played that she was beginning to feel that was actually what she had done, rather than twelve months of grueling training learning how to defend herself and how to kill, and the myriad mundane tasks of how to communicate, exchange information, and understand the maze of the structure called the Mossad. Her body and mind had never before been tested or abused by the elements as they had been during her ordeal in Israel. She had always prided herself on the condition of her body, but after what she had undergone with the Mossad she knew she was now physically and mentally fit for any challenge, and she yearned to take on whatever they might ask of her. She was more than ready.

Milledufleur stood staring out her office window at the lovely green of Russell Square, just across Thornhaugh Street which ran parallel to the building that housed her office. Recently-planted yellow and red tulips defined the perimeter of the square and provided a bright backdrop for the mallards, geese, and swans floating in the blue-grey ponds. *England, so green, so lovely!* she thought. With a soft radiant sky on a clear day it usually filled her with a pleasure unmatched by any other.

Today she was distracted. The news in the Times that morning was not encouraging for the Israelis: the PLO attacking Northern Israel from Southern Lebanon; Syria's move into Northern Lebanon coalescing with PLO elements was a move that had caught the Mossad off guard. She knew that Bashir and Amine Gemayel, the sons of the old Phalange Christian Party leader, had met with Mossad and Aman people aboard a missile boat in the harbor of Jounieh, north of Beirut. The Israelis were not impressed. More Israeli citizens dead, more casualties. *Oh, Israel! Oh, Israel!* she lamented.

She wondered if there was a connection between the attacks and Kim David's message that he wanted to see her today. She hadn't seen David since...since her seduction. *Or was it his?* she mused. Maybe there wasn't any connection. Maybe he simply wanted to see her – and maybe peace with the Arabs would suddenly break out, and maybe pigs would fly! David's call was not social.

Halfway through her training the Israelis had lost their greatest ally in the region; one month before the signing of the peace treaty with the Egyptians the Shah was deposed and replaced by the Ayatollah Khomeini. Khomeini hated the Jews. He was opposed to the very existence of Israel and was very close to the most radical of Israel's Palestinian enemies. The new regime's Revolutionary Guard had handed over the Israeli Embassy building in Tehran to the PLO, hardly a simple symbolic gesture. The mood in Tel Aviv was that, without the Shah, Iran would aid the PLO. The PLO state in Lebanon had to be neutralized.

She knew the history of the Middle East better than most. It was her profession. She was a professor of Middle Eastern studies at the SOAS College of the University of London. Sykes, Picot, Balfour, Lloyd George, Clemenceau, Bell; these were not just names on a piece of paper, they were the real-life breathing, fornicating, adulterous, scheming, self-righteous people who were the creators of the existing morass called the Middle East. She took no moral stand about the right or wrong of the historical issues surrounding the Middle East and Israel. She concerned herself with the issues and the behavior, not their morality, and of one thing she was certain: Israel's survival was not pre-destined. She believed all human activity was self-serving, or, at least, it was perceived to be even when it was folly. The situation in Lebanon was worse than folly; for Israel it was crucial.

She looked at her Rolex, gold, diamond-studded; thirty minutes before Kim David's arrival. The exquisite *montre* had been a gift from Kim before she'd left for Tel Aviv and the grueling training. The watch was much like Kim: exquisite, and in impeccable taste. *How could an inanimate object take on human-like qualities?* she wondered. *Perhaps it had been produced by artists and artisans who knew innately the traits of the buyer?*

While she waited for Kim's arrival she was entrapped in thoughts, random but still related to Israel. How could Carter, who ostensibly had coerced Begin and Sadat into a peace treaty between Egypt and Israel, stand by – even if he did not encourage – and allow the Revolution of the Ayatollahs and the demise of the Shah? Carter was supposed to be a man of religion. Maybe he equated his Christianity with the radical Islamic fervor of the mullahs. *Not a simple mistake,* she thought, *but a blunder that could approximate the blunders of the Treaty of Versailles.*

Her reverie was interrupted by the ringing of the telephone. "Allo," she answered.

"Professor Rose, you have a visitor," said the guard. "He says he has an appointment, but refuses to give me his name or identification."

She smiled. "Describe him to me. No, wait...let me talk to him."

"Allo," she said. "If this is who I think it is, tell me: what is my most intriguing physical characteristic?"

"Milly, you bloody well know that I will not repeat that in front of this, hmm...gentleman! Just tell him I'm expected!"

In another moment he appeared in front of her opened office door and she rose to meet him midway. She enveloped him with her arms and kissed him incessantly on his cheeks in the French/Arabic way. She stepped back and fiercely gripped his hands in hers as she inspected every pore of his handsome face and stared deeply into his piercing blue eyes. Except for a hint of gray at his temples, his brown hair appeared the same. His perfectly-trimmed mustache also displayed several grays, and underneath his eyes were slightly darkened circles that weren't there the last time they had met. *This man is weary and stressed,* she thought, *and no wonder!*

"You look fabulous Kim!" she lied, smiling widely and slowly nodding her head for emphasis.

He gave her a tired smile and, not lying, said, "Milly, you are even more enchanting than I remember, but, then, how could such a frail thing as a memory etch your beauty accurately."

"Kim, you are a bloody diplomat, but even if you are a bit potty, I love it. Keep the charm-offensive coming; who knows what else could come of it!" she leered naughtily.

"What! Is Mademoiselle Glace – that's what they call you in Tel Aviv, my dear – beginning to melt? Are you teasing me with the chance you will revoke your once, and once only, rule?"

"My dear Kim, I can't believe they called me Miss Ice, *quel dommage* Monsieur! What else did they say about me?" she purred.

"You know perfectly well what they've said about you; it's all in the evaluation report. And you bloody well know your evaluation was more than a bit above top notch: 'The potential to become one of our best field agents...Ice water runs in her veins...she would easily cut the throat of her mother if needed.' You were very impressive, Miss Rose, and you know it!"

She smiled and led him to a blue paisley print chesterfield at the center of her office and motioned for him to sit. She then took the wingback chair adjacent and crossed her legs. With a motion of modesty she smoothed her brown herringbone shirt. "Something to drink?" she inquired.

"Only if it's whiskey; but I suppose the dons frown on that?"

"You silly, you know the dons would never frown on alcohol; it's the lifeblood of the bloody academic life, as they say. What will it be then, a blend or single malt?"

He brightened. "A single malt, three fingers."

"One single malt, coming up!"

She rose and went to the wet bar on the other side of her office. *Poor man,* she thought. *The political infighting must be taking its toll. On top of the current crisis, that fucking crude boor, Hofi, must be giving Kim his backside. Well, the only thing the bureaucrats are united on is the survival of Israel, not the survival of their rivals.*

Survival of the fittest was the self-proclaimed ethic of the agency; there was not an inch of wiggle room surrounded by enemies who had never hesitated in their quest to kill each and every one. Hofi was a boor, but he was also a vicious animal who would do anything to anyone who would harm Israel. Kim was no boor and far from crude, but he could be just as vicious. Sharon and the P.M. knew this and gave it food to fester.

She poured three fingers of whiskey, and took a small glass of sherry for herself. She placed the amber fluid in front of him and steadied herself on his shoulder, applying a slight pressure with her hand as she slid into her chair. They touched glasses in a "Cheers." Although their time together had been brief, she felt exhilarated to be next to him. She watched him as, with eyes closed, he slowly took a long swallow of the whiskey. He sighed, then opened his eyes and edged closer as if to say it was time to get down to business.

Kim reached down and retrieved his tan weather-beaten briefcase. Unzipping the case he removed a dossier, the standard issue of the agency, dull gray, and placed it on the table in front of him. The affixed label had a single word typed on it: "CAHILL".

"Milly, as you probably have guessed, this is not a social call. I could have had someone else from the agency, or even the ministry, meet with you, but this is your first assignment as a *katsha* and you are my contribution; I feel a bit like your mentor." He raised his hand so as to stay her response; he didn't want a dialogue, at least not yet. He needed to give her instructions for her first, and, he hoped, not her last, agency mission.

"This file contains the background and the internal psychological draw up of an American with whom we want you to form a connection. The initial contact has already been arranged and will be very easy. He will be in your BCIU class here for one week. You will have him for three hours per day for five days, and during that time you must befriend him and entrap him. You will then use your abundant feminine wiles to convince him to do you a favor; not a big favor exactly, but one that could pose some...let's say, political exposure for him with the Egyptian bureaucracy, and even within his company."

She took the file proffered to her and began to leaf through the contents. "So, do you want me to ball him, or to kill him?"

"Milly, a little dramatic, what? Of course we don't want you to kill him! We need him – for a while anyway. If you have to ball him – disgusting term – I don't think you will have any misgivings about that; you might even find that could be, ah...pleasing. He is a youngish chap; some would find him attractive. But it is a job; a job that we know you can pull off with aplomb."

"So I am to, as you say, befriend our prize and convince him to do a favor for me. What, exactly, is this favor, and how long do I have to spring the trap on this Yank?"

"He'll arrive in London the beginning of April, and the first week he'll spend primarily in the Getty London office meeting staff, the usual rot. He will begin your course the following week; they want to get that out of the way quickly. He's spent the last three-and-a-half-years in Kuwait including trips all over the Gulf, even to Cairo, so he's not totally groundless about the Middle East. He just needs, or Getty's HR think he needs, an orientation course on Egypt."

She bit playfully on a pencil she had put in her mouth, as if she were contemplating turning the pencil into a gumdrop and slowly sucking the juices from it. "So, it's Egypt. When?"

"Our guess is he will be in Egypt permanently by the fourth quarter of this year. Before that time, he'll be traveling there to clean up loose ends with Getty's concession agreement, so he'll be back and forth with no discernable pattern. However, he will be here for reasonably lengthy stays and that should give you ample time to play your Cleopatra role."

"Which is, my dear Kim?"

"He will be responsible for hiring the Egyptian staff, some eighty people all told; you know the lot, accountants, admin types, geologists, geophysicists. You are to convince him to hire your two cousins. They are geologists now in Iraq, but they will be leaving soon, before Saddam attacks Iran – which we believe will be in early September."

"My cousins? I don't have any cousins, and, es-pecially, not Egyptian ones! And what's this about Iraq?"

"Saddam will attack Iran; the nutter's worried about the even nuttier Shi'a Mullahs. Iran and Iraq having a go at each other will be good for us, and we hope it's a long, drawn out tie. Kim smiled at her. "And we have made for you two highly-qualified geologist 'cousins' that you will convince your dear friend Mr. Cahill to hire."

CHAPTER 9

Sometime in late winter 1979

THE NONDESCRIPT ROOM had no windows and was devoid of all accoutrements: no pictures, no paintings, no memorabilia on the walls. It was simply a rectangle twenty feet by twenty feet with a single, steel door in or out. The military-style tables – found in most military and government offices around the world – were steel grey, and abutted each other, with eight same-style chairs four on each side. A serious-looking gathering of humorless men occupied seven of the chairs. All were senior officers of the Israeli Defense Force. Cigarette smoke was thick as a London fog, the aroma a blend of tobaccos from Turkey, France, America – but mostly Turkey – and the decibel level in the room was low. The attendees were in no mood for idle chitchat; they were obviously waiting for someone to take charge.

With an explosive bang, the door sprang open, and the big man strode in armed with files. He stopped before the seated seven and silently searched each individual face before fixing it with a knowing stare and nod of acknowledgement. He knew all of them, and he knew them well. Each had, since young men, served Israel in its skirmishes and wars with foes dedicated to their annihilation. All bore the personal scars of people who'd had brothers, sisters, children, friends, lovers obliterated by the Nazis and the Russians during the Holocaust, then by the Arabs in the 1948 invasion of the Arab nations, and in all of the subsequent wars. Now the Palestinians were increasing their attacks against the citizenry of Israel. These men were comrades-in-arms who had all experienced firsthand the virulence of their enemy. That any of them were still here was a testimony both to their steel and to the unyielding tenacity of the man who had just burst into the room. He'd been a fellow soldier, then a commanding officer, and then their General, before becoming their leader as the Israeli Minister of Defense.

He dropped the files onto the table, pulled out the chair closest to the door and sat. He gazed again into each man's eyes before, finally, sitting back and taking out a pack of Marlboros – his favorite form of tobacco abuse – and ritually pulling a cigarette from the pack. He lit it and inhaled deeply, then exhaled the smoke to mingle with that already hovering above the table. The room was still. They were all familiar with the big man's style. They knew to a man that he was about to inform them of a decision the Defense Minister had made. For the past eighteen months they had all been a part of the operational planning of a possible Israeli offensive, and they all were confident they knew what the decision would be – as well as the risks it entailed.

The big man ran his fingers slowly through his thick graying hair and took a moment to smooth his locks, then very deliberately opened the top file in front of him. He carefully removed the red-bordered document labeled "Top-Secret," closed the file folder, placed the document on top of it, and, keeping his hand on the file slowly turned it on the table.

"Gentlemen. Fellow soldiers. You all know what this is; you have all had a part in its preparation.

This is operation 'Little Pines.'" He paused briefly for effect, then continued, "Later today, at the cabinet meeting in Tel Aviv, I will recommend to the Prime Minister that we implement this plan as soon as practical. I fully expect the Prime Minister will then recommend 'Little Pines' be approved by the cabinet, giving the Minister of Defense the authority to commence the invasion of Lebanon in order to eliminate the scourge of the PLO from this earth once and for all."

The men returned their leader's stare as they all nodded a universal assent, as if that was why he had called them together. Like any effective leader he had solicited all of their concerns, criticisms, and recommendations, and he had carefully weighed them all before making his decision. Now that the decision had been taken, however, he expected – and would insist – that they, as a man, stand behind it and do all in their power to implement the plan. Any dissident would be expected to leave now.

"Anyone who disagrees, say so now." They all looked around, but none made any move indicating disagreement. The Minister nodded. "Good. Now, any questions?"

General Narkiss, seated directly in front of the Minister, raised his hand. Narkiss was the oldest officer in the room. He was leading the front lines in the 1948 Arab Israeli war and in the 1967 war, and had lost an arm and had a shattered leg as souvenirs of those conflicts. He was known to be the Minister's mentor and confidante. The big man nodded, "Yes Uzi, your question?"

"When Ari? When do we go?"

"We go as soon as two preconditions are satisfied, and we receive cabinet approval." Low laughter followed his response; they all knew the Minister already had his answer – through back door channels – or he would not be recommending a career-ending plan. Career-ending, that is, if it failed. No one could imagine the Minister spending the rest of his days farming on a kibbutz. Still, they all understood there were risks, big risks, especially if their southern flank should be attacked.

"You all know what the preconditions are and you all understand we cannot, with any precision, put a firm timetable to this business. We must be ready to make the move while the Phalange still have a chance in Lebanon and before the PLO can get many more reinforcements. We think we must be ready to go in early 1982."

"But, what about our northern flank, what about Iraq?" shouted out Colonel Rabin.

"The Mossad are confident that Saddam Hussein will invade Iran in the fall of 1980, perhaps earlier, and our military intelligence confirms that view. Obviously, if this doesn't happen we will re-think our position. But we must be ready. The scum are killing our people."

Colonel Habib, the youngest of the men and a veteran of the 1973 War on the front with Egypt, rose. "What about the southern flank? Old Sadat is stewing over his position in the Arab world; Peace Treaty or no, he could attack after we go into Lebanon."

As he rose to his feet the Minister made what they all knew would be his final comment of the meeting. "Schlomo, the Egyptians will not be a problem."

"But," Habib insisted, "Sadat?"

"Schlomo, forget about Sadat."

***

The Minister of Defense quit the room as abruptly as he had entered, and lumbered down the hall to his isolated office. His secretary greeted him perfunctorily and handed him a stack of messages, all labeled "urgent." He went into his office, closed the door, and took off his jacket. He poured himself a glass of mineral water, wishing it was a far different clear liquid. *Later for that,* he thought. He sat down and lit a Marlboro, then began paging through the messages. He came to one from Kim David and stopped and smiled. *My friend Kim.* No two men could be more opposite, yet he had no doubt Kim David was one of his closest allies. He thought back to their last meeting, only a week earlier.

Kim had just returned from one of his many trips to Morocco and London, and he had left a message for Kim to join him at his farm some twenty kilometers outside of Tel Aviv. The Minister's wife and family had gone into Tel Aviv to attend a concert, so they would have the place to themselves and time for Kim to bring him up to date. There would be time enough, as well, to enjoy some of the Polish Vodka he knew Kim would bring with him. He heard Kim's car pull up, and he eagerly walked outside to welcome his friend and instruct the soldiers not to disturb them.

Inside, the Minister ushered Kim into his study and, with a sly grin, inquired if Kim had brought "the usual" with him. "Of course, you transparent old bear; it's in my briefcase! Shall I pour us a couple of stiff ones before we get down to business?"

The Minister grunted an affirmation. "We who labor so hard for our country need a little relaxation once in awhile, don't you agree Kim?"

Kim went to the cabinet, a familiar procedure for him, and took two large-diameter, short crystal glasses and poured several fingers of vodka in each. They then sat and went through the brief ritual of each asking the other about the health of their family, before turning to the business of the moment.

"Kim, we must neutralize the Egyptians. Are you confident that your asset in London will be able to pull this off?"

"Ari, my friend, absolutely! And, my asset is not in London right now; she is in Tel Aviv – or, at least, in the environs."

"What?" exploded Ari. "Tel Aviv! What is she doing in Tel Aviv? We need her in London!"

"Relax, Ari. She will surface back at London University in plenty of time. She is nearly finished with her training compliments of the Mossad, and reports are that ice water runs in her veins. Our target will arrive in London in early 1980, where she will recruit him and do her job. Our people will then finish the job in Egypt."

"Tell me one more time, Kim, why you have so much confidence in this young woman?"

"Because of her bloodlines, old chap. Her father was Ronne-Lotz and her mother Yolande. Besides, I know her well."

"Lotz?"

"One and the same."

"Oy vey! And do you also know this young woman in the biblical sense, you wolf?"

Kim smiled. "It's all part of the job."

CHAPTER 10

Morris

ARCHIE WAS UNCHARACTERISTICALLY quiet as he drove his passengers down Knightsbridge. They passed the French and Kuwait Embassies then turned onto Brompton Road, on the way to the flat George Morris and his wife Sandra had leased when they moved from Kuwait to London. Traffic was normal for that time of day, crowded but moving steadily. His passengers, George Morris and Drew Cahill, were conversing nonstop, though not loud enough for Archie to make out much of the conversation. Archie knew his place as a driver for Getty, but he still wished he could hear all of the talk. Morris was asking questions, and Cahill was answering apparently to Morris' liking; Morris responded frequently to Cahill's answers with chuckles and the occasional "That's great!"

The Victoria and Albert Museum was off Brompton Road, and George and Sandra had immediately fallen in love with the stately neighborhood dominated by the Museum. The Morrises' flat was directly across from Thurloe Square. Archie stopped in front of Number 5 Thurloe Place, a two-story attached townhouse with a massive granite veranda from which one had an impressive view of 'The V&A.' Morris and Cahill got out of the vehicle and thanked Archie, then mounted the five steps to the veranda.

"This is magnificent! What a neighborhood to live in," said Drew. "The only word I have to describe this is: 'Wow!'"

"Wait until you've had the 'cook's tour' of the house; you'll have a double 'Wow!'" George laughed. "If I do take Stuart's place when he retires as CEO of Getty, I'm not sure that Sandra will leave this for Los Angeles."

Sandra greeted the men at the door and gave Drew a hug and perfunctory peck on the cheek. Sandra had been very close with Drew's wife during her brief stay in Kuwait, and Peg had confided to Sandra her overwhelming despondency living there. Sandra had urged Peg to work – the British School was always in need of English-speaking teachers – and Sandra felt that Drew could have done more to help keep the marriage intact. However, there would be no reconciliation; she'd had the course and Peg abruptly flew back to her home in St. Louis.

Sandra had not seen Drew since the Morrises had left Kuwait. "Drew, do you still have contact with Peg? I think about her, but haven't heard a thing."

"It's been nearly three years, Sandra. We're not hostile, but we don't correspond much. She's on the faculty at Fontbonne College in St. Louis, and lives in the West End. She does date, and I guess she's happy." He added, "Happier than when she was in Kuwait, that's for sure!"

"I liked Peg; glad she's doing well." There was a moment of awkward silence before Sandra continued, "Well, as some would say, that's history. On to other things." She smiled. "We have a surprise for you, Drew. George has discovered a pizza parlor that has just the best Chicago deep-dish pizza! How does that and a crispy Caesar Salad sound for dinner?"

Drew was elated. "Sandra, I can't think of anything better; you must be mind readers. This is great!"

"We also have some cold beer, Harp or Smithwick's. Why don't you boys have a beer on the veranda and continue your business talk while I take care of the dinner, pizza Chicago-style. The only decision you have to make tonight is which beer to choose."

George gave Drew a tour of the flat. It was impressive: Tiled foyer, a large dining room – George told him the dining room was three hundred square feet – with a massive dark oak table which could easily seat ten, a mahogany-paneled study, the living room, and an immense kitchen; all on the first floor. Three bedrooms and two bathrooms were on the second floor. George then led Drew into the kitchen and opened a fridge stocked with ice-cold beer. They both took a Harp and a mug and went out to the veranda to enjoy the beer and continue the talk they'd begun in the car.

"Sounds like you've got things moving in Egypt, Drew, and this guy Wafik sounds great. His questions to you about our plans – the basis of our interpretations of the geological data, how much seismic we're going to shoot, how many wells and their depth – it sounds like he did his homework. Also sounds like he doesn't want to be looking for another job in three years."

"That's my take. He wasn't impressed by the French, and he is banking on us to make the discoveries and go into production. Before he worked for CFP he worked for CONOCO for three years, and he likes the way Americans work. He couldn't believe that CFP pulled out after drilling a stratigraphic trap to 1700 feet and hitting oil – 10,000 barrels a day! They stepped out the drilling and put down two more wells, with some show but, in the words of the French, 'nothing significant.' That well is Block HH in our concession. I told Wafik that we have all of the CFP data and our geologists don't agree with the French interpretations; we think they misinterpreted the data, that there is plenty of sedimentary rock and the strat traps are the way to go."

"Yeah," Morris said. "Tottenham and his guys are convinced that CFP pulled a boner; we both agree with that."

"Right, and Wafik is impressed. He's not a geologist, but he's been around the oil patch a long time and talks with other companies' geologists – and the word is that CFP blew it. So, their loss could be our gain." Cahill hesitated. "George...there is one minor problem that we have to deal with."

Morris sat erect, "What minor problem?"

"Gamal picked up on this right away. It has to do with HH; since it is a prior discovery, technically it is against Egyptian law to include that section in a concession. However, Gamal feels he can handle this with EGPC, but he may have to do a favor for the EGPC General Manager."

"What fucking kind of a favor?"

"Gamal thinks, at most, that we pick up the tab for a trip to London for the GM and his wife. Alternatively, we could step out and drill sideways, like the Kuwaitis are doing with the joint field they have with Iraq, but having the concession amended would be cleaner. Since the discovery didn't lead to production and CFP has abandoned the concession, the GM, Hosni Radwan, does have the authority to amend the deal; so Gamal thinks he deliberately overlooked this to create a *baksheesh* event."

"Drew, I've been dealing with these *habibis* for a long time, and I'm sure this won't be the last favor. I hope this isn't just the tip of the iceberg. We're not the French or the Italians; our corporate governance is much tougher!" Cahill sipped his beer, giving Morris a moment to think. "I guess we could set up some bullshit meeting in London that Radwan should attend. Let Gamal handle this. We need to get them to approve the cost for 'Cost Recovery.'"

"I'll take care of it George, don't worry."

Morris frowned and finished his beer. Cahill knew there would be no record of this conversation but he wasn't worried. "I think we've got a good deal; we will score."

"I agree." Morris sat back and relaxed. "So, how did your cross-cultural adventure go today?"

"The instructor is Milledufleur Rose, a professor at the SOAS, and she is very impressive academically. Funny, Gamal met her several years ago in Egypt when he was in Cairo on leave. He attended a dinner party for Bernard Lewis given by Sadat and his wife, and Rose was traveling with Lewis. He was her mentor at the SOAS."

"I'm impressed! Lewis is a renowned expert on the Middle East. He is Jewish, you know, but with the Sadat peace thing with the Israelis, that is no longer a problem." He leaned in. "So, what does this Rose woman look like?"

Drew hesitated, "Well...she looks kind of bookish in an upper-class British way; pretty conservatively dressed, hair in a bun, and she wears black horn-rimmed glasses that cover most of her face. She's prim and proper, I guess; very organized and serious. I don't think she appreciates American humor."

Drew didn't think George needed to know that beneath the uniform he thought there was a hell of a body. Four hours with someone gave you a lot of time to examine what might lie hidden under the blanket.

"Is she married?"

"I don't think so, but I didn't ask. I'll tell you one thing, though: she knows a hell of a lot about me!"

Sandra entered and announced that dinner was served. This sat well with Drew; he was hungry, and he was anxious to get the command performance over early. He and George really got along, but Sandra was another matter; he never felt at ease with her and all her questions. She was a "Blonde California Valley Girl," that was for sure! Drew had no doubt she was devoted to George; he was just happy he wasn't George.

They enjoyed the pizza and talked about the old days in Kuwait, along with updates – George always kept track of everybody – and they had a lot of laughs discussing the foibles of the Saudis, especially the Saudi contractors who were just front men for the Palestinians and Indians who did all the work. Finally Drew checked his watch: 8:15, time to leave. The Morrises were early people, and Drew had arranged to meet Joe Harvey at nine. *Perfect,* he thought. He also had time to give Gamal a call and tell him to let it rip.

Drew thanked the Morrises, making certain to tell Sandra how much he enjoyed the Chicago deep-dish pizza. He told George he would see him in the morning before he went to the SOAS for the second day of Professor Milledufleur Rose. He then walked over to Brompton Street and hailed a cab for the Prince Albert Pub on the corner of Victoria Street and Buckingham Gate Road. Drew was glad Joe had suggested the Albert; it was just a few blocks down from the company flat that was his home while in London, and they would have an hour or so to down a few pints before the pub closed. Drew entered the pub. There was a good crowd, and the hour lent itself to a happy, boisterous atmosphere. He searched the crowd until he found Harvey, positioned at the end of the bar drinking a pint and chatting with a blonde. From Drew's vantage she looked attractive, neatly dressed in a smart business suit. *Well,* Drew smiled to himself. *Seems like the same Harvey I remember!*

Drew closed the distance and got in Joe's face while grabbing his hand and bellowing, "Joe Harvey, you old Canadian s.o.b! You haven't changed at all!" Drew smiled briefly at the blonde – "Pardon the interruption!" – then turned back to Harvey.

Harvey beamed as he pumped Drew's hand. "Drew Cahill, you star-spangled bastard; you look great! The Middle East must agree with you!"

"It's the food Joe; there's slim pickings in Kuwait. If it wasn't for side trips to Dubai and Bahrain I'd be a skeleton!" Drew turned back to the blonde. "I'm

Drew Cahill and I haven't seen this guy since 1973 – seven years!"

Harvey completed the introduction. "Drew, this is Pam. We started to talk while I was waiting for you. She's waiting for a friend to join her." Pam flashed Drew a smile and extended her hand. "I am sure that you two have a lot of catching up to do. My friend should be here in a wink, so don't be concerned about me."

Harvey recognized a brush off, but he hadn't come here to try to flip a "bird." Pam wasn't on his radar screen, at least not tonight. He'd have many other opportunities to pursue the London lovelies; tonight he really wanted to catch up with Cahill. Seven years was a long time, but he felt like it was just last week he and Cahill had worked together on the Canadian refinery scheme; it had all come to an abrupt end when the 1973 Arab-Israeli war broke out. He grabbed Drew's arm and motioned to an empty corner table. He smiled broadly at Pam, mouthed "later" emphasized by an over-the-top wink, and then led Drew through the pub's faithful to the empty table.

Drew grabbed a chair, and Joe asked him what he wanted to drink. "A pint of bitters should do it for me."

Joe returned a few minutes later, with two pints in each hand. "I figured we would have at least a two-pint chat. Besides, the bloody beer is warm anyway; I'm not sure I'll ever get used to the warm Brit beer!"

Drew smiled and clinked his glass against Harvey's. "It's really good to see you Joe." They both sampled their first pints before Drew continued. "Now, tell me again how you found out I was in London."

"It's truly a small world Drew, especially our world. It was through your SOAS cross-cultural professor, Milly Rose. Your course started today, right?"

Drew was perplexed. "How in the hell did that happen?"

"It definitely is a small world, Drew. Three nights ago I went to the Ménage à Trois and sat at the bar to check out this fabulous piece of work...you know how it goes...and she agrees to have a drink with me. So I'm thinking this is moving in the right direction! Well, she thinks I'm a Yank; so I tell her no, I'm Canadian, but I know a lot of Yanks – especially those who are in the oil business. She says, 'Well, give me some names,' which I do, including yours. Then she says, 'He's in my class,' looks at her watch, stands up, tells me she has to go, and leaves. So, that's how I knew you were here in London."

CHAPTER 11

Gamal and Milly

WELL, I UNDERSTAND *now why Drew is so insistent upon having the EGPC approve the hiring of Milledufleur Rose's cousins. After a cursory meeting six years ago – when she was with Bernard Lewis and a large entourage that had included the Sadats – and now this evening at the Mena House, having dinner with her and Drew, being near the woman is...well...a truly thrilling experience! Such a glamorous woman; intelligent, well-educated, and her* command of the Arabic language was a complete surprise! When Drew gave me her background, he mentioned that among her accomplishments she spoke Arabic, as well as French and, obviously, English. However, since Drew has only a smattering of Arabic he could not appreciate how truly formidable she is in my mother tongue.

Even at my age, this woman excites my libido; at Drew's age he must, at the very least, be simmering with lust! He could even be in love with her – and I can't say I blame him.

There are, however, several somewhat odd characteristics about the personality of this Milledufleur Rose. At dinner she sometimes displayed an almost cool demeanor towards Drew, and I feel she dominates the relationship. But...maybe these are just the ruminations of an old man. Maybe she has cast a spell over me as well, and I am simply jealous of her relationship with Drew. I am a realist, however; this woman would never look at me twice if I weren't a friend and business associate of Drew Cahill. Nevertheless...it has been hours since our dinner party, and I cannot get her image out of my mind! I still feel her presence...and I still smell her perfume. Although I can't name it, her scent will never leave me. Perhaps the next time we meet I will ask her what it is. But...to what purpose? Certainly I am not falling in love with her?! I'm too realistic to waste my time on an impossible mission! But, I have been entranced by her....

She very much reminds me of Jihan Sadat. Younger, taller and better proportioned, but still that same sort of beauty. When she speaks English she has a distinctive upper-class British accent, and when she speaks Arabic she sound like a well-educated Egyptian. So maybe her claim to be part Egyptian is true, as well as her claim to have two Egyptian cousins who are just, perchance, geologists. Where did she say they received their education? Some school in Missouri – the "something" School of Mines? Drew was very familiar with the school and commented that it was an excellent school for the earth sciences and engineering. Well, no matter. It's on their résumés.

If her account of her parentage is accurate then she has another common characteristic with Jihan: a mixture of European and Egyptian blood. This Milledufleur Rose claims that her father was Danish-German and her mother an Egyptian of Circassian blood. That would partially explain her extraordinary beauty. Circassian women were beautiful white women, prized in Turkish harems. And perhaps some of her coloration came from Italian-Egyptian blood; her grandmother's father was named Gheriani – Italian for sure. I must talk further with Drew. She is rather an enigma – lovely, but a mystery.

It was time to call it a night; tomorrow promised to be a very busy day. Gamal rang for his servant. He never – or rarely ever – ended his day without a glass of single malt whiskey and a pipeful of Turkish tobacco. His servant appeared and Gamal acknowledged his presence, "The usual, Ahmed."

Gamal would sip his whiskey and pull on his pipe while he planned his strategy to secure the EGPC approval for the hiring of Milledufleur Rose's cousins. This would not be as easy as Drew might think. The EGPC guards its authority tenaciously, and the rules are clear: they have to approve the engagement of all Egyptian personnel; in fact, they even supply a list of approved personnel for all of the oil companies. Gamal knew that this was a lifeline for the bureaucracy, a system of *baksheesh* operated to the height of Egyptian graft. He hoped that Drew had lots of money in his budget for this business; it would be expensive.

Gamal decided to start at the top of the EGPC organization. *Fewer people to pay off.*

CHAPTER 12

Khaleed

KHALEED WAS AWAKENED by the early morning call from the tower informing the faithful it was time for Morning Prayer. He rose, and was relieved to see that his wife had risen earlier in order to have his breakfast ready after he'd completed his morning ritual. As the wailing continued he pulled his prayer rug from under his cot and knelt, automatically turning eastward towards Mecca as commanded by the Koran.

He would follow this ritual another four times that day, as he would every day for as many days as Allah allowed him to breathe. His wife should be praying in their tiny kitchen, and from the sounds emanating from that adjoining room he deduced she was offering prayer to Allah. This comforted him as he pressed his forehead on the floor. He did not relish the prospect of beating his wife, as he'd had to do the day after his marriage, for not following the commandment of the Koran. Khaleed didn't enjoy the beating but it was his duty, and she had cried out in pain which told him that he had performed his duty well. The beating had corrected her behavior toward prayer.

He finished the prayer, then completed the ritual washing of his face and cleaned his teeth with a siwak before joining his wife in the dank, cramped kitchen. She greeted her husband with a nod and promptly ladled a heaping pile of fava beans into his bowl and served him a slab of freshly baked bread and a steaming cup of Arabic coffee. Khaleed's wife stepped back and motioned to him that his breakfast was ready. He grunted an acknowledgement of sorts as he ran his eyes over his wife. She was garbed and covered in the required fashion of the faithful, and this pleased Khaleed. In addition to the religious compliance, she also minimized exposing her countenance which Khaleed found less than pleasing. He would even have preferred she wear a mask exposing only her eyes; they were her best, and in Khaleed's view only, good feature. Even though she was not required to be covered when alone with her husband, Khaleed had told her that he expected she would be covered at all times except to sleep, and then only when the lights were extinguished. His wife was physically repugnant to him: her nose was oversized, her lips were thin, she had a weak chin, and she was growing fatter each day. In the year plus they had been married he had mounted her and deposited his sperm in her cavity only six times. Khaleed's duty to Allah to beget children to spread Allah's word in the achievement of *Dar-al-Islam* – when all of the world is submitted to the will of Allah – weighed heavily on Khaleed. He would have to do better, but the revulsion of her presence was too great for him to enlarge his manhood enough to penetrate. He had to think of Fawza to become excited, and then masturbate and ejaculate into that great scar between his wife's corpulent legs. He knew he had to do better. Allah must be served.

Khaleed broke off a piece of bread and shoveled it into the pile of beans. He put the bread and beans into his mouth, then spat it over the table and floor. "The beans are cold, you fat cow!" he bellowed. "I should beat you for this!" She recoiled in fright, crying fitfully. With disgust he stood and threw his towel against the wall. "I have many meetings today and tonight. I will be late. Learn how to cook!" Khaleed stormed out of the Heliopolis flat.

He walked quickly to the corner, hailed a taxi, and directed the driver to take him to the Agouza section of Cairo. Because it was a Friday and he was off duty, Khaleed wore civilian clothes; attired in a navy-blue blazer and tan slacks he could have been taken for a young lawyer or businessman. Khaleed's black hair was cropped short, and his bushy, but neatly trimmed, moustache was the only facial hair and complemented his fine and handsome features. He would go to the Al Giza coffeehouse to smoke, drink coffee, and exchange gossip with his fellow Army officers who, like him, were off duty most weekends. The Friday morning gatherings had now become a ritual for Khaleed and enjoyable, even if only because he was away from his wife. After several hours of this relaxation he would walk to the al-Hussein mosque for prayer, and then meet his friend Ahmed for lunch at the Kasr-al Nil café.

The coffeehouse was actually an old two-story house that had been converted into a haven for men to drink coffee or tea, and to smoke and gossip. The downstairs consisted of a single, large, open room, with chairs, benches, and area carpets haphazardly strewn about. Small tables were placed close to the chairs and benches, as well as close-at-hand so some of the men could sit cross-legged on the small carpets. The room was a 30-by-50-foot rectangle, with high ceilings and spinning ceiling fans that distributed the thick ever-present smoke throughout the room.

Khaleed walked through the alleyways of Agouza, which hadn't changed in several handfuls of decades. The passageways were crowded with bawabs, residents shopping, street vendors and hawkers, and patrons of the numerous cafes and coffeehouses. One only needed to know where to look to find any number and variety of food, drink, clothing, and other merchandise and services. Khaleed had been born in a small Upper-Egypt village of Mallawi, and he was still new to Cairo. The sights and smells, the ever-present din, the diverse appearances of the people populating this area were all a source of continual amazement, interest, awe – and revulsion. All manner of dress – Western, gabaliya, fez, hijabs – was on display. This was not Zamalek or the Garden City area; it was more like the Khan el-Khahili area in that contradiction of neighborhoods called Cairo.

Khaleed pushed open the massive wooden door and entered. He had to pause for several moments to allow his eyes to adjust to the dimly-lit interior of the coffeehouse and the smoke that reduced visibility and contributed even further to the dank atmosphere. Even at this hour of the morning the room was nearly filled to capacity, and the noise level approached the roar of a 747 taking off at the Heliopolis airport. The crowd was clustered in groups of seven to twelve men adorned in just about every manner of dress one could find on the streets of Cairo, and it was impossible to follow any of the conversations – one man would out-shout the other in order to grab attention to make some, usually inane, point.

Khaled spotted several men from his artillery unit at Camp Huckstep and made his way through the morass. As he approached, Khamis and Fawzi stood and greeted him in the common Arab manner – embraces and kisses on both cheeks. Watching Arab men greet each other one could wrongly assume that a warm feeling for each other existed. The two men deferentially made room for him on the bench between them; Khaleed was, after all, a First Lieutenant while they were merely Second Lieutenants. Khaleed took his a seat. After inquiring briefly about the health of his family, his two fellow soldiers returned to the heated conversation in which they had been engaged before his arrival. Even though Khaleed had no children, any question to a good Muslim that referred to a man's wife was *haram*, forbidden by Islam.

Khaleed took a cup of Arabic coffee from a traveling waiter, then sat back to take in the conversation between his two colleagues. They were having an argument over the consequences of the Muslim Brotherhood's recent success in the elections at Alexandria University which virtually assured the administration and faculty would be under control of the Brotherhood, even though this party was illegal and before that success the Brotherhood had been active mostly in Upper Egypt. One argued that this would give a negative message to the Western world, especially America, and would be against Egypt's best interests. The other man was violently arguing that any movement that would eventually provide Islam as the law of the country was good not just for Egypt, but, indeed, was the will of Allah. Khaleed sipped his coffee and carefully avoided entering into this argument; later he would tell his colleagues they must avoid such talk in public places. The Brotherhood was still illegal, and one never knew if a member of the secret police was present.

Khaleed continued feigning interest in the argument even after his attention had shifted to other men in this cluster who were engaged in an emotional shouting match about the Islamic fighters now engaging the vaunted army of the Soviet Union in Afghanistan following the Soviet invasion of that country in 1979. Some of the men argued that the mujahideen could not fail. Allah would not permit it. Islam would prevail over the godless Soviets. Most of these men were familiar with the Soviets who had dominated Egypt until Sadat aligned his interests with the Americans and threw the Soviets out. The other side of the argument was that religious fervor was no match for the Soviet tanks. Khaleed personally knew about Afghanistan, but he again chose not to enter the discussion.

The rest of the men around him were discussing the pronouncements of the Ayatollah Khomeini and whether the statements constituted a *fatwa* against Anwar Sadat. This definitely was not a talk Khaleed wanted to join in public. Khaleed was certain Allah had a mission for him – of this Khaleed was certain – a mission he would not be able to perform from inside an Egyptian jail.

Khaleed rose to leave. He had enjoyed listening to the conversations but wanted to go no further. Besides, the time for his rendezvous with his boyhood friend Ahmed neared. He bid the group goodbye, and on the way out relieved himself in the room's only toilet. The toilet was a hole in the floor combining urine and feces in a vile cocktail, and the fetid odor was disgusting. He held his breath and finished as quickly as he could, then raced outside where even the foul smog and dirt of Cairo was a welcome relief. Khaleed breathed deeply and thanked Allah, then quick stepped his way to the Kasr-al-Nil.

The Kasr al-Nile was an upscale café that sat on the edge of the Nile, a startling contrast to the Al-Giza coffeehouse. Neatly adorned tables were set for lunch and placed for the view of the Nile. The toilets were Western-style, and clean. Khaleed entered the café and immediately spotted Ahmed, who had commandeered a table on the exterior terrace with a fabulous view of the river. Ahmed rose as his boyhood friend approached. They greeted each other in the Arab manner but with true enthusiasm and warmth. Even though they were near opposites, in personality and religious beliefs, the two men had a sincere affection for each other, an affection that had been nurtured in their native villages in Upper Egypt.

Ahmed held on to his friends arms as he gave Khaleed a once over. "Very smart-looking, my friend; very trendy. I think you will prove tempting to the women of Agouza," laughed Ahmed.

"You are also looking smart, and in your case the women of Cairo should hurry inside so they are not exposed to your charms."

The friends sat. Ahmed motioned to a waiter and ordered a beer, a Stella, and Khaleed ordered tea, sweet hot tea. "I see you are continuing to indulge in alcohol, and I should leave in protest; but I believe my duty is to convince you to follow the right path," said Khaleed.

"Khaleed, just relax. A man needs to enjoy himself from time to time. Not everything can be forbidden always. Besides, I pray five times a day, give alms, beat my wife only when necessary, and only lie with prostitutes who are absent of all male ties so there can be no dishonor. Don't tell me you don't lie with that Lebanese Christian whore Fawza," Ahmed laughed.

Khaleed and Ahmed shared several fates: They had married cousins in unions arranged by their respective fathers. The fathers each owned an apartment in Heliopolis in which they allowed their daughters and their husbands to reside, free of charge, while the fathers of the brides were sensible to retain ownership and did not provide title to their daughters; they believed this to be good insurance. They were both officers in the Egyptian army, Khaleed with the artillery while Ahmed served in the infantry. They had both wanted to join the Air Force but had failed the examinations. While initially disappointed they both had quickly rationalized the situation as "the will of Allah." Even though their wives were cousins, however, they were physically different. Quite different. Ahmed's wife was exotically beautiful and dressed in the latest European fashion. On the other hand, Khaleed's wife was covered and justly so, a beastly-looking woman – but she did provide Khaleed with precious housing that otherwise would be beyond his means.

They ordered lunch and quietly talked about much of what had been the topics of conversation at the coffeehouse earlier that day. Ahmed believed the Muslim Brotherhood to be contrary to the interests of Egypt and had no viable future. Khaleed's opinion was totally opposite, but he kept his opinion to himself even with his closest friend in the world. Ahmed suspected that Khaleed had sympathetic leanings toward the Brotherhood; it was common knowledge that Khaleed's older brother Mohammed had gone to Afghanistan to fight with the Jihadists against the Soviets, and Mohammed had also been in Mecca last year during the uprising. Still, Ahmed thought fighting in Afghanistan was probably a good thing; both the Americans and the Saudis were on the side of the Mujahideen. Not a good thing, he thought, was Khomeini's *fatwa* against the Egyptian President. When pressed on this, Khaleed just shrugged his shoulders and said nothing.

"What do you hear from Mohammed?" Ahmed inquired softly.

"I heard that two months ago in February he was still alive, but I haven't heard anything since. He will be well I believe, inshallah," replied Khaleed.

Seated at a nearby table was the author of the *Cairo Trilogy*, Naguib Mahfouz. He was with four prominent Egyptians who were readily recognized by both Khaleed and Ahmed. "He is Egypt's most famous writer," said Ahmed. "Have you read it?"

"It was banned in much of the Arab world last year. No, I have not read it. You know he supports the treaty between Egypt and Israel," said Khaleed.

"Yes. And so do I. Egypt can not prosper if it is engaged in perpetual war with the Israelis. Why do you think we have so much American aid? Why are Western oil companies stepping up their oil exploration in Egypt? It is because of the treaty with Israel. My friend. I am secular and you are religious, but you are still my friend and I hope you have nothing to do with the Islamic Brotherhood. That is a dangerous course to follow."

Khaleed smiled, "Thank you for your concern." He pushed back his chair and stood. "Now, I must leave. Let's do this again next week; I will buy then."

Khaleed checked his watch. He had plenty of time before the meeting; he could walk. It was April in Cairo, still not too warm for a stroll, and Khaleed needed to relax and think before the meeting. He would cross the Nile and walk down to the Bulaq area of Cairo. The Bulaq was a stinking slum across the Nile from Cairo University. It was a perfect place for their meetings, and by the time he arrived all security forces will have left.

The denizens of this slum presented no problems for their gatherings. This truly was another world, nothing except mud brick hovels and darkened shops. They would meet in one of the darkened shops, the same one they had used for the last four meetings.

Khaleed realized the danger of these meetings, but he and the other participants were drawn together by a common and compelling goal. When they achieved their objective – delivery of Egypt from a corrupt secular state to an Islamic nation – their goal would be realized. The thought that he could be important to achieving that goal did more than inflame Khaleed; it produced a state of euphoria that even brought pleasure to his manhood. However, he was anxious: not because of the danger; because, even though they were all agreed on the objective, they had not yet devised a firm plan – a plan to rid Egypt of the heretic.

The plotters believed there was little danger they

would be discovered by the secret police; although not quit perfect, the security for the meetings was excellent. The Colonel with his military intelligence background had chosen their meeting place in that stinking slum of Bulaq well; not even the secret police would venture into this denizen of filth. Khaleed thanked Allah that fate had delivered the Colonel to the service of the Brotherhood; the structure of the Brotherhood was ingenious in its organization. Only one person in each cell knew everything. Khaleed did not even know the Colonel's name. The only member of the group who knew all of them – their names, their occupations – was the blind sheikh. The blind sheikh was not only their religious leader; he was also their political leader and had contact with many of the cells. Through the sheikh the Brotherhood was informed of their objective, and, according to Sheikh Omar, removal of the heretic was universally approved.

As Khaleed entered the hovel he was greeted by Sheikh Omar, the Colonel, and Mohammed, another religious leader. They sat at a rectangular well-worn metal table, and in addition to the three members of the Brotherhood there were two men Khaleed had never seen before. The Sheikh motioned for Khaleed to come and sit next to him. The Sheikh then led them in prayer, took command of the meeting, and with little formality introduced the two new arrivals as friends of the Brotherhood and experts in the art of assassination. They were there to assist the Brotherhood in the removal of the heretic. The Sheik explained that the men were fellow Egyptians currently living in Iraq, but they would be returning to Egypt undercover as employees of a foreign oil company. The Sheikh concluded the introduction, "They will help us to plan and to execute the heretic."

Following a deferential nod to the newcomers, he continued. "Let us now review our discussions to date for the benefit of our new friends and, also, to sharpen our thinking." He then launched into a diatribe against the heretical head of the Egyptian government.

Khaleed had heard the denunciation many times over, and knew the sermon so well he could repeat it verbatim – which he often did before he slept. It brought him pleasure to hear the impeccable logic which required Jihad in order to remove *Dar-al Harb* (the territory of war) and enter into *Dar-al-Islam* (the peaceful territory of God).

Khalid had of course taken instructions on all of the Koran and its meaning by the Imam of his village. His attitude towards war and nonviolence could be summed up briefly: There is no Islamic tradition of nonviolence and no presumption against war. War is simply the last resort in responding to the *da'wa* to disseminate Islam, made necessary by the refusal of nonbelievers to submit to Islamic rule. In his mind, there was no such thing as Islamic pacifism, and those who are martyred for spreading the word are immediately with Allah in paradise.

The Sheikh once again reviewed the reasons he had issued a *fatwa* against the heretic, and as he continued on his voice became more and more emotional until tears flowed from his opaque, sightless eyes. It was a compelling case: there was no choice; it was required by the Koran and the teachings of his Prophet. Sheikh Omar finished, his face flush and beaded with sweat. He then sat slumped and exhausted in his chair.

The Colonel took over the meeting. "We are united in our commitment to exterminate the heretical President. We have discussed bombing his house in Giza, or Tahra Palace in Cairo, or his house at Mit Abu el-Kom, or his Rest House at the Barrage. The difficulty with this approach, however, is severalfold: First, he is protected by the Americans, who randomly move him from place to place so we cannot know where he will be with any certainty. Secondly, we may incidentally kill many of the faithful. This may be permitted by Jihad, but on a political basis it may not be a popular move." The Colonel nodded to the two newcomers as he continued. "I've been in discussions with our friends here; our brothers have been trained by the Iraqis and by Hezbollah in Lebanon. Please, brothers. Share your thoughts with us."

The assassins both stood as the Colonel passed the nonexistent baton to them. They did actually look enough alike to be brothers. Both appeared to be in their late thirties, and they both wore bushy black mustaches, Iraqi-style. They had fine Arab features, and both were tall, well-proportioned, and wore neatly-tailored double-breasted Western-styled suits, one light tan, the other navy blue. Both wore silk ties done in the upper British class style. The shorter but apparently older of the two men began to speak. He spoke softly in an upper-class Egyptian accent, and got to the point quickly. "We have been studying this matter in detail, and our conclusion is that the assassination must take place when he is making a public appearance. He will be shot. There is to be a parade celebrating the October 6, 1973, War against the Zionists. The parade of the Egyptian Army will pass by the reviewing stand just across from the offices of the Egyptian General Petroleum Company on the 6 October 1973 Boulevard." He stared in silence at Khaleed for several long seconds before speaking again. "Khaleed, you will be in that parade. We will work very closely with you. We expect to be in Egypt by the end of this year; that will give us ten months to finalize the plan. We will make certain that your machine-guns are fully loaded and several of our Sudanese Brothers, in army uniforms, will be with you. You will kill the heretic. You, Khaleed, will be Allah's instrument. *Allahu Akbar!*"

Khaleed's heart raced and he swelled with pride. He rose, and in a strong but quavering voice exclaimed, "I am Khaleed al-Islambouli and I will kill the Pharaoh! I am not afraid to die!"

The two assassins gave each other a slight nod, and an even slighter smile. They were satisfied.

***

Khaleed was intoxicated with the joy of realizing he would be a martyr for Allah and would be in heaven with all of the pleasures promised by the Koran. He felt he might explode, and he needed to release this swelling. He ran to the bridge to cross back over the Nile and return to Agouza; he felt drawn as if he was being propelled by some outside force. He sped down the warren and past the coffeehouse where he had begun this glorious day. She was in a brown-brick, narrow, two-story building. He banged on the door, yelling her name. "Fawza! It is Khaleed. I am here to be with you!"

She appeared at the door and beckoned him to follow her up the stairs to her bedroom. He watched her as she swayed up the stairs ahead of him; she moved like a skilled belly dancer. Her crimson shift was nearly transparent and he could easily see the outline of her red bra and underpants, as wafts of her bittersweet perfume floated over him further penetrating and inflaming his every sense. By the time they reached the top of the stairs and stood swaying arm in arm, Khaleed was floating in an exploding sensual world like he had rarely experienced. She embraced him warmly and felt his rigid organ. She put his hand on her breast and whispered in his ear, "Welcome, my General," as she swabbed his mouth with her tongue. "You are more excited than ever, *mon* General," Fawza cooed. "Come with me. Fawza will pleasure you as you will." She took his hand and led him into her faintly-lit bedroom, to the circular bed dominating the room. She stopped and slowly undid his tie, unbuttoned his shirt, zipped down his fly. Khaleed struggled feverishly to remove his shoes and pull down his pants. Fawza slipped her shift from her shoulders. It fell to the floor as she undid her bra and revealed her olive-colored breasts. She pulled his head to her breast, moaning slightly as Khaleed began licking the erect nipple, then louder as he pulled her breast as far as possible into his salivating mouth. She removed the red underpants then laid back spread-eagle on the bed, Khaleed's erection was so hard it ached. He had to hurry. He came alongside her, put his head between her spread legs, and began to lick her love canal. She was panting and encouraging him to suck harder on her. She then turned on the bed which allowed her to take his manhood into her mouth, where he exploded in a stream of hot semen.

Khaleed cried aloud as he came. She smiled at him, "You are so strong, *mon* General. Now relax and smoke with Fawza. Relax. Inhale. We will take our time before we pleasure each other." She lit the hashish-laden cigarette and put it into his mouth. "Inhale deeply, my hero." He did as directed, and was soon lost deep in a euphoric state in which he began mumbling and responding to her prodding questions.

After several hours, Khaleed washed, dressed, and wobbled out of Fawza's apartment into the noisy streets of Agouza. The last influences of the hashish ebbed as he walked through the crowded streets and thanked Allah for this Christian Lebanese concubine. She had no male ties, making her lawful for his pleasures. And, even though his friend Ahmed has introduced him to Fawza, he knew that Ahmed was no longer visiting her. Ahmed always related his encounters to Khaleed, and he now had other prostitutes he used. Khaleed had no intention of telling him of this or of any future encounters with Fawza.

As he walked Khaleed visited other compartments of his mind, compartments that allowed him to live in a world absent Fawza; he knew as he needed he would have her again. It would be more than a year before he would have his chance to kill the heretic. There would be time for many visits. Khaleed was sated with pleasure. He had his destiny.

Fawza poured herself several fingers of cognac and lit a Marlboro. She was pleased with her effort with Khaleed, and now she had time to relax before the arrival of her next visitor. Time to have a hot bath. She must rid herself of Khaleed's smell.

Her next visitor wasn't an Egyptian Army officer; he wasn't even an Arab. She drew a hot bath liberally adding lilac-fragrance bath salts, and immersed herself in the sudsy, fragrant, hot water. She took a scrub brush and with an even pressure rubbed her skin until she had cleaned every part of her lithe body. Finished with the chore part of her bathing ritual, she laid back and dreamily enjoyed the random thoughts that filled her head. As she sipped the cognac, she wondered how fast Khaleed would choke if he knew she was not a Christian Lebanese woman, but, in fact, was Yolande Harmer, a Jewess from Haifa. She smiled, then turned her thoughts to her next visitor. He was an employee of the Mossad.

CHAPTER 13

Luncheon with Grandmère Rose

MILLY WAS HOME from class early and was reviewing term papers turned in by her graduate class. Drew was back in Egypt, and that was a plus; with no need to act out her charade she could enjoy herself. *Thank God this is nearly over!* She looked forward to spending a relaxing evening alone. The heat in her flat dispelled the chill from the damp, rainy weather London was experiencing, and she poured a glass of Chardonnay, leaned back on her overstuffed divan, and relaxed. She had a sheaf of papers to review, but, instead, she sipped the wine and thought back to memories of Grandmother Rose.

Milly had told Drew she was a product of her Grandmother's creation, both good and bad. Rachel Rose had programmed Milly from an early age, and Grandmother Rose detested Milly's father. Michael Ronne-Lotz had abandoned Milly's mother as soon as she'd informed him of her pregnancy, and Milly couldn't imagine what would have been her fate if Rachel and John Rose had not adopted her immediately after her mother had died in childbirth.

Lotz's mother, a German Jew, had seen the warning signs of Nazism and Hitler, and had taken Lotz as a baby and emigrated to what would become Israel, but at that time was British-controlled Palestine. Milly's grandmother had often listed many reasons to hate Lotz, a former Israeli spy who was now a selfish, failed businessman. During the time he was recruiting Milly for the Mossad, Kim David had told her that her father "saved our nation in 1967." Milly had responded, "Saved your nation, not mine; I'm British. You're the Israeli, not me."

"But Milly, you're a Jew."

"Not so anyone would notice."

My God, she thought, *Kim was nothing if not relent-*

less. His recruitment of her to the Israeli cause had been complete; she was now totally committed to Israel's survival. Perhaps she enjoyed the thrill of the game, the excitement of being a part of a movement that she could influence but which, also, could fail. Whatever the attraction, she was now actively working on Israel's behalf with the Mossad – just as both her mother and her father had done.

She'd had many "luncheon meetings" with Grandmother Rose, but one, in particular, stood out. She was in school in Scotland, and it was Easter break. She recalled it as if it was yesterday – not some 16 years ago.

***

She'd arrived at Euston Station early and had decided to walk to the Grosvenor House, in London's West End, and enjoy the wonderful weather of spring in London. The grass was green, the sky a greenish-blue and cloudless. Yellow and red tulips were arranged in neat rows throughout Hyde Park, and the sweet smells of spring influenced everything. Even the honking of the cabbies' horns seemed intent upon playing a melodious tune. At Easter time in London the finest in fashion was on parade, especially on the fashionable byways of the West End. She had just turned seventeen and now thought of herself as a young woman, a proud young Englishwoman, and she relished this change from the hills of Scotland to the fascinations of London. The monthly luncheons with Grandmère Rose, as she preferred to be addressed by Milly, had recently become less onerous. The luncheons were still somewhat uncomfortable, but she knew they were necessary and she accepted that she could never repay her grandmother for providing her years of support, care, and concern.

Milly entered the lobby of the Grosvenor House right on time and glided over the plush carpeted entry to the restaurant, where she was greeted warmly by the maître d'. "*Bienvenu*, Mademoiselle Rose; it is so good to see you again! You are blossoming into a charming young lady."

With her dark eyes flashing Milly smiled broadly at the fawning maître d'. "Jean, thank you for your kind words, and it is always good to see you."

Jean returned the smile and beckoned her to follow him. "Your grandmother has not yet arrived; allow me to show you to your table."

The table was in front of a large bay window overlooking Marble Arch. Jean seated her and inquired if she would like a drink while she waited. She ordered a Perrier with lime, and in less than a minute she was sipping her mineral water and waiting.

Her grandmother was habitually late; however, if Milly was late by even a few minutes her grandmother would soundly berate her. So she was never late for the monthly luncheons with the matriarch.

She never knew what the main topic of the lecture would be, and today she was especially anxious. She nervously pulled at her neatly-trimmed black hair and tugged at her navy-blue school uniform jacket. Did her grandmother know what she had seen in her grandmother's flat last month? Was that what she wanted to talk about? *Oh God! But, how would she know?* she thought. *But then, how does she seem to know everything?* The more Milly thought about what she had seen, the more anxious she became. Tapping her foot on the carpet, she again checked her watch. Now fifteen minutes late. Longer than usual!

The restaurant at the Grosvenor House was filling with customers, largely businessmen attired in the usual business uniforms and the occasional group of dowagers or younger socialites. As the tables filled closer and closer to her, she began to feel hemmed in and anxious. She reached in her jacket for her pack of Players; when she had turned sixteen her grandmother had allowed her to smoke, but only in prescribed areas and certainly never while walking on public streets.

Milly pulled a cigarette from the pack and quickly

lit it, then took a small draw and exhaled through her nostrils – à la Marlene Dietrich. She sat back. As the room filled so did the decibel level, and this served to relax Milly; at that level of noise no one would be able to overhear their conversation. Of course Grandmère Rose, being the mannered lady that she was, always spoke in muffled tones...at least in public.

Milly turned her head in time to see that Jean was escorting Rachel Rose to the table. Milly stood politely to await her arrival, and as they drew closer she scanned her grandmother for any sign of aging. She found none. Rachel Rose walked slowly and gracefully with the poise of a much younger ballerina, and her flaxen hair showed no signs of gray. Milly smiled inwardly. *No doubt only her hairdresser knows!* Perched neatly atop her head was a tan tam with a small brown feather on the left side, and her navy- blue double-breasted suit neatly but modestly displayed her still shapely frame. In contrast to Milly, she had sky blue eyes, and she wore a light red lipstick and just a tinge of eye shadow and mascara. Except for a diamond-studded broach pinned to the left lapel of her suit, she wore no jewelry. Milly marveled at how striking her grandmother still was even at age sixty-five. Milly always wondered where her dark hair and dark eyes came from; certainly not from her grandmother.

After thanking Jean for his effort and ordering a pink gin, Rachel Rose gave her granddaughter a polite but characteristically reserved greeting. "Milledufleur, you are ripening into a lovely young lady. Grandfather Rose would burst with pride over his granddaughter."

"You mean adopted granddaughter. You have always made that point, and you have frequently reminded me of how much I owe to Grandfather Rose. I understand that." She hesitated, then continued, "Even after five years, I still miss him; I know you miss him, too, Grandmère."

Her grandmother picked up the menu without responding. "Shall we review the menu? Then we may gravitate to our discussion of the day, *n'est pas?*"

"Surely Grandmère, but I know what I'll have: the lamb."

"Good choice. I'll try the sole." She looked up from the menu. "It's local you know."

Milly leaned closer. "But, Grandmère, what is to be the topic of the day?"

"My dear, it is, of course, where you will attend university. I've decided that it should be the School of Oriental and African Studies at the University of London. Bernard Lewis is there, you know."

Milly relaxed. This was a topic she could handle.

"So I agree...like I have a choice?" She smiled at her grandmother. "Actually, the SOAS program at London University appeals to me; I've bested the Arabic and Hebrew languages, and in school have concentrated on Middle Eastern history. But what's so special about Bernard Lewis?"

"My dear, he is the preeminent Middle Eastern scholar, and of special importance to you: he is a Jew!"

Milly frowned. "But Grandmère, why would it be important to me that he is a Jew?"

"Because, my dear, you are a Jewess."

Milly was instantly confused. *A Jewess? No, I am English, not a Jew!* She had no overt reaction, and certainly she felt she had no prejudices...*But a Jew? No, I am English!* This was beyond the pale; she was seventeen and in her parochial view of the world, she was English...wasn't she? Rose was a product of the establishment, a society dentist, an inheritor of great wealth. He was a member of English society. Her grandmother was a Circassian-Turk who had emigrated to Egypt; Circassians weren't Jews. After her husband, Nagiub Gheriani, had died, her grandmother had moved to England and married John Rose. *What is this nonsense about being a Jew? My father wasn't a Jew, my mother wasn't a Jew! So what is she talking about?"*

Grandmère Rose sighed. She took a sip of the pink gin in front of her, then signaled Jean and gave him their luncheon order. She told the waiter that the young lady would have her lamb well done, even though she knew that Milledufleur preferred lamb cooked medium rare. There was no objection from Mme Rose; she would save her objections for bigger issues. Or so she thought.

Milly sipped from her Perrier and lit another cigarette. She was determined to resolve this issue of her being a Jew. Grandfather Rose certainly was not a Jew, and as she was growing up there had been no outward signs that Grandmother Rose embraced any Jewish practices. One of her classmates was Jewish, and she was overt in the rigors of the Passover rituals.

Grandmère Rose told her that it was important that she now acknowledge and embrace her Jewish heritage. "You are now a young lady, and you will soon be pursuing a university education and concentrating on Middle Eastern studies under the tutelage of Bernard Lewis. In these times there are advantages to being an upper class, well-educated Jew, and I have dedicated my life to seeing that you receive the best education and advantages possible. Your mother, my only child, was headstrong, and she wound up abused by Michael Ronne-Lotz.

"Grandmère, I know the story about my father; over the years you have repeatedly emphasized his failed moral character and the horrible way he treated my mother."

"My child, your father is a Jew. More important, however, is the fact that your mother was a Jew. I also am a Jewish woman. It is time you understand this fact and recognize and appreciate the opportunities it provides you. I have had numerous conversations with Professor Lewis about you. He is impressed with your academic and linguistic achievements. There are few with your academic background who also speak Hebrew and Arabic fluently, as well as French and English. Also, your Grandfather Rose has made significant contributions to London University's School of Oriental and African Studies, and the importance of this is well-recognized by the University and by Professor Lewis. Believe me, these are factors that separate you from most other people. The world is now experiencing regret because of the holocaust. The United States is more than ever Israel's protector, and many other people now support Israel's position in the Middle East, and this increase in world support impacts our world. You may have opportunities to make significant contributions in this area. Not many will have this chance."

"But Grandmère, I don't feel Jewish in the least!"

"My dear, feelings are not relevant in this instance. It is opportunity and seizing it that are important. Do not worry about how you feel about being Jewish. Just accept the fact that you are very beautiful, intelligent, and Jewish. "Rachel Rose smiled. "I am pleased that you agree with attending the SOAS."

"Grandmère, I am most anxious to enroll at the SOAS and study under Professor Lewis. I am grateful to you . . ." Milly sat up straighter, lifted her chin, and made eye contact with her grandmother before she continued, "and to Grandfather Rose for providing this opportunity."

Rachel Rose sat a moment in thoughtful silence before she acknowledged her protégé's gratitude and acceptance of her offer. Milly listened to her grandmother in silence, and continued to watch her even after her grandmother's eyes had left hers.

Their lunch was served a minute later, and as they ate their conversation was reduced to comments on the fashions of the day and other mordant subjects. The main event had been concluded.

It was early afternoon when they exited the Grosvenor Hotel, and the busy city street was full of cabs, limos, and other vehicles. As they reached the intersection the elder woman was intently lecturing the slender young lady on matters of decorum and dress, and the woman failed to see the speeding black vehicle as she stepped down from the curb. The other pedestrians did not fail to see the cab, and their screams shattered what had been a tranquil spring afternoon.

Out of the screaming throng the girl leapt to the street beside the woman and pushed her back to the sidewalk, both of them narrowly missing being obliterated by the black London cab that was now screeching to a halt. The cab finally stopped some twenty feet past where the woman would have been if not for her companion, who had propelled her backward to the safe region of the concrete sidewalk by the force of her thrust. The girl couldn't maintain her balance, and the end result of her saving action was to tumble atop the elderly woman. The two were face-to-face on the sidewalk, and the woman struggled to remove the girl from her, screaming at her rescuer, "Oh my God; look what you have done!"

While the elderly woman may have been temporarily at sea, the crowd of pedestrians voiced praise and congratulations to young Milly, who was being saluted for her bravery by the still shaking cabbie as he helped her to her feet.

"Thanks-be to the Lord, young lass! That was the closest call I've had in my twenty-one years of driving a cab!" He then assisted the people helping the elderly woman to her feet, and solicitously inquired as to her condition. She graciously thanked the cabbie for his help and assured him she was shaken, but uninjured. She now realized Milly had, quite literally, saved her life, and as she regained her composure she quickly turned her attention to her granddaughter. She pulled Milly close, and with eyes teeming with tears of both pride and gratitude – emotions seldom expressed by Rachel Rose – she embraced her granddaughter as she whispered a very sincere "Thank you!" As a matter of fact, emotion was seldom a condition that affected Rachel Rose; she prided herself on her reserve and *savior faire*. They had stood her well with John Rose, while they were in public at least. Of course, what had gained her marriage with John Rose was not her behavior in public, but, rather, her performance in private. There was no reservation in private, only the uninhibited passion of the courtesan that she truly was.

"Oh, Milledufleur, your quick thinking and action saved my life! You are a precious flower! What is this? Your knee is bleeding! Let me have a look."

"It's nothing Grandmère, just a scrape. We can go into the hotel and wash it off. I'm sure they will be able to find some iodine and a plaster."

Rachel grasped Milly's arm and guided her back toward the entry to the Grosvenor House, all the while assuring her granddaughter that, although she was unscathed by the adventure, she was emotionally in a state of shock.

"Let's get your knee tended to, and then I'm going to the bar to have a splash of brandy to ease my nerves; pity you are too young...but no, you are 17. You shall also have a drink! Maybe a spot of claret would do. I'm sure that you and your friends occasionally go off campus and sneak a bit, *n'est pas?*

That caused Milly to smile, and she assured her grandmother that she was, indeed, wise. After the cleanup of Milly's knee, replete with a large orange plaster which Milly thoroughly detested, Rachel escorted her into the Oak Room – the most splendid of six bars in the Grosvenor House.

***

I can't believe old Rachel, queen of the frost, is actually allowing me to have a drink in public! She must have hit the pavement much harder than it seemed! And she has never expressed emotion with me before, so what gives? Not a new leaf! Who's kidding who? The only time I've ever seen her express emotion is when I was home from school last month, when I got home early for my piano lesson and walked in on her disgusting bouncing of my piano teacher. Imagine! A sixty-something woman balling a thirty-something puffster...but that's Rachel! It took me a few seconds to realize what was going on. I'd never experienced a sexual act before, and it forced me to sneak up to my room and relieve myself. Aida and the other girls at school talk about masturbation enough so I slid right into it. And they were right! It does feel so very good!

She is a real pisser, that one! SOAS is for me, she says! Although...actually, I do agree. So why argue? I wonder why she never told me before that I'm Jewish. And why does she tell me so little about my mother? She just repeats the same old phrases: "Why, she was just beautiful, my dear. Just like you."

CHAPTER 14

Gamal & Drew

DREW CAHILL DEPLANED and went through customs and immigration. He'd made this trip so often recently that the Egyptian civil servants smiled and exclaimed "Mr. Getty!" as they perfunctorily checked his passport and his Egyptian work permit/temporary residence permit. He then headed to the Swiss Air baggage claim where he was greeted by the ever-smiling Ahmed. "It is so wonderful that you are back, Mr.

Cahill; I hope you are rested."

"And it's always good to see you, Ahmed. Yes, I am rested. There's not much jet lag, it's almost north to south. Let's get my bag and drop it at the Zamalek Marriott; I've a meeting with Gamal Hashem as soon as we can get there."

"Oh, Mr. Cahill, you have so many meetings! You should rest more."

Drew laughed. "Just get me there, Ahmed; you won't have to wait."

Ahmed grinned from ear to ear. He was happy it would not be a late night.

***

Ahmed pulled up in front of Gamal's mansion and Drew exited the car. After the usual display of eternal gratitude from Ahmed, Drew proceeded to the massive oak door and knocked. The door was opened by the black giant, who greeted him with a smile and "salaam alaikum" and led him to Gamal's den.

Gamal, as usual, was nattily attired; he wore a dark blue double-breasted suit with a yellow handkerchief in the breast pocket, a white starched shirt, and a solid dark blue tie. He genuinely liked Drew Cahill, and he greeted his client warmly as he offered a seat.

"Before dinner let us have a libation or two, the usual?

Drew nodded an affirmation and Gamal gave his black giant the drink order.

Gamal and Drew exchanged brief pleasantries – they had seen each other just two weeks earlier – until their drinks arrived. They exchanged toasts, *"a te santé,"* *"à la vôtre,"* and each savored the first taste of his drink. Gamal sat back, drink in hand.

"So, Drew, I gather that your meetings in London went well."

"As well as they could, I suppose, but it's now 'crunch time.' Thanks to you, Gamal, the HH block problem has been solved and Getty Los Angeles is now ready to sign the concession agreement, and as soon as that agreement has been signed by both EGPC and Getty the clock starts: three years to drill 3 wells in the Gulf of Suez. It may sound like a lot of time, but, believe me, it will be tight!"

"Drew, I know that George Morris has the utmost confidence in your ability to get this done, and I will help you any way I can. I understand this is important for you and Getty, but it is absolutely critical for Egypt's future. I want you to succeed, but my country must – and I emphasize 'must' – find oil for its economic future."

Drew nodded. "I'll review with you the game plan

we agreed to in London, but let's talk about this over dinner. Swiss Air does take good care of its regular fliers, but it's now been almost seven hours since I've had food and I'm starving! What restaurant surprise do you have for me?"

Gamal gave a huge grin and his eyes sparkled. "I do have a surprise for you! It's a new – actually, a very new – place, opened just after you left for London, and it is only a ten minute walk from here. I've tried it; took Anwar Hammis, and we both loved it. It's named *La Tour Eiffel*."

"Another French restaurant in Zamalek; sounds great Gamal!"

"It is not exactly French; it's more French-style. The owner, Jacques Plantes, is French Canadian; an interesting fellow, and the food is fantastic."

"Sounds good. So you took Hammis; good move getting close to the EGPC Finance VP. You are a clever man, Gamal!"

Gamal acknowledged the compliment with a smile, then downed the last of his drink. He rose and informed his servant that he and Mr. Cahill were leaving for dinner at La Tour Eiffel Bistro.

"We can go now."

The evening was pleasant, and the aroma from the Zamalek Eucalyptus trees and flowering shrubs was a happy bonus to the fine weather; a perfect night in

Cairo. As they strolled Drew gave Gamal a summary of the London meeting with George Morris and his staff, and Gamal occasionally asked a question or gave a nod of acknowledgement as Drew detailed the Getty game plan for exploration in Egypt. Gamal was impressed by this group of Americans and their work ethic, especially when contrasted with the Egyptian work ethic – or the lack of one.

Good architect! Drew thought as they reached the Bistro. While new, the building looked old. It was a simple one-story on the corner of the block, he guessed about 120 feet long and 60 feet deep. The white stucco exterior was framed with large, rectangular, mahogany-encased windows, and the entrance was about half the length. Over the doorway was a *La Tour Eiffel* sign that included a miniature depiction of the Tower. As they entered they were immediately greeted by the owner. A mahogany bar with an ornate backbar ran the side of the Bistro, and the traditional bar stools were about 50% full of patrons. The main areas of the Bistro were filled-in with both rectangular and circular tables, again of dark wood, with red-cushioned seating. Most of the tables were already occupied, and conversations in Arabic, French, German, and English dominated the atmosphere. Jacques Plantes escorted them to the back where they could have some privacy; he had correctly assumed they did not want to share their conversation with the community.

Plantes seated them and insisted they accept a drink "on the house." Gamal accepted for the both of them and asked Plantes to join them for the cocktail, but the owner deferred to another time. Drew was pleased the man had not joined them. After Plantes left, however, Gamal explained to Drew that while Plantes was a French Canadian, he was also an Egyptian. In fact, he was an Egyptian Jew. His mother was Egyptian and had married Plantes' father in Montreal.

Their waiter, attired in a tuxedo, greeted them, served their "on the house" drinks, explained the menu, and suggested a few minutes to make their decisions. Drew was anxious to tell Gamal what was afoot, and as soon as the waiter had withdrawn Drew began talking.

"Gamal, we spent the last two weeks interviewing the British and American crew that we will be sending to Egypt. The agreement will be signed in Los Angeles within two weeks, and the EGPC will sign right after Getty. Then the 3 year clock starts. Have you been talking to Wafik? We need to hire him as Manager of HR so we can get our people down here."

"Yes, Drew, I've been in constant contact with

Wafik. He has resigned from the French firm, and we have already had several sessions with EGPC personnel. Mr. Hammis has told his people that they are to give us priority treatment. Further, I have sent the letter you wrote in London to Mr. Radwan and Mr. Hammis. As General Manager of EGPC Mr. Radwan has the authority to authorize the work permits and residence visas for the British and American personnel."

"That's great!" Drew grinned at Gamal. "And I assume that includes me as the Getty General Manager?"

"Your assumption is correct. EGPC is very pleased that you plan to hire 75 Egyptian staff in addition to the 25 British and American personnel. Based on your earlier talks with them they were expecting a little less, so they are very happy. I don't need to draw you a diagram; you know how the system works in Egypt: everyone benefits."

They both had a laugh at Gamal's remark. Their waiter arrived to take their dinner order, and Gamal recommended a plank steak and a bottle of 1974 Puligny Montrachet. Drew was impressed, not so much by the choice of wine but by the fact that the restaurant had it. *Plantes must have connections,* he thought.

They sipped the complimentary Scotches as Gamal told Drew that the résumés of the non-Egyptian crew had been sent to EGPC and had already been reviewed. "The only one that was questioned was the choice of John Teh as Manager of Accounting. I explained that Mr. Teh was not only an American-born, U.S citizen of Chinese descent, but he also is a CPA, has an M.S. in accounting from Stanford, and has 10 years of experience with Getty."

Their dinner arrived and they continued their conversation as they ate and drank. The résumés of the Egyptian personnel had been reviewed by George Morris, and by James Tottenham and his Manager of Exploration, Paul Haricort. They had picked the ones they wanted to interview in Cairo, and as soon as the contract was signed the interviewing of the Egyptians would begin. Wafik had already contacted the top people and had set up a schedule. The recruiting was on the critical path of the exploration program. The EGPC people were happy with the non-Egyptian staff, but Gamal knew that they would be very involved with the selection of the Egyptian personnel. Gamal had explained the reasons to Drew again and again: not only was there economic benefit to Egypt because the oil companies paid 50% higher than market by Egyptian law, but, also, the senior staff of EGPC had relatives, friends, and, yes, even lovers, they wanted to have hired. Everyone familiar with the "Egyptian System" also knew that the "kickbacks" would enrich the EGPC top ranks. Gamal reminded Drew that the baksheesh had been invented by the Egyptians and over the centuries had been perfected by the Egyptians.

His long day was finally catching up to Drew and he was bushed. He suggested they call it a day and pick it up the next morning; also, Tewfik would then be available so they could plan the recruiting and housing for the expatriates. They had secured an option to rent a newly-constructed office building in Maadi, a newer suburb of Cairo where most of the oil companies had offices. Since the early days of Egyptian exploration and production, the international oil companies had developed the Maadi community infrastructure – including the schools. Money had proved to be a necessary tool for the infrastructure development, and Egypt had come a long way since the early days of exploration. It was not yet in the same league as Saudi Arabia and the other Arab Gulf states, but it was now a growing part of the world's oil business.

Drew was also anxious to get back to his hotel because he had promised Milly he would call her. She would want to know what progress he had made in getting her Egyptian cousins a job with Getty. This wasn't a slam dunk, he knew, but he would talk to Gamal and Tewfik in the morning. Getty had agreed to spend $30 million over the three-year period, and he had estimated that the three-year cost of the Egyptian staff would be about $4.5 million – or 15% of the $30 million. That was almost a moot point, since they were required to have an Egyptian labor component. Of course, the 75 could probably have been pared down to 70, he estimated, or $300,000 less. *Well,* he thought, *there is no crystal ball, and the 15 admin and accounting staff are essential.* The Egyptian accountants were generally given good marks by the expatriate oilmen, and the Egyptian geologists and geophysicists would be essential to the interpretation of the seismic data they would shoot to compliment the data package they had bought.

He bid adieu to Gamal and strolled back to the Cairo Zamalek Marriott. He liked what the Marriott people had done in the restoration of the former Khedive's palace, which now formed the lobbies, bars, and the casino. *Classy,* he thought. The rooms, however, were just typical Marriott hotel rooms. As he walked he was thinking of the problems he would have to face, not just during the start up but also for the exploration phase. The start up and setting up of the administrative systems was not his favorite work, but once that was settled down he looked forward to the drilling program. That's what he knew how to do and that's where the payoff would be. He had confidence in the Brit geologists and geophysicists. Michael Sullivan was Tottenham's best man. While Tottenham was a stuffed shirt, he was a first-class professional. Of the 23 Brit staff the 19 geologists/geophysicists were the key. This was make-or-break territory. The Brits had four of the six petroleum engineers, and the two Americans were seasoned oilmen that Drew had worked with in Kuwait.

He walked through the lobby and headed to his room after briefly contemplating a drink at the bar. It's too late, and I have to call Milly. *It was a call he was anxious about.* He took off his jacket and threw it onto the sofa, then sat on the bed and rang the hotel operator to place the call.

Milly picked up on the second ring. "Allo," she said with her upper-class English accent which excited him so.

"Hello Milly, it's Drew."

"Well, I was beginning to think you had forgotten about me."

"Sorry to be so late; it was a long session with Gamal. I had to bring him up to date on the meetings with Getty in London, and he'd also been busy in Cairo – especially with EGPC. We covered a lot of ground."

"How is Gamal?" she asked.

"He's great, and he sends you his regards." He

knew what her next question would be, and although he wasn't eager to continue he knew it had to be addressed. "Milly, this simply was not the time to raise the issue of your cousins with EGPC; Gamal thinks it's better later, maybe tomorrow."

"Are you merely avoiding me, or do you think there will be a problem?"

"Milly, this is not exactly by the book; it may take a little while."

"How long is a little while?"

"I'll call you tomorrow, miss you."

"Je t'aime, a demain."

Merde, she thought as she hung up. She knew they had some time, but not forever. She had a sense of the Egyptian bureaucracy, but, still, why would this be difficult? She felt if it was, Kim would be pushing her to move faster. She contemplated her next move, but feared she had already played out this hand.

Drew sensed Milly was nervous about this; he knew that she had made a promise to her grandmother to take care of her family and, after all, they were her grandmother's cousins. Milly had explained in detail what the depressing economic conditions were for them if they couldn't get jobs with an expatriate oil company, and he admired her loyalty to her grandmother and to her extended family. However, he was getting nervous about Milly's cousins; what if he just told her he couldn't get this done? If he couldn't get them the jobs, what would she do...other than never see him again! Would she end their arrangement? The truth was, he didn't know. He wondered if he could handle this. How in the hell did he get into this pickle! Tomorrow he would talk again to Gamal; now he needed sleep.

***

If you could have one friend in the political jungle of Getty, Mort Bistrisky was the friend to have – even if he was the head of HR in Los Angeles. Mort had been in on the call to Burdick when Morris had gotten for him what Drew still considered his 'pardon' from the hellhole of Kuwait. Drew was looking forward to spending a relaxing dinner with his friend. Additionally, if it hadn't been for the HR policy, he would not have attended the cross-cultural course conducted by Professor Milledufleur Rose. He thought back to their first contact outside of the class.

She strode across the floor with the glowing chandelier reflected in her eyes as it beamed a path of pulsating light on her and lit her way. She was spotlighted as a star entering on stage. He was aroused. He'd been sitting in the partially-darkened room watching each new entrant, and he had picked her up just as she'd stepped onto the dark-planked floor. He watched her promenade across the floor, stride by lovely stride. The room was now nearly half-filled but none of the denizens were close enough to smell. To his delight, she kept coming.

As she neared he sensed he knew her, but he didn't recognize her until after she'd pulled out a chair from the table just *en face* his and sat down. She gracefully crossed her legs and turned her head slightly, but enough to make eye contact. She was close enough that he could taste her perfume; it was both sweet and musky, like strong Arabic coffee. The pungent odors emanating from the kitchen were in sharp contrast to her smell keening his consciousness. As they made eye contact, recognition sparked between them. She uttered an audible gasp, and, even in the candlelight, he blushed.

What is she doing here? he thought. He knew why he was here. The guys at the office had told him this was a great spot to meet some birds; he thought it was time for some company.

She wondered if her unmistakable gasp had belied her now-fulfilled expectation. She knew her information was solid, so she knew she would find him here sooner or later. To her relief it was sooner. She blinked then parted her lips in a coy smile exposing well-formed and pearl-white teeth. She mouthed a soft hello. He nodded and tried to think of something clever to say. He sat there grinning like a dunce for what seemed an eternity to him before iterating one of the classics of all lines.

"It is Miss Rose, is it not?"

"And it is Mr. Cahill, is it not? Now that we've circumvented the possibility that we aren't who we think we are, I believe it is time for you to say something that will make me want to join you?"

Before Cahill could respond, she rose, smoothed her black cocktail dress, and slid up to just inches from his seat. She moved like the graceful feline that she was, then stopped and stood smiling as she examined her quarry with steely grey eyes. Cahill clumsily pushed his chair back and tried to raise himself with grace to meet this transformed Miss Rose. As he reached the limit of his stature he stared down at her. This close, her scent was intoxicating. She was intoxicating. He began a visual perusal of this exquisite woman as he parted his lips and tried to speak. "Uh…well, I didn't expect to see you here," he managed to stammer.

"Are you going to ask me to join you, or will you just stand there shaking your head?"

"Oh, sure, sorry…it's just that I didn't expect to see you here…I mean, like…in a place like this. Oh shit! I didn't mean it like that!"

"Mr. Cahill, nice speech, but I'm still standing. If you prefer, I could take another table."

"No! No, not at all; please join me."

He pulled out the chair next to his and assisted her, waiting until she was fully settled before sitting down next to her. He was careful not to get too close; he didn't want her to think that he was the typical Yank: "Overpaid, oversexed, and over here." *At least, that was what they used to say,* he mused. "Could I stand you to a drink, as you Brits would say?" he asked.

"You are an international, Mr. Cahill; true to your résumé. Yes, you may 'stand me to a drink,' although I would prefer to remain seated," she grinned condescendingly. "Gin and tonic, *s'il vous plaît.*"

He didn't have to look far for service; in anticipation of their need, a well-groomed young Brit sporting a resplendent evening coat with black tie, inquired as to how he may be of service. Cahill, asserting his position, gave the fawning and condescending waiter his reply. "A G&T, no ice, and whiskey with water, plenty of ice; oh, and make that a Bell's."

"So right," the waiter responded. Cahill wondered what was 'so right' about a couple of fucking drinks. These Brits are *a-case-and-a–half,* he thought, grinning outwardly.

"You seem amused, Mr. Cahill; care to share the source of your mirth?"

"It's nothing. I just get a kick out of some of your British phrases; they tickle me. But, one thing: Since we are not in the classroom now, can't we get rid of the Mister and Miss monikers? My name is Drew and the syllabus has you as Milledufleur Rose, but my guess is that very few ever call you Milledufleur. Am I right?"

She smiled as she carefully removed a pack of Players from a small black accessory bag. She put the cigarette between her red lips and proffered a gold lighter for him to light her smoke. She nodded in thanks as she exhaled a stream of smoke, blue in the reflections from the chandelier. *He is surprised,* she thought. She wasn't; her intelligence was too good.

The rather pompous waiter arrived with their drinks perched neatly on a tray. "Madam, the gin, and Monsieur, the whiskey, I presume," he stated with assurance as he set the drinks in front of them. "Voilà!" As the waiter departed Milly continued to study Cahill as he stirred the drink in front of him. "Cheers," he said as he raised his glass and stared into her eyes. A chill ran through him. She raised her glass in response and engaged his stare. As she sipped her gin she leaned back in her chair and crossed her legs, slowly enough to reveal a very shapely thigh.

"So, as you prefer...Drew. And you are so right: the only person who called me Milledufleur was Grandmother Rose, and she's gone now. She always called me Milledufleur. Most of my friends, however, call me Milly. Not a very imaginative derivative, but much simpler." She set her drink on the table. "So, Drew, have you ever been to the 'Ménage à Trois' Club, before tonight that is?"

"No, but the guys at the Butler Place office told me it was a good place to go for...ah...dancing, and the lot. And they said the food isn't too bad for a club. How about you; have you been here before?"

"Oh, for sure; they have a decent band and I like to dance. It's good exercise, and I find it refreshing. And there is always a good supply of youngish dance partners, young professionals like yourself. London, as you know, has always been a Banking/Finance and Insurance mecca. Lately, with the advent of the North Sea oil and gas plays, the energy world is also well-represented here: young men like yourself, Americans, French, German, Scandinavians, well-educated and well-paid. There were even rumors that Jean Paul Getty turned up here from time to time, but that was before I ever came here. And you know about rumors."

Drew wondered about Milly and the Ménage. According to the Getty guys, if you couldn't score here you couldn't score anywhere, and they insisted it was not "pay for play" – if you excluded dinner and drinks. *God, she was beautiful!* He couldn't believe the transformation, from Professor of Middle East studies during the day to an absolutely seductive doll at night. *Like night and day,* he thought. *From a female Clark Kent during the day, to Superwoman at night!*

She had absorbed all of the information about Drew Cahill in the Mossad files she'd been given. She knew he was ambitious, had been married briefly to a St. Louis woman (Peg nee Riley), and had no children. The marriage had been a casualty of the Kuwait experience, a very common occurrence for Americans. She believed the American women were not cut from the same cloth as the English, the European, or, even, the Canadian women. The Middle East environment was not conducive to American women, who she believed were generally not as tough and were more selfish. Further, she had been doing the Business Community for International Understanding (BCIU) seminars for four years and had been exposed to a smattering of decent examples of Americans, British, and Europeans, and she felt the American men were pushovers compared to the Brits and the Europeans. She had no doubts about her ability to seduce this American; that could happen as quickly as tonight. However, she was determined to complete her mission and that would be a more difficult play. She definitely would need all of her wiles and her wits about her.

The band began to play "Satin Doll" and she smiled at him. "This is one of my favorites. Care to dance, Drew?" He mumbled something which she construed to be "yes," and she took his hand and led him to a spot in the middle of the dimly-lit dance floor. The dance floor was sparsely populated because of the relatively early hour. She knew that sometime after 10 p.m. but before midnight, the crowd would expand greatly; as the desire to find a companion for the rest of the evening would grow as the hour grew later. She turned and took his arm and placed it in the nape of her back, and pulled him towards her until they were in a tight embrace. She put her head on his shoulder and began swaying to the beat. As he felt her body moving, his body and his heart inside began to throb.

He was excited by her touch, by the feel of her skin, and the pulsating rhythm of her torso moving against his. "So, Mr. Drew, you do know how to dance. Do you enjoy this, dancing with me?"

"Enjoy is an understatement; if I enjoyed it any more, I'd explode!" She pulled him even closer and nuzzled his cheek as they continued to dance until the song climaxed then ended the performance. She lightly kissed his cheek and mouthed "thank you," then led him back to the table.

She paused to allow him to help her into a seat moved as close as possible to his. "Thank you for the dance, Drew. You have promise as a dance companion, better than most Americans I have met. You could be a challenge to me."

He wondered how many Americans she had danced with before him. Indeed, how many French, German, and, even, English men. However, he quickly dismissed these thoughts as provincial. She had been running her course for several years, and she had to have met a number of oilmen during that time, and, yes, possibly had even had a drink or a dance or two with some of them. And anyway, he hadn't exactly been celibate since Peg had left him.

They ordered another drink, and she asked him how he liked the course – and if he felt it would be beneficial to him. Drew considered his reply carefully; he didn't want to insult her intelligence or be too dismissive. He wanted to be both polite and honest. He explained – and she well knew – that he had spent a number of years working for Getty in Kuwait, and that during that time he had also travelled to Saudi Arabia, Lebanon, Bahrain, Dubai, Abu

Dhabi, Jordan, and Iraq – before the 1980 Iraqi invasion of Iran, of course. He had even been to Cairo several times on recruiting trips.

Getty employed some 5,000 Arabs in the Neutral Zone of Kuwait, he went on to explain, and while the vast preponderance of Arabs were Saudis, what he considered to be the producing group were not the Saudis, but Jordanians (mostly Palestinians with Jordanian passports), Iraqis, Iranians, Egyptians – and the majority of these producers were Palestinians without passports. They were accommodated by the Saudis and Kuwaitis because of their competence, while at the same time they were at the mercy of the host countries. The Palestinians formed the core of the professional group: doctors, dentists, geologists, engineers, accountants, and the personnel people. These peoples, he believed, were, indeed, a large component of the Israeli-Palestinian "troubles."

"I know you've been exposed to the Arab/Muslim world much more than the vast majority of your countrymen, but do you think this session has given you any different views of the Egyptians? Do you think the Egyptians are the same as the rest of the Arabs you have met over the past 5 years?"

"Milly, you are an academic specialized in this culture. I'm not in your league by any stretch, but my take is that Egyptians are in a class of their own. I'm not sure they are even Arabs. Egyptians have thousands of years of their own culture, and then they have been under the rule of different cultures including the conquering Muslims and, even, you Brits. But my sense is that they have an existence that is unique, and it's Egyptian."

Milly stretched out her hand to him and gave it a firm squeeze. "Drew, you are perceptive; definitely not the 'Ugly American' you Yanks have been labeled by some." She released his hand and picked up her bag. I like your company, Drew, but I am famished, and despite all of the attractions of the Ménage, the food is not one of its strengths." She smiled at him. "Let me treat you to dinner. The Connaught Hotel has an excellent menu, and I think you would enjoy it."

He had heard of the Connaught but had never been there – and the Morrises probably hadn't either. "Well, why not," he replied.

"On y va," she said, and proceeded to usher him out of the Ménage à Trois. She knew the atmosphere at the Connaught would be much more conducive to her plans for the night. They settled the bill and she led him to the street, where she secured a cab for them. They nestled closely in the taxi, and after she had given the driver his instructions, she pinched

Drew's leg and kissed his ear and cheek, then murmured, "This could be an interesting night."

It could be much better than interesting! Drew thought. He believed he was being seduced, and, if so, knew he would go quietly into the night.

CHAPTER 15

Milledufleur

AS WAS THE whole of Getty London, Drew was pleased that the concession agreement between Getty Oil East Gharib and EGPC had now been signed. This was a measure of at least a little relief. Even though the EGPC had agreed that the costs already incurred during the preceding two months would be subject to "Cost Recovery," there could still have been a glitch by the bureaucracy that might have killed the deal. They all now knew that the big and only unknown left was would they discover "commercial quantities" of oil in the Gulf of Suez.

Drew had drawn up a number of timelines – even a critical path timeline – using the PERT chart organization. Each time he did the analysis the critical path went through the shooting of seismic and the interpretation of the data. The seismic shooting had to be completed by July 1981. This information would tell them where they should drill the first of three wells. The seismologists had to finish the interpretations by 15 September so they could get the three wells drilled by December 1983. They had a drill rig contract and were hopeful to drill the first well by 15 September 1981. The concession was signed 1 March 1981 so they had until 1 March 1984 to decide if they had a commercial play. Using their Getty Monte Carlo simulation program they needed over 100,000 barrels per day production. Not an elephant by the 6 Sisters standards, but considering that its Kuwait production was 70,000 barrels/day, for Getty this was bigger than an elephant; it was more like a mastodon.

Drew wanted to shoot the seismic right away. He knew the availability of a seismic boat to do the shooting was currently not a problem – there was capacity available in the area – and rather than risk the boat not being available when needed, he wanted to fix the boat now to cover the seismic shooting and have a safety margin built in. The cost of the boat fixing was nothing compared to the $30 million Getty would have to eat if there were not enough reserves to get a payout.

The London Getty exploration group had estimated from the EGPC data that their exploration block could have reserves over a 20 year period of 500,000 barrels. All they had to do was find it. Drew knew that George Morris was betting his career on it and, by, extension Drew's career. Morris could probably survive a write off of $30 million; Drew knew he couldn't. Morris might not become the President of Getty Oil, but he would most likely be able to finish off his days in his present position in London. Drew, however, would be out of Getty. His career would be over, and he would be picking at whatever might be available. Actually, though, this did not bother him; it only helped him become more focused. He was not going to lose.

**

Drew was pleased that Wafik had gone ahead with the renting of an apartment for him in Zamalek weeks before the concession agreement was signed, and had also leased an office in Maadi for the exploration group – all 75 Egyptians and 25 Expatriates. Wafik had also started the interviewing of the Egyptian staff, and they could now begin hiring immediately. He, Gamal, and Wafik had a meeting scheduled with the EGPC General Manager and its VP of Finance and Accounting, to, hopefully, finalize the hiring of the two Egyptian geologist/seismologists who had left Iraq shortly after Saddam Hussein had invaded Iran in September 1980. They were now in Kuwait on *laissez passé* temporary permits, but they would be out of their jobs with Kuwait Oil Company very soon, and they needed jobs in Egypt. Milly had asked him to help her cousins get jobs, and Drew sorely felt he needed to provide this help to Milly.

***

Ahmed picked Drew up at the Zamalek flat at 8 a.m., then picked up Wafik and Gamal and headed for their 9:30 meeting at EGPC. They had less than 10 miles to travel as the crow flies, but Cairo traffic was dense and unpredictable. Ahmed, however, was the best at getting through this kind of traffic, even driving on the sidewalk when necessary. As they rode Wafik and Gamal continued to update Drew on the hiring approvals for the Egyptian staff, and they reiterated that the EGPC were pleased with Getty's decision to increase the size of the Egyptian staff beyond EGPC's initial expectations. Drew wondered silently if this unsolicited move by Getty would help his efforts to hire Milly's Egyptian cousins. He was anxious about his position with these two hires. He was confident that they had an excellent relationship with EGPC, but did his case make sense? What would he do if he faced stiff opposition from EGPC?

Ahmed turned onto the street named for the Egyptian crossing of the Suez Canal which had launching the October 1973 Arab-Israeli War. With little regard for the actual outcome of that war the Arabs and Egyptians looked upon the event as a great victory. Each year on 6 October the great event was celebrated with a full military parade for select political and military attendees, and each year the magnitude of the "great victory" grew in the minds of the Arabs. Ahmed drove them past the reviewing stand on October 1973 Street near the rather modern EGPC building complex, and they entered the EGPC parking lot at 9:10 a.m., in plenty of time for their 9:30 meeting.

Drew wanted to again go over his position with Gamal and Wafik, so rather than wait outside until the scheduled time they decided to convene in the lobby of the building. They entered and announced to the rather attractive and well-dressed female receptionist that they were early for their 9:30 meeting with Messrs. Radwan, Hammis, and Rahman. She greeted them warmly in both English and Arabic, then gave them their visitors' passes and bade them sit wherever they chose in the large and well-appointed antechamber. They declined her offer of coffee, explaining they faced the prospect of having to accept numerous rounds of coffee during the upcoming meeting.

Gamal and Wafik both sat enface a coffee table adorned with twin vases of bright lilies, while Drew gripped the folder containing the files of Anwar and Saleh Mabruck, Milly's cousins, and paced. Both Egyptians sensed he was very nervous about this meeting; Drew was in a state they had not seen in him before today.

Gamal had met Milledufleur several years earlier when, as a new member of the SOAS faculty, she had traveled with Bernard Lewis to Egypt for meetings with political and cultural members of the Egyptian establishment. He recalled she was an extremely attractive woman with a warm personality. He wasn't certain about the depth of the relationship Drew had with her, but he could well imagine.

Wafik finally asked, "You seem a bit out of sorts today Drew; is there something bothering you? Something about today's meeting?"

"There's nothing really bothering me, Wafik; it's just that I am very anxious to get all of this administrative stuff finished, and these two hires are the only open items remaining before we can move on."

"It will be finished soon," Wafik tried to assure him. "I've had informal conversations with Anwar Hamiss about the staffing, including these two that you've asked EGPC to include on the approved list. They only want to be sure they won't be criticized. They do agree with your argument that fast, accurate data interpretation is critical to tour drilling success, and it's not that other oil companies have not proposed their own candidates. It's just not often done."

With a higher sense of the importance to Drew of this approval, Gamal said, "I basically agree with Wafik, but as I've said repeatedly we should not overstate the case. Let them come to the conclusion that this is just good insurance. In the case that Getty doesn't discover commercial quantities, Getty bears all the cost of exploration and that could be $30 million. No risk to EGPC. In the event commercial quantities are found, then Getty is entitled to complete cost recovery. However, the biggest bonus goes to Egypt. Now math isn't my forté, but it seems to me that we are talking here about something that is less than 1% of the recoverable cost, while it could quite possibly be a reason that oil is discovered."

"Gamal," said Drew, "I thought you said that we shouldn't overstate the case."

"Hardly overstating," replied Gamal.

Drew was nervous; he could shoot holes in his own case. *These natural traders will use any opening to get an advantage. What trade off will they want?* he wondered. *More importantly, what would Getty's internal auditors say?* And what would Milly do if he didn't get the approval? Would this be the end of their short but intense relationship?

"Relax," Wafik said. "I know these people better than almost anyone; they will be cooperative, especially if you invite them and their wives – or maybe no wives – for a dinner at the Mina House and a show of Fawza, the famous Egyptian belly dancer."

They all chuckled, and that moment of mirth gave way to the arrival of Waafa Sabaagh, secretary to the EGPC General Manager, Omar Radwan. She was even more attractive than the receptionist, and better dressed in a snug one-piece pale blue silk dress with a simple band of pearls dropping from her neck to her bodice. She also greeted them warmly in both English and Arabic, and then led them out of the reception area to an elevator bank. She bade them enter, then pressed 14 for the top floor of the building. They followed her to Radwan's office where she bid them adieu as they were greeted warmly by Radwan, Hammis, and Rahman. The Egyptians embraced in the Arab manner, with a hug and a kiss on both cheeks, while Drew kept his Western demeanor as he gave each of his hosts a firm handshake while maintaining eye contact.

Radwan's office was befitting that of a top bureaucrat of an important oil agency of the Middle East. It was spacious, some 40 feet by 50 feet and rectangular in shape, and the thick, plush, light beige carpet was adorned with bright-colored Egyptian woven rugs strewn throughout. The office provided a view to the east where outlines of the pyramids were visible, and it offered a shot of the 6 October viewing stand, which would be full of dignitaries on the upcoming namesake date as they celebrated the Arab victory over Israel. An impressive view in any case.

In front of Radwan's desk was a circular mahogany-trimmed table with ashtrays and glass coasters placed conveniently, and six leather-bound chairs, three aside, awaiting the participants. Radwan sat in the middle, with a window view, and was flanked by his two staff. The Getty people sat across with a large and very impressive oil, depicting a familiar

Paris scene of the opera house circa late nineteenth century, on the wall behind Radwan's desk for the viewing pleasure of his guests. No doubt the very expensive work was a gift from CFP (Compagnie Française des Pétroles). In fact, the entire office was adorned with the best artifacts, French, German, Italian, Japanese, and, even, American, that money could buy. The European companies had little problem "gifting" the higher-up EGPC bureaucrats with expensive items in exchange for their assistance in securing approvals and-the-like from that all-important Middle East oil agency. The American rules, however, made it difficult for American companies, like Getty, to participate in this "gifting," and there were no Getty pieces in the office – at least not yet.

Gamal opened the dialogue of what would prove to be a rather lengthy meeting. He began in Arabic, as was polite, but soon switched to English in which all were proficient. He thanked them again for taking the time to discuss the Getty request to secure EGPC approval to hire two geophysicists recommended by Getty's General Manager, Drew Cahill.

As Gamal talked, Drew focused his attention on Omar Radwan. He'd had several meetings with the EGPC General Manager, all of which had been courteous and professional. *Of course, Getty had a lot to offer the Egyptians – like 30 million reasons to be friendly!* Both Drew and Morris believed that Getty was probably the only serious bidder for the CFP abandoned concession. Tottenham and his crew had studiously examined the data package and they believed that there was a significant play, just not big enough for "majors" like CFP.

Radwan seemed to be listening intently to Gamal's presentation. In his early 50's, Radwan was old enough to understand the game and young enough to need more years to secure a reasonable pension package. He was a big man by Egyptian standards, a bit overweight but far from obese, and he had a well-trimmed mustache with tinges of grey that matched the grey in his receding hair. Drew felt that Radwan had the presence of a senior diplomat, which, in a way, he was. He nodded at the points Gamal was making in his lawyer's summary, but Drew couldn't read Radwan. He was like the proverbial Sphinx. Gamal concluded his comments and turned to Drew to continue.

"Gentlemen," Drew began, "there isn't much that I can add to my associate's brief. You all understand the importance of an early interpretation of the data and conclusions from the seismic shooting that we are ready to contract. Your approval of that contract is appreciated and indicates that you all understand the importance of the interpretation of that data to confirm what we believe could be a sizeable play. By virtue of their education and experience in similar deposits, the two seismologists we are presenting for your approval will give us more depth than we currently have. And, as Gamal has pointed out, the cost is very minimal."

As Drew concluded, the EGPC contingent nodded in an outward sign of approval.

Radwan stood. "Thank you for your efforts. Of course we must support your technical work; however, there are some factors we must consider. We have approved your expatriate and Egyptian staffing. Now you ask to increase the Egyptian staffing by two additional people who do not come from the candidate list we gave to you. This is rarely done in these situations. Please give us a few minutes to discuss this in private."

The EGPC contingent left the room to discuss Getty's request. Drew was visibly nervous and paced around the room. He stopped in front of Gamal.

"What do you think they'll do?"

"Drew, we've discussed this several times. They are not likely to deny your request; however, in order to avoid setting a precedent not to their liking, they will most likely deny 'Cost Recovery' for your geophysicists. You will have to decide if you can handle that. Obviously this is only a problem if you have a commercial discovery; if not, 'Cost Recovery' is academic. Also, I think they will expect some favors for themselves personally. This could be regularly-scheduled dinners at the finest Cairo restaurants, and this would of course include their wives or mistresses. Not inconsequential, but I think you will be able to handle it. I may be able to help you in this regard; after all, as your attorneys we sometimes must do some entertaining on your behalf."

"Gamal, you are a smooth one."

Drew was not blown away with Gamal's reading. The 'Cost Recovery' could be a problem for him later, but he was convinced: no cousins, no Milly. And he wasn't prepared to not have her, maybe not ever, but, certainly, not now.

They waited, making small talk until the EGPC contingent returned. Radwan presented the EGPC response. It was practically verbatim what Gamal had suggested to Drew. Gamal winked and smiled.

"Gentlemen, we have a deal. Our attorneys will draft the wording and I'll sign it. Let me now suggest dinner tonight at the Mina House." They replied in unison, "The continuation of our friendly Egyptian-American relationship!"

Drew couldn't wait to tell Milly that her cousins were in.

CHAPTER 16

Interlude and Aftermath

DREW'S CALL THAT they had approval of her 'cousins' from EGPC was more than pleasing, it was glorious. She had succeeded in a major part of her assignment; they were now almost home free. She finished her afternoon lecture, and, with Drew in Cairo, knew she could now relax and enjoy the rest of her day. She'd arranged to meet Joyce Brian for drinks at the Grosvenor Hotel. Of the people Milly knew, Joyce was as close to being a friend as anyone could be. Joyce had been at the SOAS for five years as an Assistant Professor specialized in North African Studies from the end of WWI and the Treaty of Versailles. She was about Milly's age, and, like Milly, played the field.

Joyce was an attractive blonde, on the short side with a shapely figure, more cute than voluptuous. She was, as contrasted to Milly, an English lass through and through. She and Milly shared some of the same interests, namely academics and men, and prior to Milly's leave on "sabbatical" they often would get together – along with her friend Mary Greer – at various meet and greet places, including the Twilight Club and Milly's favorite, the Ménage à Trois. Since they both hadn't seen Milly in quite some time, she had also invited Mary Greer to join them, and tonight she was looking forward to some catch up. Mary wasn't an academic; she was a financial analyst at Barclays who supplemented her income by doing occasional duty as a hostess at several London "swamps." Mary wasn't in the same league as the two other women, but she did possess a "rack" and a lovely ass.

It was a pleasant day in London, and Joyce enjoyed the walk to the Grosvenor. Since she was the first to arrive for their meet at the Grosvenor Bar, she informed the maître d' that there would probably be three and they wanted the table overlooking the Park and Marble Arch. Joyce ordered a Chardonnay as she was being seated, and Milly arrived just as the waiter finished pouring the wine. Milly indicated she would have the same.

"Good to see you, Milly! You know, even though we teach at the same University, it is such a large campus we seldom come across one another; as a matter of fact, we haven't seen much of each other since you returned from your sabbatical – a kibbutz in Israel, right?"

"Right," said Milly, "and I have never physically worked so hard! Now I know and appreciate how dedicated the Jews are to the survival of Israel; it certainly has given me new insight into my Jewish heritage. My Grandmother always emphasized to me the importance of embracing the fact that I am, first and foremost, a Jew."

"This is a facet of your personality that I, at least, had not noticed prior to your sabbatical. It always seemed to me that we both worship at the same hedonistic altar. As responsible members of society we have always believed in an orderly behavior for the good of society and nation...at least 'good' as we define it. So I am a bit surprised that a religious component has entered your world."

"Quite the contraire, my friend; religion has nothing to do with anything. My embrace of Judaism is an embrace of the culture, and, more importantly, of the cause for the survival of the Jews as a race. I don't believe in an eternal reward; like many Jews I know, I believe our heaven or hell is how we experience our life during our time here on earth. I do believe in guilt, but not in some esoteric sense; only if we are not supporting our heritage. In a sense we are a tribe, and we all must do what we can to survive."

Joyce looked at Milly as if she was seeing her for the first time. "So having indiscriminate sex with multiple partners doesn't rise to your guilt standard?"

Milly grimaced, then laughed. "No, and it seems to me that it doesn't for you, either!"

Joyce joined in her banter. "Well, my Protestant ethic does at times prod me with a sense of guilt – although usually only after I've had too much to drink and the chap is an inconsiderate, beastly sort."

They both laughed, and they continued this back-and-forth until Mary Greer arrived. She was seated by the maître d' and she also ordered a Chardonnay. As he took her order the maître d' was visibly flustered; these were three outstanding women and it was probably a good thing they couldn't read his mind. Then again, it was the effect they expected to have on any male who was still above ground.

When the maître d' had departed, the three women settled fully into their get-together as if it had been a very long time since they had last seen each other – although it really hadn't been that long. However, there had been some interesting changes in their lives since they had last been together, and they leapt quickly into catching up.

The most significant change was in Milledufleur's life. Since Milly and Joyce shared a common academic environment, Joyce was sometimes involved in the SOAS Cross Cultural training programs aimed at oil company clients, and both Joyce and Mary were now more than interested in Milly's program – especially the scuttlebutt they had heard about Milly's newest student, an American oilman. Joyce and Mary began to bombard Milly with questions, until she finally signaled for a time out and suggested they have dinner at the Polo Lounge on Conduit Street, just off Regent Street and down from Berkeley Square. They all agreed it was a good idea; they could eat while they talked and checked out the clientele.

The Polo Lounge, featuring a sporty equine-like atmosphere, was a West London standby. A lounge ran along the interior while the restaurant was street side. The women arrived in tow and were seated promptly in the cozy restaurant. It was early, shy of six o'clock, and the place was less than half full.

The maître d' greeted them and volunteered that he hadn't seen the three ladies there together in a while, and welcomed them back with a gusto that appeared sincere. He also informed the three that, in addition to British patrons, they were now attracting a large contingent of Scandinavians, French, and Italians, men of course. There were also, in fact, a few femme fatales at the bar.

The three women were in an upbeat mood, but Mary seemed the most enthusiastic about the state of play. "This looks very appetizing," she said as she looked around, "and I'm not talking about the menu."

"I don't know about you two, but it's a long time since lunch for me and I'm famished!" said Joyce. "Let's eat before we do any preying."

The three agreed. They summoned the waiter and ordered what Joyce and Mary, at least, were hoping would be fuel for the fire. Milly was just pleased that her cover for the Mossad training had held up so well, and she had fully expected that she would meet with a barrage of questions from her friends about Drew Cahill and about her involvement with that young American oilman. She'd known he would not be a secret, and that fact in no way would imperil her mission; if anything, it would be helpful. She was still uncertain how she should handle questions about him, but she suspected that her involvement with the American was common knowledge amongst her friends and associates alike. The best approach, she decided, was to be direct; and, after all, she suspected that Joyce and Mary would both love to have an encounter or two of their own with this particular American.

"So, my good friend, Miss Rose," Joyce began. "Tell us all about your re-introduction to your Jewish faith; are you a born-again Jewess?"

Milly tried to look stern as she ordered a second round of gin and tonics for the three of them.

"Drink up!" she said, holding her nearly empty first-round G&T aloft. "Who knows where this could go; my new beau is away, and, as they say: 'while the cat's away....'" Milly and her two friends drained their glasses.

"Listen, I'm not a born again anything but I am a Jew, by culture and election. I am deeply committed to the nation of Israel and to the Jewish people. Thanks to their grit and the support of the United State, there is an Israel and the Jewish people are prospering. I don't want to be melodramatic, but this gives me a cause, and I will fight to preserve Israel and the Jewish people everywhere."

In the silence that followed, the waiter brought their next-round drinks. Mary gulped her G&T then ran her tongue over her teeth as she winked at a middle-aged businessman at the bar.

"So, Miss Rose, does this new awakening, so to speak, mean you will abandon your lustful ways and possibly settle down and marry that gorgeous American hunk?"

"Mary, you are so classy. I'm not about to marry anyone. Drew is good company and great in the sack; that's it. I'm just letting this play out. He is not my man, just a date. I haven't changed in that regard... and hopefully never will."

The middle-aged businessman winked back at Mary as he raised his glass in a symbolic toast.

"Looks like you could have your encounter there," Joyce said.

Mary grimaced, but not so the businessman could see. "Only if he's the last bloke around...I don't think so!"

They all laughed then turned to their food so they could get fueled for the hunt they were anticipating. The three approached dinner as they approached life: with a hedonistic, self- gratification gusto. The chitchat continued as they leisurely enjoyed the dinner, but Milly couldn't help wondering how her friends would react if they knew that she was working for the Mossad, and that, rather than being a date, Drew Cahill was, in fact, her target. She was certain they would be more than shocked. She was confident that they hadn't a clue; they no doubt had bought the sabbatical-on-a-kibbutz – hook, line, and sinker.

Joyce looked at Milly with renewed interest, as if to discover a link to her thoughts. She said, "In all candor – and I'm sure Mary agrees – I think your renewed commitment to your faith has brought you closer to Cahill. He is very attractive and quite a catch; you make a lovely couple. I know I would trade places with you in a heartbeat! I'm afraid the train of life has passed us by."

"I appreciate what you're saying, and I do have a high regard for Drew. We are taking it one day at a time, but I do enjoy his company and hope to continue. Who knows where it might go?"

Milly was pleased with the exchange; she just wished time would go by more quickly.

CHAPTER 17

M. S. Bistrisky

IT WAS THE summer of 1980, not a bad time to be in London.

Mort Bistrisky arrived at Los Angeles International Airport and immediately headed for the American Airlines First Class Lounge. Mort was looking forward to this London visit. He and Drew Cahill were friends, and he knew George Morris pretty well albeit more on the professional rather than personal level. He and Morris had a lot of respect for each other's capabilities. Besides, Morris owed him a dinner for his help getting Mike Burdick to go along with Morris' decision to bring Drew out of Kuwait to run the Egyptian campaign for Getty Oil East Gharib.

Mort walked quickly to the American Lounge where he was greeted warmly by the always attentive American Airlines ground representatives. Traveling to Europe and to Africa Mort flew American whenever he could; Asia, however, was a different kettle of fish. The American carriers could not beat Cathay Pacific or Singapore; their flight attendants were young, well-dressed, and very attractive. The American carriers were unionized and the overseas routes, especially the Asian routes, were staffed by "Golden Oldies."

Mort handed his passport and ticket to Ms. Casey, the American ground stewardess. "So good to see you again, Mr. Bistrisky. As requested, you have an aisle seat on our Boeing 747, Seat 2B. We will board in 45 minutes, so you have plenty of time to relax and enjoy a pre-flight libation in our lounge. We should arrive in Heathrow at 7 a.m. London time." Ms. Casey gave him a grand smile. "Have a great flight, sir, and as always, it is our pleasure." He thought she was lovely.

Mort entered the lounge and took a seat as far away as he could from the other patrons. As they imbibed and grew in self-importance the decibel level increased, and Mort didn't want or need idle conversation. He had a lot on his plate and wanted to think.

He picked up a copy of the Los Angeles Times and turned to the editorial and features articles, where he found an article entitled "The Muslim Brotherhood and Anwar Sadat." The article had been jointly written by Bernard Lewis and Milledufleur Rose. *Small world,* he thought. He'd met Lewis at Princeton after Lewis had left the SOAS, and, of course, he had met M. Rose on several occasions. Jeremy Brown, the London Getty HR Manager, had suggested to Mort that they consider using the SOAS as their cross-cultural trainer, and he and Brown had interviewed her. Following the interviews and meetings with the SOAS, Mort had decided that London University would work for Getty; he'd felt that Getty would get the deal in Egypt and that the SOAS would be very helpful in the training of the Getty group. In fact, Drew Cahill had already completed the course with Professor Rose and the SOAS, and Mort now needed to talk with Drew, for several reasons. He needed to share some things with Drew concerning M. Rose, and he wanted to get feedback from Drew.

Before he'd finished reading, Ms. Casey approached and told him his flight was boarding. She and her colleagues then ushered the nine first class boarders out of the lounge and directed them to the waiting 747. Mort felt pleased on two counts: one, within 9 hours they would be in London, and, two, he would not have a seatmate en route. He guessed Ms. Casey had seen to that, and he thanked her warmly. She was great.

The flight crew, including the pilot and the co-pilot, were all smiles as they welcomed their customers aboard. Mort made himself comfortable in his seat, then took the L.A. Times article from his briefcase and prepared to continue reading the Lewis and Rose article. He was distracted, however, by a hovering, solicitous, middle-aged flight attendant inquiring if he preferred orange juice or champagne. He opted for champagne as he prepared to read, eat, drink, and sleep across the continent and, then, the Atlantic. Mort's solicitous aging flight attendant returned with champagne and a selection of the day's newspapers for him. Mort took his champagne, selected the 14 June 1980 Wall Street Journal, and thanked her. She returned his thank you with a perhaps too beaming smile.

"Anytime, Mr. Bistrisky. Also, we have a wonderful standing rib of roast beef; I could put some away for you if you'd like?"

"That would be great Ms. Green," he replied.

"Please call me Julie," she said, smiling even more broadly.

He sipped his champagne as he leafed through the Journal, then stopped at an article headlined "More Controversy in Israel with the PLO." He sped through the article and noted that the PLO was allegedly raiding Jewish settlements along the Israel-Lebanon border. Mort shook his head. *This is ominous.*

Mort was a Jew, and his sympathies were with the Zionist movement, but he was, first and foremost, an American. The political risk for Getty in Egypt had been reviewed in painstaking detail by the Getty operations people, as well as with outside advisors, before the decision had been made to aggressively pursue the Egyptian concession. Getty, as did all oil companies, constantly lived with the risks associated with operating in potentially hostile environments. Getty had pulled out of Ecuador after two of their drillers had been abducted and then assassinated. They had also quit Angola because they had judged the risks too high primarily because of the politically instability of the Angolan government. Getty as an operating group believed that Egypt had a stable government and it was more than likely to remain stable. Their meetings with the U.S. State Department gave them confidence that the United States considered the relationship strategic. They were aware of internal rumblings within Egypt concerning Sadat; however, the consensus was that if for any reason Sadat should step down, the government would continue to function and their investment would be safe. Some even believed Egypt could be more stable without Sadat. Mort didn't think their position would be better without Sadat, but he concurred that Egypt would remain stable.

There was general concern because of the political advances of the Muslim Brotherhood, but the Getty conclusion, buttressed by the State Department's position, was that the Muslim Brotherhood did not have the depth of support nor the financial power to be more than an irritant. While Egypt's population was largely Muslim, there was also a sizeable Christian Copts and Jewish population, and the general belief was that support for Islam was more cultural than religious. Getty believed that the educated Egyptian society was secular and was much more interested in economic development than in being an Islamic state.

Mort, like most Getty management, realized that they had to expand the reserve base. Kuwait was a large producer but the threat of nationalization was real. Reserves in the North Sea would be declining over time; all North Sea reserves were "farm ins," Getty had little or no operational control. Reserves in California were steady, and prospects in Australia and Western Canada were promising but they didn't have the potential of Egypt. Getty needed to generate additional and larger reserves if they were to grow as a company. Mort had a lot of confidence in the Morris-Cahill team, and he wanted success as much as anyone including Morris and Cahill.

And he hadn't come to the party without gifts. Mort had an MBA from the University of Chicago, and a Law degree from Northwestern. He had no plans to practice law, but he believed legal training was a definite asset. Mort's wife had finally told Mort in no uncertain terms that, with one child and another on the way, it was time to start making a living. Mort had been heavily recruited, but he thought Getty gave him the best chance to reach the top of the pile and make some serious money in the corporate jungle. Since the death of Jean Paul, management had become more aggressive and had instituted lucrative incentive pay packages. At age 39, Vice President of Human Resources was not insubstantial. Mort and Cahill were the same age.

Julie was making a patrol of first class again. She stopped alongside Mort and asked if he would like a drink before dinner.

"Sure, I've still a long time. Make it a Dewar's with lots of ice and some water; in fact, make it two. And I'll have wine with dinner, a Cab."

"My pleasure, Mr. Bistrisky." She brought the drinks quickly. "Do you travel to London often?"

"I do, and expect to be doing it more in the future."

She smiled, "If you fly American we'll probably see each other again. My flight schedule has recently been adjusted – you know, seniority – and I love London." She bestowed her widest and brightest on a captive Mort as she started for the galley. "Dinner should be about 15 minutes, enjoy your drinks."

Mort sipped his Dewar's and picked up the day's WSJ as he waited for his dinner. As he scanned the paper he thought of the celebration at Getty Los Angeles Headquarters two weeks earlier, the day the Concession Agreement had been signed. They'd anticipated the agreement would be consummated, but, still, they had all breathed a sigh of relief with the signing. Now the real work loomed, and Morris and the London Getty staff had gotten a flying start. Thanks to some heads up thinking by Drew Cahill and Morris, the British and American staff were ready to go, and they were already finishing the recruiting in Egypt.

He had recruited Drew for Morris. Cahill had been working for Getty in California when Morris called Mort pleading with him to recruit what Morris had called "an ass-kicking drilling leader" for Kuwait. Mort had originally brought Drew into Getty, and he knew immediately that Cahill was the man for Morris. The trick had been convincing Cahill that this was a great career move for him. As head of HR, Mort was acutely aware of the difficulty recruiting for Getty's operations in the Partitioned Neutral Zone of Kuwait, and Mort always thought back to that time with a sense of satisfaction. He had pulled it off; he had landed Cahill. Of course, Morris believed Mort was the moving force. Truth was, it had been a joint effort.

Mort was busily scribbling notes in his ever present notebook when Julie brought his lunch-*cum*-dinner. Julie set his tray.

"You look like you are working away," she said.

"Just trying to organize my thoughts for the meeting. After dinner, I'll want to get in some sleep – or at least close my eyes."

She smiled. "I'll make sure no one disturbs you. Where do you stay in London?"

He didn't know why she cared, but politely told her he would be at the Connaught.

"Oh, I've heard that's a really upscale hotel! We

have to stay at the London Hilton, and actually share a room. Of course, that's better than staying out at Heathrow; nothing much to do out there."

"Some solace to that; Heathrow is pretty desolate." With that he put his nose into the prime rib, savoring the cut and the flavor.

***

Mort slept during most of the cab ride in from Heathrow. In a Cockney accent the cabbie announced they would be at the Connaught in 10 minutes or so. *Well,* Mort thought, *in the Connaught by 9 a.m., time for a shower, change of clothes, and coffee, then a cab to the London Office with plenty of time to make the 12 noon meeting.*

Mort was accorded the usual warm greeting by the Connaught front desk staff, and the porter took his baggage and escorted him to his room on the third floor. "Welcome back to the Connaught, sir. I see you'll be with us for two nights before you return to America."

"Good to be back; this is a great hotel." The porter nodded in agreement. "I'll take a shower straightaway, and would you please bring up a pot of black coffee."

"Of course, sir."

Mort toweled off after the shower, donned the Connaught Hotel robe, and poured himself a cup of coffee. He then placed a call to Butler Place.

"Good morning; Getty London. How may I direct your call?"

"Hello Mary, this is Mort Bistrisky. Would you find Drew Cahill for me?"

"Well, of course, Mr. Bistrisky, and welcome back to London. Please hold."

"Hey, Mort! Just in?" Drew greeted him in his flat Midwestern accent.

"Drew. Good flight, just had a shower, and I'm ready for the meeting. I've gone through the agenda; seems like you guys are sitting on go."

"Mort, we are ready! The London guys are raring to go; we just want to make sure everyone is on the same page. Looking forward to seeing you! Listen, just want to confirm that Morris is taking us to dinner tonight – you'll never guess where."

"Okay, Drew, where?"

"The dining room at the Connaught! Wimpy's is more George's style, right? Listen Mort, we both know George is an early dinner; he'll get out as soon as possible. If you aren't too jet-lagged, you and me can head for the Audley Street Pub; it's only a block from the Connaught."

"Would not miss it, Drew; I'll have plenty of time

to sleep on the flight back. And, this will give me a chance to talk to you about Ms. Rose, Milly as you call her."

"Sure…but what about her?"

"I've known her for four years or so – totally in a professional sense – and I just want to share some of my impressions of her."

"Sure. And I'll save you a seat at the meeting. See you soon." Drew wondered about the "impressions", Mort wanted to share with him.

Mort dressed quickly, blue suit, white button-down-collar shirt, and red tie. The Brits always wore suits in the office, but even though Getty paid their English staff more than the English oil counterparts, the Brits didn't have the income to dress as well as the Americans, and Mort's Hickey Freeman suit would stand out compared to their somewhat wrinkled and frayed outfits. Mort knew this embarrassed the London crew, but he also knew they would manage with their ever-present "superior air." He exited the hotel and the porter quickly summoned a taxi. Within 15 minutes he exited the cab and headed to the Butler Place meeting room. It was still several minutes before 12 noon. The room was abuzz with conversations going on at the same time, raised and excited voices. The crowded room, the higher than normal temperature, and the under-powered English air conditioner, all combined, resulted in an uncomfortably warm room, which, however, did nothing to dampen the enthusiastic spirits.

Mort greeted the Getty London staff warmly, starting with George Morris, then his counterpart Jeremy Brown, the London HR Manager, then Drew, then James Tottenham, the London Exploration Manager, and, finally, Paul Haricort who would be the in charge of the Getty London exploration crew in Egypt. Mort knew that Haricort ranked very high in Drew's book; the direct report to Drew in Egypt with a dotted line to Tottenham would be workable. George Morris would assure that.

Brown stepped up, clanking on a glass, and called the meeting to order.

"Welcome to all," Brown greeted them in his clipped English. "And a special welcome to our Americans: Mort Bistrisky, Getty Los Angeles VP of HR, Drew Cahill, who will head up this joint American and British crew, and...uh...also, Egyptian colleagues who aren't here today because, well...actually...because we haven't hired them as yet!" Brown chuckled at his version of British humor, and was joined by a spattering of polite chuckles. He then continued. "Actually, that is one of the reasons for this meeting: to establish the plan for the hiring of the Egyptian staff who, as you know, will include geologists, seismologists, accountants, human resources, and secretarial support staff. We took a bit of a risk by hiring the local HR manager, Wafik Tewfik, ahead of time, and he has been on to the EGPC who have given us a list of EGPC-approved personnel along with their resumes. Wafik and Gamal Hashem have already talked to the group and have set up schedules for interviews. As soon as our people are on site, the hiring begins. We are organized!

"Now I turn this meeting over to George Morris, our Getty London office General Manager. George!"

George stood and faced the gathering. "You all know I'm a man of few words, and I won't fail you now." This got a chuckle from the crowd before he continued. "In all seriousness, getting this concession is one of the most important events, possibly even the most important event I've seen in my many years with Getty. Thanks to all of you, we are now in a position to get the 'Elephant!'"

When the self-congratulatory applause and enthusiastic comments died down George outlined the game plan for the rest of the afternoon, and they then divided into several working group sessions, with George, Mort, Drew, Brown, Tottenham, and Haricort forming their own group.

When the meeting ended, shortly before five,

George, Mort, and Drew grabbed a cab to the Connaught for their early dinner. They had reservations at Angela Hartnett's MENU, the finest of the many excellent dining choices at the Connaught.

When they had been seated, their waiter – attired in black tuxedo and white tie – took their drink order: three Glenlivets, neat. The drinks arrived promptly, and George picked up his drink and nodded to Drew and to Mort.

"Mort, I promised you this dinner. First, we got the deal, and, most of all, for you going to bat with Mike Burdick in L.A. so I could hire Drew to run Egypt. Now, cheers to us, and onward to victory!" The three lifted their glasses together and drank.

As they put down their glasses, George stared intently at Mort.

"And another reason for this dinner is payback to you for recruiting this miserable son-of-a-bitch into Kuwait! I will never forget that phone call to you more than four years ago – when I nearly begged you to get me the best exploration guy around. You got him, we drilled, and we hit three wells in under four years. And these were not step outs; they were wildcats! For that, you Jewish bastard, I owe you! The company owes you!"

Mort was taken aback by Morris; this wasn't exactly George's style! *Maybe it's the Glenlivet,* he thought.

"George, I appreciate the compliment, but I was only doing my job. When you called and wanted a top notch driller I knew we had him onboard. I knew Drew was your man. However, you sealed the deal when you promised Drew that it would be no more than four years in Kuwait; that you'd bring him out and get him a good position with Getty. So, cheers also to you!"

"I think I have something to say here," said Drew. "I'm not going to volunteer to do this, but I think I do owe you both a dinner. Mort, along with George's arm twisting you got me to go to Kuwait, but you both got me out, and, more importantly, the job of running Egypt – which is going to make us all a bunch of money! And George, I followed your advice: I saved nearly everything I made during those four years, and I've been buying Getty stock. It's gone up 30% over four years, and once we hit pay dirt in Egypt, it will be worth even more! The only thing I lost was a wife, but maybe that was for the best. Peg and I weren't really that compatible, and I think we're both better off. So, I raise my glass to the both of you!"

As they finished the drinks their waiter announced with a flourish that he was ready to serve them, which he did, and they continued their chit chat while attacking their food. "God, this prime rib is great!" said George. Mort and Drew smiled and winked at each other.

True to form, after they finished dinner George checked his watch and proclaimed that it was getting late for him. "Besides, Mrs. Morris will want to have a nightcap and have me go over the day with her. Can't disappoint her, can I boys?"

Drew and Mort headed a block south to the Audley Street Pub. The Audley Street was one of the favorite watering holes of the Getty London office staff, and a popular after work hangout in the upscale Mayfair area. It was just 6:30 when they entered the pub, and the crowd had withered since the earlier peak. Drew pointed to a table in the rear. "Mort, grab that table, and I'll get the drinks; what do you want?"

"Pint of lager," said Mort. He headed for the table in front of a window framed with red drapes. Drew brought their drinks and sat across from Mort.

"Well, cheers and good to see you," said Drew. They both downed a good portion of their pints before they returned their glasses to the table. "Well, George was true to form. His wife doesn't cut him much slack – but I get the impression he likes it that way."

Mort smiled. "I agree. So, Drew, good meet today. I have to give you credit for being totally organized.

You must be anxious to start the drilling. When do you think you'll punch your first hole?"

"Mort, we'll beat the schedule! We have a fix on a seismic boat and we'll start shooting right away. Schlumberger has the boat positioned; we'll have two of our best seismologists sit the boat and we'll start the interpretation right away. We should start drilling within a month."

Mort smiled. "You are fast."

"The fastest," said Drew.

Mort downed most of the remainder of his drink before he spoke again. "How did your training at the SOAS go with Ms. Rose?"

"As you know quite well, Mort, I have taken these courses before – I'm not exactly a novice at this – but I was very impressed by the course organization and depth. Professor Rose is brilliant. She spent a lot of the time reviewing Egyptian history, but she concentrated mostly on the period prior to and after the British occupation. She also spent a lot of time dealing with the current government, especially Sadat. I think she is very high on the Egyptian people."

"You know, Drew, her mother was Egyptian, and when her mother died Milly was adopted by her Egyptian grandmother; she had immigrated to England and married a very wealthy and socially prominent English Dentist, John Rose. I first met Ms. Rose four years ago; Jeremy Brown persuaded me to come to London and meet with some of the key faculty at SOAS, including Ms. Rose who was a full professor of Middle Eastern studies. She was a protégé of Bernard Lewis, rated by many as the most prominent Middle East scholar. I met him at Princeton, where he'd moved after he left the faculty of the SOAS. He told me she was one of his most brilliant students. What he didn't tell me was that she was also very beautiful."

"Okay Mort, so where are you going with this? Like, so what? I know she is super intelligent, and I guess she is a looker. What is it that you want to tell me about her?"

"Look Drew, We've known each other a long time. Peg and my wife got pretty close when you and Peg lived in California, and they still talk. Peg seems to be getting along well back in St. Louis, and Hannah thinks that if a divorce can be civil, your split is it. By the way, she sends you her best. She always liked you a lot – as I'm sure you know. You are a bit of a rake, Drew." Mort smiled at his friend.

While the crowd had thinned, Drew recognized several of the women at the bar from Getty's London office and he appreciated the fact that the noise level was still high enough for him to talk with Mort without fear of being overheard.

"Glad to hear Peg and Hannah are still friends," said Drew.

"Just as you and I are friends, Drew. And I'm talking to you as your friend. You have a hell of an opportunity with this deal, and I wouldn't want any off-the-wall factor to mess up your career. Let me tell you what I know and what I surmise, okay? First of all, in addition to being drop-dead beautiful, a brilliant academic, and well-connected in the U.K. and in Egypt, she also has ties within Israel. She is a Jew, you know."

"Mort, you're Jewish also. Look, I've visited Israel on a couple of occasions for fun and games, so what?"

"The 'so what' is that I'm not a Zionist; I'm just an American who happens to be a Jew. I hear lots of rumors and talk – maybe smoke, maybe not – but she could be a Zionist and more than just an Israeli sympathizer."

"So, what are you saying? That she's some kind of fucking spy?"

"Drew, calm down; I just want to let you know what I think. You're spending time between here and Cairo, and soon it will be more time in Cairo than in London. Sure, George will give you time to come to London to blow away the dust, but it's going to get more intense. Drew, you have a great perch within

Getty, and you know there are people in Los Angeles who are jealous and would like to have your shot."

"Mort, that is always the case; the politics gets intense. So what?"

"You are young, single, and, let's face it, you aren't a monk. She's a real beauty; who wouldn't be attracted to her! My advice to you is simple: do not let her draw you into any kind of a compromising situation. I'm very serious, Drew; don't do her any favors other than buying her dinner and flowers."

Drew was taken aback. *What the hell? Is he talking about Milly's cousins? Gamal knows about the hires, and Wafik knows, but...so what?* We need people to interpret the shootings! He also knew there were no secrets in their world.

"Thanks for your concern, Mort – you are a good friend – but, really, there isn't any problem here. I do know a lot about her. She told me who her parents were, and that when her mother died in childbirth she was adopted by her grandmother and John Rose, and that he is a prominent member of the English upper class. Mort, I'm not going to tell you I'm not attracted to her; I am. I do enjoy her company, but don't worry. Look, I know you're tired; let me buy you a nightcap and then get you back to the Connaught. I'll see you tomorrow before you head back to L.A."

Drew watched Mort take the elevator to his room, then went to the concierge desk and made a phone call. "Allo," she said.

"Milly it's Drew. I'd like to see you now. Okay?"

"You know where I live. I was hoping you would ring; it's early, and I've saved something special for you. Hurry."

He could feel her over the phone, and he couldn't have hurried any faster. He flagged down a cab.

"Lowndes and Belgrave."

There was no traffic at that hour and they arrived in minutes. Drew gave the cabbie a big tip, bounded from the car, and rang her flat.

"This should be Drew Cahill, "she answered. "If it is, come up quickly; if not, go away before I call the police."

"Don't call the constable; I'll be up in a flash!" He took the stairs in twos, and was greeted by Milledufleur Rose from behind her partially open door – open just enough that he could see she was wearing a flimsy black negligee which came down to just above her knees – and nothing else. She stepped aside as he entered her flat and quickly closed the door. She smiled and took his hand as she led him into her well-appointed and comfortable den.

"I trust no one is following you? You do look flummoxed."

"It's been a long day: the program was kicked off, the concession is done, and we're going to find that elusive elephant! I've been most of the day with Mort Bistrisky; he sends his greetings."

"I like Mort. He's a smart one, and ambitious as all hell; just like you. Pity we didn't have a chance to catch up with each other. So, if the Concession Agreement is now part of American, British, and Egyptian history, you'll be in full staffing mode."

"That's right. I'll be back to Cairo tomorrow."

He was always aware of her presence, and this night even more so than usual. The lights in the room were dimmed, and as she reached the sofa the soft light of the alongside table lamp picked her out. Her black hair molded her beautiful eyes, mouth, and light olive complexion, and her illuminated negligee gave him a preview of an inviting landscape. He wanted more.

"So, what is it that you have saved for me?" He was surprised; his voice sounded normal.

She very slowly slipped the gown from her shoulders.

"Nothing you have not seen before."

She paused, then let go of the gown.

"But I think you like it." The gown floated to the floor.

"Oh God!" was all he could manage that time.

She undid his belt, then pulled down his trousers and briefs and gently pushed him onto the sofa. She first knelt beside him and took him into her mouth while arousing herself with her hand. She then mounted him. As she took him inside of her she began moving her hips, slowly at first, and then increasing the movement. She began to scream. "More! More! God, I love your pecker! More!" The frenzy increased until they both finally released in a spasm of orgasm.

She lay beside him and kissed him gently, her tongue exploring his mouth. He was exhausted, and all he could offer was a weak "You are so wonderful," and, later, "I love you, Milly." She smiled and massaged his chest.

Drew slept, but Milly only dozed briefly, then freshened up and donned a soft-green silk robe. Drew awoke as she was laying out one of the white Connaught Hotel robes he had recently left for their use at her flat, and after he'd showered she led him to the pantry. "Let's have a nightcap while you tell me all about your day, including more about Mort and your plans for Egypt."

"Milly, Mort thinks you could have an involvement with the Israeli's. I told him that was a stretch, but he wants me to be careful, and to not do something stupid that could screw up what is a very promising career."

"Now why or how could I do that?"

"Look, now that Gamal and Tewfik have worked a deal and EGPC has given Getty permission to hire your cousins, everything is in the works. However, this hire does mean my ass is hanging out a bit, and Morris would not like that. However, if we score all will be well. Besides," he laughed, "after tonight, I would have hired all of your cousins!"

"Drew, you are fabulous. What you have done for my cousins would have made my grandmother very happy, and my obligations to the family have been served. For this I thank you. And besides, Drew, there won't be any problems; you said yourself that they are experienced oilmen. They can help you find your elephant."

Drew sipped his drink. "That is possible. The critical path is through the interpretation of the seismic data, and two more experienced eyes could make a difference. At least, that's what I tell myself."

"Come on, My Yank." She took his hand and led him to her bedroom. "I know you have to get moving early, but you have to sleep somewhere; it might as well be here. I promise not to bother you, too much."

Later, after Drew was sleeping soundly, she lay thinking. Again she wondered why the Mossad wanted these two "cousins" hired by Getty. Surely not because they wanted Getty to find oil! *Were they worried about Sadat?*

CHAPTER 18

Acquisition and Change in the Oil Patch

MILLY WAS REVIEWING her notes for the next lecture when she was interrupted by the clang-clang of her phone. She'd given instructions to her secretary that she only be interrupted for important calls, and since important calls included Drew Cahill, she hoped this was Drew.

"Allo," she answered.

"Milly, it's Drew. I hope this isn't a bad time, but

it's been almost two weeks since we've talked, and I miss you."

"Drew, it's okay; we can talk. I haven't seen you for almost a month now! I know you've been busy, but it's a long time. In fact, I was just thinking I should take a plane to Cairo just to make sure you are alive and well."

"Actually, that's why I'm calling. Morris wants me to meet him in London this weekend. He says it's urgent, but he doesn't want to talk about it over the phone. So, I'll be there and you and I can see each other later this week!"

"That's super, Drew! And if you come in Thursday night, I could take Friday off and that would give us more time to re-connect, so to speak."

"Re-connecting sounds like a great idea; I always enjoy connecting with you!"

"Drew, you are so naughty, but I love when you are naughty."

He took a deep breath and gulped. Even though miles apart he swore he could smell her and feel her, and he could hardly wait for Thursday night. He thought about their last night in Zamalek, at the Cairo Marriott. *Lucky we didn't get arrested for indecent and lewd behavior!*

"Drew?" He realized she was asking him a question. "Do you know what's behind George's urgency?"

"I don't know, but there's been a lot more noise than usual on the grapevine. He sounded a little nervous, not the smooth and glib George we've come to know and love. I'm going to try to reach Mort; he may have a clue. I'll take a room at the Connaught, then I'll come by your office – say about 4 on Thursday?"

"You are going to stay with me," she said. It was not a question.

"For sure; I love your place, and everything that's in it. The room at the hotel will make me reachable for Getty business; they'll take messages when I'm not there."

"Good idea. I'll see you on Thursday at 4."

He hung up and quickly called Gamal, Wafik, and Paul Haricort; he wanted a meeting asap in his office in Maadi. He then buzzed his secretary and told her to put in a call to Mort Bistrisky at his home in Los Angeles.

"It's 8 p.m. there; he should be home."

Drew's secretary buzzed him right back. "I have Mr. Bistrisky on the line."

"Thanks, Jehan." He picked up the phone. "Hey Mort, glad I caught you. It's been a long time since we've talked."

"Pretty good timing, Drew; Hannah and I were just on our way out for dinner. Say, this phone connection sounds pretty good, much improved over the last time we talked!"

Drew chuckled, "It should be; you don't want to know what it cost, though. I had to hire a retired Egyptian army colonel as a consultant to get a decent phone line. Christ! That's how it works here, though: baksheesh, baksheesh! Damn, you'd think this country would be rich with all the payoffs! Anyway, it works.

"Listen Mort, I got an urgent call from George; he wants me to come to London this weekend. Meetings with George and the London guys aren't unusual, but they are usually scripted with agendas. However, Morris wouldn't give me a reason for this command performance, and he sounded a bit edgy. Have you heard anything?"

"Nothing that I can tie into a meeting between you and George. You know about the Pennzoil takeover offer that was rejected by the Board as frivolous?"

"Yeah, that was all over the place. It gave the stock a little temporary kick, but things settled down after the money guys figured it wasn't anything but a publicity stunt by Pennzoil."

Mort went on. "Well, there have also been some rumors about possible mergers, but those are always around. The stock price has been steady, and other than the merger talk it's quiet. I do know that there have been some visits by Texaco brass with our Chairman and Mike Burdick, but I've been told those meets have been about possible buy-ins to our North Sea plays."

Drew's radar turned on. "Who told you that, Burdick?"

"Well, yes; it was Burdick."

It's Bullshit! thought Drew.

"Thanks Mort. Let me know if you hear anything that you can tell me. Oh, and is the Sarah C. Getty Trust still managed by that New York attorney, Lansing Hayes, friend of our Chairman, Sid Petersen?"

"Yes it is. I've heard that he's very ill, however, maybe on his deathbed, and as I understand it, he's incapacitated. But what does that have to do with anything?"

"Nothing Mort, talk to you later." Drew got off the call quickly; he needed to think.

Christ! thought Drew. *Burdick is as full of shit as a Christmas goose! North Sea Getty concessions buy-ins by Texaco? Mort should know better than that! They're not even close to being big enough for Texaco! Christ, those Getty plays are old, and pressure and production are declining; that's one of the reasons we're in Egypt and Togo. If Texaco is interested they're interested in a lot more than the North Sea plays.*

Drew sat quietly as he pulled the pieces together.

He had just decided that he strongly believed that Texaco's real interest in Getty was to take over the entire company, when Jehan interrupted his thoughts as she knocked on his office door before coming in. *Well, at least I trained her well.*

"Yes Jehan?"

"Messrs. Gamal, Wafik, and Paul will be here in half an hour. Do you want me to reserve a meeting room?"

"No. We'll have the meeting in my office. Thank you, Jehan."

Jehan buzzed him a moment later on the intercom. "There is a Miss Rose on your line; she says it's urgent."

"Yes, Milly? No problems I hope?"

"Drew, the Israelis have just bombed the Iraqi reactor at Osirak!"

"Jesus H. fucking Christ! Now what?"

"Drew, is that a question or a comment?"

"I guess it's a bit of both. Really, though, this isn't a big surprise. Since Saddam invaded Iran last September, he's been telling the world that he's armed with sophisticated weapons, and that the Iranians had better be careful. The question is: Why now? Why didn't they wait until the reactor was further along and the Iraqis had spent more money? What does your G-2 tell you is happening?"

"Drew, who really knows, but what we do know is that the war between Iran and Iraq isn't going to be over very soon. The reactor could have been a game-changer; it might have forced the Iranians to rethink their position. That is now unlikely for quite some time. "

"Milly, I'm not speculating; these political scenarios are beyond me. My guess is this will not impact us in Egypt, but it will give me and Morris a little more to talk about when we get together on Saturday." His voice became lighter. "I have some people about to arrive, so Milly, think of a great place for you and me to have dinner Thursday evening."

"I thought you wanted me for dinner."

***

Gamal, Wafik, and Paul Haricot arrived right on time, and as soon as they were all seated in his office, Drew began.

"Gents, we've got a bit to cover. Let me tell you what's up, and what might be up. First of all, I just learned that the Iraqi nuclear reactor site has been taken out by the Israeli Air Force, I suspect with U.S.-made F-15s. Gamal, Wafik, what is your take on this?"

Wafik immediately deferred to Gamal.

"It's not a surprise, and it won't have any impact on Egypt. The Iraqis don't have the capability to retaliate, so it's moot. The good news is that this will probably keep the Iraq/Iran pot boiling for a few more years."

"That's what I've heard from another source," said Drew. "So, let's move on now. As I've told you, George wants me to meet with him in London this weekend. Meeting Morris in London is no novelty, but he sounded different about this one, and it's unusual that we don't have an agenda. So, what I want you all to do is to review our current state of play for our program: the situation with Egyptian personnel, our expats, the seismic program, and when we can start drilling. He, and, I'm sure, Los Angeles, will be looking for this."

Haricot started off with a status of the exploration program: the seismic shooting was finished, and was on schedule and on budget. He estimated they would be finished with the interpretation by 1 September 1981. What they had finished so far looked very encouraging, and it confirmed the conclusions reached by the Getty London exploration group on the "data package" provided by EGPC. They were now more certain than ever that the French had blown the interpretation. They had also chosen locations for the drilling of the first two wells, were narrowing the choice for well number three, and, if the money held, also for number four. Negotiations were also near a "fix" on a drilling rig, and if the status quo held they could be ready to start drilling on 15 September, possibly earlier.

"That's great; looks like we'll beat our deadline for the first well." Drew was pleased.

Next, Wafik gave a presentation on the staffing. All was in place, including the two late-add Egyptian seismologists with experience in Iraq who had been brought in by Drew, and Wafik volunteered that they were more than pleased with the contribution to the data interpretations provided by the two men.

"This looks good. I know George and Los Angeles will be satisfied with the progress you've made," said Drew. "I'll be here until Thursday morning, then I fly to London. If anything comes up let me know right away. Good job, and for those of you who can make it into Zamalek tonight, I'm buying dinner at the Don Quixote."

While Drew was having dinner with his guys in Zamalek, another dinner meeting was taking place in a far different part of Cairo. The Blind Sheikh, the Colonel, and the two Egyptians were meeting again with Khaleed in the slums of the Bulaq. The Colonel looked directly at Khaleed. "Khaleed, you are to take part in the 6 October victory parade; it is important that you be in that parade as part of the Egyptian Army. You will be there, will you not?"

"Inshallah," he replied.

"Inshallah. We will meet with you the evening before the parade, and we will have a very special gift for you," said the older of the two Egyptian brothers.

"Today is the 7th of June," said the Blind Sheikh. "We should meet again in July, August, and September, and then, finally, the evening before the 6 October victory parade. That is when you will be given the special gift by our Egyptian brothers."

Khaleed was thrilled; this would be his entry into paradise. He left the meeting and hurried to see Fawza; the swelling in his pants needed to be released. She was sent to him by Allah, of that he was certain.

***

Drew and his dinner companions were in a good mood, and why not? It was a beautiful night in the still graceful older-lady ambiance of Zamalek, and like all good restaurants in Cairo, the Don Quixote contracted with an international vendor for their supply of lamb, beef, veal, and, even, pork. This assured them a quality supply of meat not generally possible in Egypt, so it was well worth the price, and their clientele gladly paid the price. The Quixote did likewise with their wines: limited quantity, but high quality.

Drew ordered the wine and suggested either the veal piccata or the lamb shanks. Gamal and Wafik ordered the lamb while Haricot and Drew opted for veal. The wine, Burgundy, a Chambolle Musigny, 1977, was produced by their waiter with a flourish. Drew did the tasting ritual and pronounced the wine *très bon* in a poor excuse for a French accent, which elicited smiles from Gamal and Wafik. Haricort, as most Brits, didn't have a clue.

Drew stood and proposed a toast: "Here's to our great team, both here in Egypt and in London, and including Morris and Tottenham. Also, here's to the Getty shareholders who are supplying the money for this great venture. May the 15th of September be the beginning of our discovery of the elephant we know is beneath the waters of the Gulf of Suez." He looked at his group and said, "Did I miss anyone?"

Gamal stood and added: "Here's to our many friends at the EGPC, for their fine cooperation." He took a sip of the wine and exclaimed, "This is a damn fine wine!"

They enjoyed the dinner, the wine, and the companionship. Drew put Paul in a car for his return to Maadi, then he, Wafik, and Gamal strolled toward their homes in Zamalek. When they arrived in front of his residence, Gamal asked them in to join him for a nightcap. Wafik begged off, but Drew readily assented. He wanted to talk to Gamal privately. During dinner he had decided to bring Gamal in on what he thought could be the reason Morris had summoned him to London: the takeover of Getty Oil by Texaco.

***

Only hours after Drew had phoned her, Milly had received another call from another gentleman; a gentleman not an American. This call was from Kim David.

"Hello Kim, and where are you calling from?"

"Not a very enthusiastic response from my favorite Middle Eastern Studies muse. I thought you might have at least asked me how I am rather than just 'Where are you?' However, to answer your question, I'm not far from your office, and, even if you didn't ask, I am well and very busy."

"Today must be my lucky day: first a call from Drew Cahill and now from you. Are you going to pop in for one of your 'quickie' visits?"

"I'm pleased to hear you are keeping our Mr. Cahill close. As for your question, hmm...a quickie would be super…and you do have a couch in your office, don't you. If you can do it, I could pop in straight-away. I'll be there in a flash."

Milly wasn't sure how long a "flash" was, but with-in minutes the receptionist phoned to inform her that a Mr. Kim was here to see her. "He says he has an appointment with you, but I'm not aware of any appointment. What do you want me to do?"

"Send him up; he knows the way."

Kim walked through her half-opened door and closed it behind him. She went to him and embraced him warmly. "It is good to see you Kim." She smiled up at him and lied, "You don't look any worse for the wear."

He held on to her as he scanned her face and body. "And you look ever more beautiful, my dear. Tell me, do you have time for that quickie?" She slowly pulled away as he eyed the couch in her inner office.

"Kim, my dear, a 'quickie' isn't part of your vocabu-lary. So take a seat and tell me what's on your mind."

"It doesn't have to be quick my dearest, you may take as long as you like. But, for now, bring me up to date on Mr. Cahill, and, of course, on your two "cousins" now working for Cahill in Cairo."

"You probably know more about what's going on in Cairo than I do. They are there, and have been for a while. From what Drew tells me they have settled in nicely, and they are recognized as very good geophysicists. Congratulations on your selection."

"I just get them there after the professionals have done the selecting."

She was right, of course. He knew the day they entered Egypt and the hour they took their desks in the Getty operation. He also knew of their meetings with the Brotherhood in the Bulaq slums of Cairo. She knew nothing of those things.

6 October was closing fast, but not fast enough for him; there was still plenty of time for mistakes and for agreements to unravel. There was still time for visits to the Israeli military by the Egyptian Vice President and the former head of the Air Force. Mubarak could tell them that he couldn't, or wouldn't, keep their secret agreement that Egypt would not attack the Israelis if Israel proceeded to invade Lebanon. If that happened, they would all be given their heads to hold in their laps.

Kim leaned forward, and when he smiled she recognized the gleam in his eyes. "I forgot just how adorable you are, young lady; Cahill is a lucky man to have become your prey. He must be putty in your hands."

"Not quite putty, my dear."

"*Touché.*" Kim relaxed and got back to business. "So, Cahill will be here Thursday. Not unusual for him to visit London on business, but you said he was nervous about this visit, about the timing and such?"

"He's been very busy with the program and is very pleased with the results they've gotten. He believes they will be ready to drill their first well by 15 September. As a result of his workload, however, we haven't seen each other in a month. He's anxious to come to London, but he's worried. I'm guessing he thinks Getty could be taken over."

"Possible, but that should be no problem for our concerns – as long as the 'program' continues, at least for a while."

"Till when?" she said. "The 6th of October?"

Damn smart woman! he thought, and changed the subject.

"So, Milly, I do have time for dinner tonight. Where should I take you?"

"Kim, you are a dear, but I suspect dinner is not where your interest lies."

"You are a bloody mind reader. So, let's just skip dinner and get on to the main event. Your place, or mine at the Connaught?"

"Kim, I need to take a pass today. Cahill will be here in a couple of days and I must be 'a woman in need' for him, rather than a woman who has been sated by one of the world's greatest rakes. I need to be a woman who is in heat; an actress sometimes needs to use all of her props."

"Very commendable, my dear." Kim rose to leave. "In any case, I've some calls to make. I will be in contact, more frequently now that we're approaching the end game. Let me know how your reunion goes."

As soon as he was back in his room at the hotel Kim put in a call to his friend and comrade-in-arms in Tel Aviv.

"Ari, it's Kim. My guess is that you are in need of having that last great Polish vodka I brought you replenished very soon."

"My friend, you are so right; I could, in fact, use some right now. Are you going to be in Tel Aviv soon?"

"Ari, I'm leaving for the airport now. I'll be there as quickly as ELAL can get me there, and I will see you tonight. I want to bring you up to date." Kim rang off and took a cab to Heathrow.

Ari wondered what news Kim would be bringing to him. "Operation Little Pines" had been approved by the Israeli cabinet, and Ari had the authority to launch the invasion at his discretion. From all reports he had received so far, Kim's agent was proceeding right on schedule, and he hoped Kim wasn't going to tell him something different. 6 October was close, but there was still plenty of time left for unplanned and unforeseen events to derail their plan. This thought numbed him, and then the old war horse did something that was uncharacteristic for him: He prayed. And he prayed not just for this operation; he prayed for Israel and its survival.

Ari called his wife to tell her he would be late; he was about to have an unexpected visit from an old friend.

"Tell Mr. David 'hello' and 'shalom,' and, Ari, please go easy on the vodka. You and your friend do have a track record at these meetings. You are getting older, Ari; your friend is much younger."

Ari responded wisely, "Yes dear."

He looked forward to seeing Kim, but he had plenty of work to do before Kim arrived. He had lunch with General Narkiss and Colonel Habib, and it was definitely a working lunch. They again went over all of the plans for the incursion into Lebanon, and Ari informed the two men that the Prime Minister had not gotten any flak from the Americans over the Israeli bombing of the Iraqi nuclear reactor at Osirak. In fact, the Americans thought it was a good operation; good riddance was the consensus.

Kim arrived at 7 p.m., and as soon as the two old friends had shaken hands and embraced, Kim brought out the bottle.

"So," said Ari, "you did bring the Polish vodka!"

He beamed. "Let us have a drink before we get into your update. I must inform you, however, that my wife has warned me against becoming too enthusiastic with you and overdoing the vodka drinking – to which I, naturally, agreed."

"Ari, I do not want my friend to be in hot water with his bride; I can brief you quickly and make sure you have a reasonably early night. But first, let's have that drink."

Ari agreed and took the bottle to the pantry to prepare their drinks. The men raised their glasses in a toast.

"First I prayed for our survival, and now I'm toasting with you and drinking to success. Our operation must succeed; we can't live with this constant shelling from these psychopaths! We must neutralize Sadat before we move against the PLO in Lebanon. If Sadat isn't taken out, we can't chance this move. We don't have a good fallback position, and for certain he will attack our rear in order to regain his standing in the Arab world."

"Ari, we are in agreement." Kim finished his drink, then continued. "Let me review the situation with you. As you already know, our two agents are firmly embedded in the Getty Cairo operation. Their cover is working and should hold. Milledufleur Rose, our agent in London, entrapped the Getty general manager and convinced him to secure EGPC approval for their hire. Milly tells me they are respected by the Getty group. They are pros. They have also infiltrated the Muslim Brotherhood in Cairo. The Brotherhood believes it is their mission, their jihad, to execute Sadat as an apostate, and their chosen instrument of execution is a religious fanatic named Khaleed Islambouli. Khaleed is from a small village in upper Egypt, and he is obsessed with the idea that his own heroic death in performance of service to the Brotherhood will be his means to the promised eternal reward. He is characteristic of suicide bombers: he relishes his own death. The plan is simple and will work. Khaleed is a First Lieutenant in the Egyptian Army, and he will be marching in the 6 October parade. He will be carrying a submachine gun loaded with live ammunition, 35 rounds, not the blanks the rest of the army paraders will be carrying. Sadat will be seated in the sixth row with his wife and Hosni Mubarak, and they will be sitting amongst military and political dignitaries. Because the teachings of the Koran allow sexual relations between a woman nonbeliever and a Muslim man, Khaleed regularly visits a whore who he believes is a Christian Lebanese with no marital ties, making her a legitimate object. What he does not know is that she is not Lebanese, nor is she Christian; she is

Jewish and she is a Mossad agent. She plies Khaleed with sex and marijuana to loosen his tongue."

Ari smiled at his friend, encouraged by what he was hearing. He asked Kim if he wanted a refill, and Kim nodded his affirmation. Once their glasses were again filled Ari asked Kim to continue.

"Khaleed will be walking with his unit, and when they get to where Sadat is seated they will stop. That is when Khaleed will shoot Sadat. No one else will be a target. He is to empty his gun on the apostate before he himself is grabbed. We believe Khaleed will be dead shortly thereafter. Mubarak, the Vice President, is very cooperative.

They finished their second drinks in silence. Ari's voice was subdued when he finally spoke.

"You have done much and the plan is solid, but there is still a long time between now and the 6th of October – plenty of time for things to unravel. We will not know until early on the 6th if the operation has been a success. If it is, then we go; if not...we don't have many options left."

"So right, but remember: it was the Brotherhood who developed this plan. They concluded that Sadat moves constantly between three residences and is heavily guarded by the Americans, as well as by his Egyptian guards. The parade is open, and there he will be an exposed target. None of the Egyptian army personnel in the parade will be issued ammunition; it is their security policy. If our two agents get the loaded submachine gun to Khaleed without difficulty, then it will work.

"Your Milledufleur, she has done her part well; she will finish up shortly with the American, Cahill?"

"For certain. Rest assured, Ari, our agents are very good, and every detail is being attended to. Now let us have a nightcap and give you an early evening."

***

Drew's flight was on schedule. *Kudos to Swiss Air,* he thought. He was thankful that Swiss Air routed their London flight via Zurich; it was a little longer than a direct flight from Cairo, but more reliable and much more pleasant. He checked his watch; it looked like he would be at her office before 4 p.m. *Perfect!* He was anxious to see her; a whole month was too long, but he'd had to get the program moving. He knew that these programs needed constant pushing, and it had paid off. They were now at a good place.

He got out of the cab at the SOAS School and entered her building, where he announced to the bland, dour, and unfriendly receptionist that he was there to meet with Miss Rose, he was Cahill. She rang Miss Rose's office then told him he could go up, and before she could give him directions he informed her that he knew the way. He ran up the stairs, and Milly was waiting for him by her open office door.

"Drew, it's wonderful to see you."

"God you look great!" He embraced her and gave her an open-mouth kiss. She responded, but she then pulled away. "Later. Not here, not now. We have plenty of time tonight and tomorrow."

Drew turned back to the door. "Let's get out of here. I have a room at the Connaught; we can walk over, I'll check in, and then we can get something to eat and a cab to your place, where we can plan tonight and the next day."

"I've a better idea," she said as she followed him through the door. "I'll explain it to you as we walk." She took his arm. "Tomorrow will be museum, art gallery, and London-park day. I know you will enjoy it; I am an excellent tour guide, and you will see things you would never find on your own. As for tonight, we will dine in. I have ordered a divine dinner from Harrods, and it will arrive at 6 p.m. No need to visit a wine merchant, Harrods will do the selection; they are exquisite purveyors. Further, there is an excellent old film on the telly tonight, 'Casablanca' with Bogart and Bergman. How do you like my plan?"

"Your plan is great, except, you seem to have left

out one activity."

"I did not leave it out; I just didn't mention it. Didn't think it was necessary. Besides, it's not an activity; it is the *raison d'être*. It will be the appetizer and dessert, you will be my main course." She squeezed his hand as they walked. He was trying his best to remain serene, but he knew it would be a losing battle.

She waited in the lounge while he checked into the Connaught. Dinner was arriving at her place at 6, and she wanted to be there in plenty of time before it arrived. She was as anxious as he, so they wouldn't need much time before dinner.

"Milly, dinner was awesome! You were awesome; this was all so much better than going out to a five star restaurant!"

Milly took his hand. "Let's get into something comfy. I've the robes that you pinched from the Connaught, one for each of us. You do remember that night?"

"I will never forget!"

They snuggled on the sofa, sipping their after dinner drinks. "You haven't mentioned a word about your upcoming meeting with George Morris. Is the concern all behind you, or are you still nervous about a Getty takeover?

"I didn't want to ruin dinner, but, sure I'm concerned. There seems no other plausible reason why George would want me in London yet be so silent and nervous about the agenda. I feel reasonably certain there is a takeover in the works. We all know that Gordon Getty believes the stock price doesn't reflect the true value of the company. He feels he could double his already substantial holdings. So, between Gordon and the Sarah C. Getty trust, if the price is high enough, there seems no way the Board could do anything other than sell."

"What does this mean to the Getty employees, and, especially, to you?"

"I really don't know; I've been thinking through it, and as usual there are just a few options. Before I left I had dinner with Gamal and our guys, and after dinner I met privately with Gamal. We had a long talk, and his thinking has helped shape mine."

"You're wise to consult with Gamal. He is connected and he knows Egypt. So, tell me what Gamal thinks and what you think."

"It's pretty straightforward, not many twists possible. First, if this is just noise and there is no takeover in the offing, then it's the status quo. We keep on with the program and start drilling September 15. But – and this is a big 'but' – we feel this is by far the least likely outcome."

She sat back and looked intently at Drew. "So what

do you feel are the most likely outcomes?"

"We think there is a takeover by Texaco in the works, and that it is already pretty far down the curve. If that is the case, Texaco would most likely pick up the Getty reserves in Kuwait, the North Sea, Norway, California, Alberta, and Australia. These are all in production. The operation would be simple, and it's a quick way to increase their proven holdings. Texaco gets rid of all Getty personnel, closes Los Angeles and London, then folds the operation into their structure. Big economies of scale are possible, so it's a good way to help pay for the acquisition. The other way is for them to sell all the Getty non-oil subsidiaries and the fairly meager retail gas outlets. Getty owns ESPN, Getty Minerals, and substantial wine acreage in California. If you do the math, they could probably pay nearly double the present market price and still get an attractive payback."

"What about Egypt, and Togo?" She had no interest in the potential deal except for its effect on Egypt; this was her only game. If there is to be a takeover, how soon would it be? *Could the Egyptian part hold together until after 6 October?*

"Not sure; Getty is on the hook for Egypt, but compared to what Texaco would be paying out in a takeover, $30 million wouldn't even amount to a rounding error in the deal. Texaco might drill if they believe the deposit in Egypt is commercially viable, but if they have no interest, then Getty would just forfeit the $30 million to EGPC – and no drilling, no employment."

"So what's your guess?"

He said, "Depends on how they like the play in Egypt, it might get at least a look. They would explore."

"And that could take how long?"

"My guess is that they know enough now to make a decision. I'll probably find out when I meet with George early Saturday morning."

She had known Cahill personally for a year now, and she knew everything there was to know about him on paper. The Mossad files were nothing if not thorough. Although she had never spent that much time with any other man – not even with Kim David – what did she really know about Drew Cahill? She thought he was an attractive man, but, then, so were many others. She knew he was kind and easy to be with, and she knew what attracted him to her – and it certainly wasn't her resume'. However, if she never saw him again she knew she wouldn't shed a tear – well, not more than a couple, in any case.

She stood and smoothed the Connaught robe. "Another drink, or more dessert?"

"A bit of each please. You were right, Harrods did a

great job with the food and wine."

"Why do you do what you do?" she asked as she brought the drink and dessert to him on a tray.

"For a number of reasons: One, I know how to do what I do, and I do it well. Two, for the money; it's much more than I could earn working in Los Angeles, Houston, or New York. And finally, I want to be President of Getty, and I have a good chance. Morris is a shoo-in to be the next CEO of Getty – if we score in Egypt, that is."

"What if there is no more Getty; then what will you do?"

"They'd probably need me to either close it down or to bridge the gap, and that could take a month or more. Then they'd have to pay me off – a year's salary – and I have a lot of Getty shares which will, of course, be sold. I'll probably go back to the states, look around, and get married."

"Get married? Didn't you try that once and it didn't work?"

"But that was before I met you."

She was flabbergasted. She looked at Drew as if this was the first time she was seeing him. He couldn't be thinking about them. He couldn't possibly be thinking of her in a permanent relationship – or could he? She didn't – or, they didn't – ever talk about anything of a relationship nature. Maybe that was it; he had just assumed this would go on and on. This wasn't comfortable – not the final outcome, but the timing.

"Milly, how about you tell me what you want to do with the rest of your life?"

Merde, she thought. She just wanted to get through the next three weeks or so, not wax emotional about some starry-eyed future together.

"Quite frankly, I love what I do and where I do it. I can't imagine doing anything else, anywhere else."

CHAPTER 19

The Final Gambit

DREW SLEPT FITFULLY. He knew there could be only two possible outcomes, and he was anxious; either would have a major impact on his life. Change was not what he wanted. He wanted to be President of Getty Oil and marry Milledufleur. Period. But probably not in that order. The last two days with Milly had been, to his mind, perfect. He loved being with her. Even the "cultural" tour of London museums and art galleries had been fantastic; she knew everything. It was no wonder he loved her so; she was perfect.

George is always in the office early, even on Saturday, Drew thought as he headed quickly for Butler Place. It was a bright and lovely Saturday in London in June. The sunshine and the fragrances of the blossoms picked up his spirits. *How could anyone be pessimistic on such a summer day!*

They had been smart to spend the last two days relaxed, in a low-key mood; he felt that he and Milly had more meaningful discussions than at any other time in their relationship. He had made it clear to her that he loved her and that he wanted to marry her. It was also clear to him that she would not relish moving to the states. He felt there had to be another option, but he had no way of knowing until he met with George. *Onward and upward,* he thought.

He arrived at the London Getty office and took the lift to George's floor. The door to the office was open and Morris was standing by his work table going through a sheaf of papers. He saw Drew and motioned him in. They greeted each other warmly, as the old friends they were.

"Drew, great to see you; you look relaxed and well-rested. Thanks for making the hurry-up trip. I wish I could have been more specific over the phone, but the subject matter is complex. You'll see what I mean. But first, how about some coffee, and we have some breakfast pastries if you'd like."

"Thanks George. I'd love a coffee, but I'll pass on the pastries; I've had breakfast."

"That's one of the reasons we both stay fit, regular exercise and sensible eating regimens. Of course, I have 15 or so more years on you."

"George, you look great, but, of course, I give Sandra a lot of the credit for keeping you in line. And how is Mrs. Morris?"

"She is both excited and nervous. So am I."

"I'm just nervous, George; I'm not sure what this mystery trip is all about. My educated guess is that a Texaco takeover could be the reason for this meeting, but it could be many things. I really don't know."

"Drew, that's why I like you, you're sharp. A takeover by Texaco is exactly the reason we are having this meeting. This has been in the works for a while, but for obvious reasons they wanted to keep it very quiet and I think that has worked well. There has not been much, if any at all, talk about a takeover as far as I can tell."

"So what's the deal, and why am I here?"

"This is an asset play, Drew, except for Egypt, and that's why you are here. They want the current operating reserves in Kuwait, the North Sea, Norway, California, Alberta, and Australia. Los Angeles will be closed, as will the London office. However, they like the discovery potential in Egypt a whole lot, and Drew . . ." Morris hesitated dramatically, then continued, "Drew, they want you to run it."

Certainly this was one of the scenarios that Drew had speculated could happen, but right now the air had been sucked out of him; he needed some structure to hang onto. What does run it mean, what happens to Morris, if they close Los Angeles is Mort out?

George sensed that Drew was unsettled; who wouldn't be! "Drew, here's the deal in a nutshell: I'm going back to California as soon as we can clean up some details. As you know, we all have Getty stock accumulated in our employee stock purchase plan. I have more than most because I also augmented the shares awarded with my own purchases; I've some 40,000 shares. Based on the buyout terms, that is worth about $5 million, plus the settlement of one year's salary." Morris smiled at Drew. "Now you know why I said Mrs. Morris is excited. Most of the guys at my level will be happy, but obviously not everyone will be as excited; after some severance and stock uptick many people will be pounding the pavement – but then, who said life is fair. In general, though, they are some pretty talented people, and they'll survive."

"Whew! Yes, I expect Sandra is very happy! You'll be able to keep body and soul together with that kind of a payoff. And you'll probably get into the consulting game before too long."

"I haven't thought about it much, but I do think I'd like to do some consulting, possibly even some teaching." Morris poured himself a cup of coffee and refilled Drew's while he talked. "Texaco's London Office is control for their operations in the Middle East, Africa, and Europe. They are not too far off the Getty organization, except they're much bigger. Their Managing Director in London is a Brit by the name of James Millington, not a bad guy, younger than me but older than you. He really likes the looks of the Egyptian play, and he really likes you. He says he met you years ago, when you where part of the Atlantic Richfield operation and their North Slope elephant."

"I do remember him, rather short, neat, with black hair combed straight back, and a British Public School accent," said Drew.

Morris added, "He wants to see you today; we'll have lunch at the St. James Club, then you and he will break off and look at the details. Now I'm not negotiating for you, Drew, but I do strongly recommend that you meet with him after lunch. By that time you both should have figured out if you like each other. I do know they will offer a four-year contract of about $250k base with the standard allowances for expats in overseas operations. Plus, they will offer you bonuses based on success and levels of success. So I recommend that you talk. What do you think?"

"Why not, sounds interesting. Besides, if I don't I could be going back to the States much earlier than anticipated, and ,while not destitute, there could be other complications."

George grinned. "Like the Jewish Professor Miss Rose?"

Drew blushed a bit and nodded his head.

"Oh, by the way; it's all gray now."

"What's all gray now?"

"His hair."

The meeting between Cahill and Millington did get underway at the conclusion of the lunch with Millington, Cahill, and Morris. The lunch was relaxed; they were all on their best behavior, and the three men seemed to get along quite well as they shared stories of action, suspense, and boredom in the oil patch. Cahill and Millington were sequestered in Millington's well-appointed office; it was apparent to Drew that not all the money from operations went back into the ground. As their discussion progressed Drew was impressed with the

Texaco thoroughness. After three hours Millington asked if Cahill had any other questions.

"I think you've covered it well; it is best to keep the Egypt team together, especially the Brit geologists and geophysicists. No sense in starting over."

Millington nodded in agreement. "Do you think we will be able to keep the group intact?"

Drew said he thought they could do so with very few exceptions. *Hell,* he thought, *this is a good deal for all of them, even for Milly's Egyptian cousins.*

"So Andrew," said Millington, "do we have a deal?"

"Well, governor, it looks like we have a deal. I'll have my Egyptian lawyer vet this, but aside from some legalese, we are there. Also, I'll run the plan by EGPC, not for approval but for their information. They will be happy about the acquisition."

"When do you return to Egypt?"

"Tomorrow, and I'll ring you on Tuesday, but essentially we have a deal."

They shook hands. They were both pleased with the outcome.

"Andrew could I stand you to a stiffy?"

"Thanks James, but I have some personal details to attend to and an early flight tomorrow. We will be seeing a lot of each other I'm sure, and I will take you up on that offer soon enough."

Drew stopped at the receptionist desk downstairs

and called Milly.

"Milly, I've great news; they want Egypt and me! I won't have to head home with my head down. And best of all, there is a future for us. I can be at your place in 15 minutes."

"Hurry darling, I can't wait."

Milly was pleased. Drew will continue the operation and her "cousins" will stay in place. She didn't think Kim would be surprised, but he will like this. He will definitely like it. She even thought Grandmother Rose would like it. It was due to Grandmother Rose that Milly was aware that she actually did have cousins in Egypt, even if those cousins of hers were not Anwar and Saleh Mabruck. She wondered if Grandmother Rose would approve of what she was now doing. *Well,* she thought, *it was she who planned my education and my training under Bernard Lewis at the SOAS.* It was Grandmother Rose who had shaped her life, for good or not.

Drew arrived at her flat in less than 15 minutes. She embraced him and beckoned him to relax on the sofa as she snuggled up to him. "Drew you are so excited, but I don't know anything of what's going on other than what you so quickly said over the telephone. Does this mean the status quo for you in Egypt?"

"It's not quite the status quo; Getty Oil is history.

Texaco will swallow up its operating assets and furlough all the people except for Egypt, which I will continue to run with a four-year contract. If we do discover oil and in the quantity we believe is there, I'll be more than financially independent – and we can live anywhere, even London!"

"Drew, I don't know if you are super brilliant or super lucky – maybe both – but as you often say, who cares? I am more pleased than you will ever know." She sat up abruptly and looked at him with concern. "What will happen to George Morris and to your friend Mort?"

Drew shrugged. "Morris will be in 'fat city,' as we say; he has $5 million from his Getty holdings, plus his severance pay from Texaco. He and his wife will return to California sooner than planned. However, and more important for George, he won't be returning as President of Getty. That was pretty much a *fait accompli* before Texaco, especially if we hit big in Egypt – which we will. Mort, however, is a different story; along with thousands of others he'll be furloughed. He has some shares and he'll get a severance payout, so he won't exactly be destitute, but he will need to get another job. He will, but he had a good-go at Getty. This means life will now be more complicated."

"But doesn't this mean that you won't be President

of Getty after George, as you planned?"

"Well, obviously there is no more Getty; it's already a part of history. Getty is gone, and I wouldn't put money on me becoming President of Texaco. Texaco is a much bigger company, and I don't have any relationships there except for James Millington – and I started working for him today. President there would be more than a long shot; Getty was probable, even likely."

"How about I fix you a drink then take you to dinner. I know you have to get up early tomorrow so you will want to get to bed early." She smiled at him. "I am."

Over dinner Drew explained his plans for the coming months. Everything hinged on the 15 September date for drilling the first well. The well wouldn't be very deep, 300/400 feet at most, and they would have some showings quickly; however, it would take longer to determine more precisely what they had. The Texaco London organization was pretty much comparable to Getty's, so there wouldn't be time lost with internal bureaucratic fumbling. For the first well, all needed approvals were in hand; and as for the rest, Drew explained that James Millington and his exploration people would visit Egypt in early June to "press the flesh" – as Millington would say.

The exploration group would be focusing on the

locations for wells 2, 3, and, possibly 4. They had gone long and contracted the drilling platform contract so that was behind them, and the platform would be in place before 15 September. The rest of July and August would be spent assuring the best spot to drill, and he estimated his schedule would have him in Egypt 3 weeks out of 4, with the fourth in London. He also estimated that, following the startup of drilling the first well, he would probably be in London the first week in October. Because of this schedule he pressed Milly to spend more time that summer in Cairo, emphasizing this would give her an opportunity to get to know her cousins. Although they covered much in conversation, they finished dinner early then returned to her flat and went to bed.

The summer dragged on; it was, as usual, hot, very hot, in Cairo. The visit by Millington and his staff went well, he thought – but then, why shouldn't it? They all had jobs, and with Texaco supporting the operation the confidence level, which had been high, was now higher.

Milly told Drew that she would visit him in mid-August, and he was elated. He planned a dinner party with Gamal, Wafik and his wife, and Paul and his wife, and because this was to be a very special occasion he booked a dining room at the Mina House.

Milly's flight was scheduled to arrive on Saturday at 4 p.m., and Drew arranged for his driver to pick him up at his Zamalek flat at 2 p.m., explaining to Ahmed that this was a very important visit by a very important lady. Ahmed assured Mr. Cahill he would never be late, and he wasn't.

Drew caught sight of her as she was exiting customs and immigration. As he hurried to meet her he thought, probably for the hundredth time, *She is absolutely adorable!* He had tried to buy an engagement ring that could complement her beauty, but without success. *She is already perfect,* he realized. He introduced Ahmed to her, and as Ahmed gathered her luggage he was all over her and gushing about how lucky Mr. Cahill was to know such a beautiful lady.

Ahmed broke all traffic rules speeding his passengers to Drew's flat. Once there, Drew reminded Ahmed – for the third time – that they had dinner reservations at the Mina House at 8; Ahmed assured him they would be there with time to spare. Drew was excited; he couldn't decide if he would give her the ring before or after dinner. While Milly was freshening up from her flight he secured the ring in his trouser pocket and began to rehearse a variety of speeches to accompany his presentation of the engagement ring.

Ahmed drove to the Mina House, arriving 20 minutes early. Drew was pleased; this would give them plenty of time to check out the room and the view of the Giza Pyramids and the Sphinx. As they entered the Mina House they were welcomed by the hotel manager. The manager was certain that he had met Mr. Cahill on previous occasions; he was also certain that he had met Miss Rose a number of times. Gamal arrived shortly after Milly and Drew, which was fortunate for Drew as Gamal and the hotel manager were old acquaintances. By the time Gamal had finished with the hotel manager, not only was Drew destined to be the next President of Texaco, but Miss Rose was certainly a member of royalty.

The night was clear and bright and the view from their dining room was spectacular. There was no doubt in Drew's mind that this was to be a magical night. The rest of their party arrived right on time, and the feting began in earnest. Drew was always impressed by the Egyptian ability to elevate the atmospherics to a highly festive mood. Dinner was fabulous; the toasts were many, camaraderie flourished, and all passed a wonderful evening. Even Milly was impressed. Finally, as toasts became more frequent and grand, the evening wore down. The celebrants embraced one and all and wished each other well, the party broke up, and they all went their respective ways.

Drew had Ahmed drive him and Milly to the area of the pyramids. "We won't be long Ahmed; we just want to stroll a bit before ending this evening."

As they walked along the antiquities he took her hand. "Milly, this has been one memorable night; I hope it will become even more memorable." He stopped and kissed her gently, then held her as they continued on. "I'll be in London for meetings and then to review our preliminary drilling results and we won't see each other again until the first of October. I will miss you more than ever, and I don't want this night to end." He stopped and turned to face her, taking her left hand in his. "You know I love you, and I want to marry you." With that he produced the ring and slipped it onto her finger. "Drew, this is unexpected, I don't know what to say! We really haven't talked about marriage, I'm not sure I want to be married, period."

"Milly, this will work! You know everything about me, and the more I learn about you the more I love you! I'm not talking about living in the States; I can understand your reluctance to do that. We can live here; split time between London and Cairo. Just think about it. Keep the ring and we can talk about it when I see you in London October 1st."

She shook her head. Thank goodness it was less than two months to go. She would talk it over with

Kim when she saw him back in London. *My God, we're close!* she realized. Two weeks left in August, then September and the first few days of October; and after tonight she wouldn't be seeing Cahill for another six weeks. For her that was a plus. She should be able to do this standing on her head. As soon as she returned to London she would see Kim David and get his thoughts about this new development with Cahill. Aside from that, though, there wasn't anything else to plan; 6 October would either work or not. She was certain the Mossad had a backup plan, but she had no clue as to what it could be. They weren't about to tell her, not yet anyway. She only knew this had to work. Israel had to survive.

Scarcely talking, she and Drew meandered amongst the sands. She twisted the ring on her finger several times, remarking that it was indeed lovely. This was enough for Drew; surely she loved it, and him. When they returned to the waiting car, she suggested they have a nightcap at the Marriott then return to Drew's flat. She didn't have to ask twice.

***

It had been one of the hottest summers Drew had experienced, as hot as Kuwait, and Drew and his team were glad they were now into September; it would offer some relief from the August burnout. The drilling platform was in position, ahead of schedule. Drew and his exploration team would drive to the Gulf of Suez on 7 September, then take offshore supply boats to the platform. The drillers would already be onboard taking care of the final details. The American drillers were ready to start drilling on 11 September – which was not just a convenient date, but was also a birthday present for Drew.

There wasn't anything more Drew could contribute to the program at this stage; all of the analysis and planning were in the book, and the coming weeks would tell if they had it right or not. Drew, however, knew he had to be on the platform as they sank the first hole. It was mostly a matter of show, but he had to be there.

The drive to the Gulf was hot, tedious, and dusty, but spirits were high and they kept busy talking about past campaigns they had all waged. This would be the crowning moment, and nervous was a weak word. To a man, they were anxious. Even with the detailed planning and reviewing, they all knew being dead-nuts-on was never a given; they could be yards off and not know it. Luck was never discounted; they all had enough projects under their belts to understand this. However, they anticipated the drilling would be smooth. Also they were ahead of schedule, and this was a good sign to all of them. As they boarded the platform they all observed the waters of the gulf were calm, very calm.

The drilling did commence on 11 September, and it was easy going; they would be at their targeted depth within a week. Drew turned forty filled with anticipation.

***

Ahmed was on time to drive Drew to the Cairo airport. Drew couldn't wait to get on the plane; things were progressing so well that he sometimes could barely contain his excitement. The results from the drilling were encouraging, very encouraging. There was no doubt there was oil in the rock; it was too soon to tell how much, but the consensus was, considerable – and Drew knew Millington was high on the results. Texaco London should confirm what the Egyptian exploration group believed; they had a play on their hands. In addition to the excitement of the drilling, there was Milly. It had now been a month since they had been together, and phone calls were no substitute.

Drew phoned Milly as soon as he had deplaned and cleared customs. He told her he would check into the Connaught but he wanted to see her tonight. She readily agreed.

While she waited she thought back to her meeting with Kim David right after she had returned from Cairo. Kim had anticipated the call.

"Milly, I'll come to your office straight away, or, if you prefer, I could come by your flat later this afternoon."

"Kim, come by my office as soon as you can; I need to talk to you sooner than later."

Kim arrived shortly after the call. Milly explained that she was uneasy. Cahill had asked her to marry him and had given her an outlandish engagement ring.

"So, what is the problem? He will be here on 1 October, the plan is to have a regime change on 6 October. Everything is in order. The plan will be operational; all you need to do is to continue the bewitching of Mr. Cahill until the plan is executed. After that we don't care what you do with Cahill, although marriage is obviously out of the question. We think you have handled this assignment extremely well, and we have many other assignments for you that should prove exciting. After 6 October you can demurely break it off, or you can tell him to fuck off, rude letter to follow. The train will have left the station."

"Then I shan't worry any further, my dear. I shall occupy him like never before, and he will never know until it's over. Actually, sex with Cahill isn't bad."

"So there are some benefits; not all work and no play?"

She smiled at him and her intention was quite clear. "Come see me when it's over – that is, if you are still in London."

***

They met for dinner at one of their familiar haunts, the Ménage à Trois. Drew was beaming, almost walking on a cloud. The meeting with Millington and the Texaco staff had gone extremely well. While it would be a little longer before they could state with certainty the absolute amount of reserves, they all now knew that this would be big, very big.

He tried to explain the atmospherics of the meeting, the general sense of excitement over the results to date. "There is no doubt among us that we are on track to success. Jim Millington is confident, and also very, very pleased that they picked up this drilling project – and he is now off the hook for hiring me. This bodes well for us both."

"Drew. You've been talking nonstop about the deal, but you haven't touched the prime rib – which you adore – yet you have managed to belt down three scotches. I don't want you to drink any more; it might interfere with what I've planned for you to-night." This got his attention, and he managed to focus on her completely as she continued.

"Put quite simply, I will screw your ears off. Six days from now you'll be back in Egypt, but when you leave London you won't be able to walk."

Drew beamed. "We're out of here!"

She carried out her plan, and Drew was the very willing beneficiary – and he was certain that she loved him as much as he loved her.

Their week was active and frenetic, and Drew knew that he was having the best time of his life. Business was good and their evenings were full. Drilling continued in the Gulf of Suez, and the feedback continued to be that this was indeed a play. The exploration team could hardly wait to drill the second well.

Drew had meetings at Texaco's White Hart Lane office on the 6th, which would be his last night in London; he had an early flight to Cairo on the 7th of October. *God,* he thought, *I need a break from her; she is insatiable!*

The meeting at White Hart Lane began promptly at 9 a.m. GMT. Millington had his senior exploration personnel, geologists, seismologists, and his petroleum engineers there, as well as Mrs. Peters, his private secretary. Drew had met with this group often since the Texaco takeover, and they had developed a good working relationship, no doubt enhanced because they all were aware of James Millington's respect for Drew Cahill's capabilities. Millington summarized the work to date.

"Gentlemen, the first well is to final depth and it looks great. Drew is returning to Cairo tomorrow, and his group should finish their interpretations within weeks. I know you will have your conclusions ready at that time as well. Then we will get on to the 2nd well. I don't want to jinx the program, but we are looking good, very good."

The meeting went on for several hours, but it was now essentially over and they were filling time before breaking for lunch. Just before noon Mrs. Peters was called out of the meeting, and she returned minutes later visibly shaken. "Gentlemen, it was just announced on the BBC that the President of Egypt, Anwar Sadat, has been assassinated at the 6 October parade in Cairo." The air was literally sucked out of the room, and the room was filled with disbelief and shock.

Drew gasped. *This couldn't be good!* He had no personal relationship with Sadat, but he believed Sadat was a good friend of the United States. He could immediately imagine a raft of problems without any upside. He did know that Gamal knew Sadat and influential members of the Egyptian bureaucracy. He also remembered that Milly knew Sadat, or, at least, had met him when she was Bernard Lewis' protégé when Lewis was at the SOAS. Drew needed to talk to Gamal and to Wafik right now. He also wanted to talk with Milly, but that had to wait until after he had feedback from Gamal and Wafik. He wondered if Gamal had gone to the parade. Gamal had told Wafik not to go. Drew shot after Mrs. Peters and told her he needed a line to Cairo. It was urgent that he talk to Gamal and Wafik immediately. Millington cornered Drew; they needed to know how this could affect their project. Drew assured him he would get the feedback quickly.

Within minutes Mrs. Peters had both Gamal and Wafik on the line. Wafik had stayed put, but Gamal had been at the parade; however, he had left early, shortly before the shooting. He had driven to the Getty Maadi office which was close to the parade grounds. They were both on the line when Drew grabbed the phone from Mrs. Peters. He dispensed with pleasantries and went directly to the heart of the matter.

"What the fuck is going on; are there riots; how will this affect us?"

"Drew, stay calm. There is no uproar here." Gamal's tone was relaxed and soothing as he went on.

"I got a call from EDPC, both Radwan and Hammis, assuring me that all is under control. They told me there will be no effect on our deal; they still believe it is good for Egypt. They stressed that since Vice President Mubarak is now the President of Egypt, if anything the relationship with Texaco/Getty will be even stronger. They informed me that the only casualty was Sadat. A bullet did glance off a step and nip Mubarak's calf, but it was a superficial wound. No one else was injured. Apparently the killer shot Sadat 20 times before the security police grabbed the killer. The shooter was an Egyptian army officer, Khaleed Islambouli, and he was a member of the Egyptian Brotherhood. It is believed he acted alone."

"Christ," said Drew. "You make it sound like rather than an assassination, this is just an orderly changing of the guard! I guess that's one way to avoid a recount."

Neither Gamal nor Wafik caught Drew's attempt at irony. They went on to stress that Mubarak was a solid supporter of not only the U.S. but also of long term peaceful relationship with Israel. Gamal again pointed to the long term stability of (now) President Mubarak. Wafik explained to Drew that he and Paul had called an emergency staff meeting and explained the situation to both the expatriate and Egyptian staff. Wafik thought it went well. The only staff members who hadn't attended were Miss Rose's cousins, Anwar and Saleh Mabruck. In fact, they have been absent since yesterday afternoon.

Wafik went on to tell Drew that Radwan wanted to talk to Drew and James Millington, and he suggested Drew phone Radwan as soon as this call was finished. Drew agreed. He then reminded Gamal and Wafik he was flying to Cairo in the morning, and suggested that Gamal and he have dinner in Zamalek tomorrow evening. When that had been arranged, they all rang off.

Drew found James Millington and related the conversation, and they then placed a call to Radwan at the EGPC. This was also a calming conversation. Radwan assured them both that everything was fine. He then set up a meeting with Drew upon his return to Cairo. Millington was considerably more relaxed, but he made the point that he would be much better once Drew was back in Egypt.

Once Millington was satisfied, Drew excused himself explaining that he needed to make an important personal phone call. He called Milly's office, and the receptionist told him that Professor Rose had been called to attend an out-of-town meeting; she was not available. She added that Professor Rose thought he would call, and she had left a personal letter for Mr.

Cahill.

Drew ran to Milly's office, and arrived breathing hard. Milly's prickly receptionist handed him the letter and showed him to a visitors' office where he could digest the contents in private.

The bright October sunlight streaming into the room and brightened it, and his spirits lifted. The envelope was addressed to "Andrew Cahill, Esq." and Drew anxiously ripped it open. The letter was hand-written on her personal ochre stationery. As he read her letter he shook his head in disbelief. He then re-read the letter, and his shock and disbelief turned first to anger, and then to puzzlement. He could not believe or accept the words that leapt at him from the page. The contents were brief and terse:

> Andrew, or Drew as you prefer, I have been called away for an important meeting out-of-country. In any case, we will not see each other again. Please do not bother to look for me; it is highly unlikely you will find me, and even if you did, you would not like the consequences. You have your oil concession and business with Texaco. As you have told me many times, this is what you really want. So pursue it. Who I am

and what I want is incompatible with you and with your world. Marriage was never a possibility.

You will find the ring you proffered to me that night in Giza. You might find other uses for it, I certainly won't. You will quickly discover, if you haven't already, that your relationship with the EGPC and the new President Hosni Mubarak will be solid, lasting, and predictable.

Adieu,

Milledufleur Rose

Drew paced the room as thoughts raced through his head, and he did not at all like where the ones pushing through for his attention were taking things.

Over the several minutes he went from shock to anger. *Damn it,* he thought, *she used me!* He recalled Wafik's comment about the absence of Milly's cousins, and he was slowly realizing that he had been a pawn in her plan – or in someone's plan – to get her two cousins into Egypt. He was now beginning to understand that she had played him like a fish, and that he had taken the bait, hook, line, and sinker. The cousins – if that is who they really were – were gone, he was sure of that, and she was gone. Sadat was also gone, but the Egyptian government was solid and totally behind the Texaco deal. Also, the peace with Israel would prevail.

Drew needed to think, and he certainly could not get his head back on straight surrounded by the SOAS offices. He left the office and hailed a cab to the Connaught. He still had a room for tonight and a plane reservation to Cairo tomorrow. Everything as it was, except...she was gone. At the hotel he headed for the bar in the restaurant lounge. It was after lunch, and the bar was empty except for one lone woman at the other end of the bar. Drew ordered a whiskey with ice. The single malt was having a calming effect, or so he thought.

Morris had a clue about Milly, but James Millington does not; that is a plus, he thought. The more he thought about Milly the hotter he got. No doubt he'd fallen for her, and he'd believed she felt the same. *Damn fool!* He was pissed that she had played him for a fool. She was a great actress, and he had no doubt that acting was all it was – and that now over. He needed to figure out what to do next. He needed another drink and called to the bartender for a refill.

The woman at the end of the bar smiled. "You're Drew Cahill," she said. "I know you from Getty. I'm Maria Arnold. Mind if I join you?"

Drew shrugged. "Why not?"

She took the seat next to him, shook his hand, and identified herself as a senior geologist for Getty's North Sea minority holdings. She had been with Getty for seven years before the Texaco takeover and her termination. Drew bought her a drink as he listened to her lament. It was a bit of a relief to have someone distracting him from his own thoughts for a while.

"Well, Maria, it's no bed of roses for any of us. Let's drink to our survival."

She took the drink placed in front of her by the bartender and raised it in the gesture of a toast to Drew before she drank.

"Drew – if I may take the liberty of calling you by your first name – from my perspective your survival looks pretty good, maybe even better than when you were leading the Getty effort in Egypt. Reporting to Texaco's Managing Director and leading the exploration group that you put together for Getty looks like a pretty good deal from where I sit. I don't have a job and I'm not sure when I will have one. My guess is, your lament is that Miss Rose may not be at your beck and call. As my mother used to tell us, there are many street cars; if you miss one, there is always another one."

Drew laughed; it reminded him of sayings his father had shared with him when he was a student. "Did you know Milly Rose?"

"I did meet her several times, but I can't say I knew her. She is a very attractive and intelligent lass, and it was no secret that you and she were 'an item,' as they say. However, the rumor was that she was growing tired of you."

This was like a shot to his stomach and served to increase his anger. "Well, the Getty London world was a small one! What else did they say?"

"Does it really matter? I don't imagine you will have a difficult time in the dating world. You are an attractive man with, as they say, a future."

Drew looked at Maria with new eyes. What he saw was a well-dressed, tall, mid-thirties woman with brown hair, blue eyes, and a well-formed body. Drew realized she was very attractive, and she became more appealing as the minutes went by. He was becoming interested in Maria.

"I'm flying to Cairo in the morning. If you can, let's have dinner tonight; you pick the restaurant. I'm sure you know some good ones."

She gave Drew a big smile as she took his hand in a shake. "Mr. Cahill. That is a date."

"Great! By the way, have you ever been to Egypt?" Drew's spirits were growing much brighter; after all, she was right, he did have most of what he wanted. And Maria was interesting. London was in his travel plans. *Who knows,* he thought.

IT WAS BRIGHT outside, humid and uncomfortable; a real summer day in Chicago. Inside the Rush Street bar it wasn't as bright, and it certainly was a lot more comfortable. Still, it was too bright to be sitting in a bar and drinking early on a Saturday afternoon. The bar was empty save for two men, casually dressed, and the bartender, white shirt, black tie, black vest. The thirty-foot backbar was dark mahogany, replete with carvings and mirrors above the bottles of liquor neatly arrayed across its full length. Atop the backbar were two TV's, one at each end, blaring the latest – or not so latest – news from the Fox News channel.

Two men were seated at the right end of the bar, and, not having anything better to do, the bartender stood in front of them doing what bartenders often do, engaging the men in conversation and the occasional shaggy-dog story. The bartender had a seasoned look, probably the result of imbibing too frequently of his wares over the years. He was younger than his two customers, but he wasn't at all as well-preserved. His customers both had manes of nearly-white hair, neatly cropped, both had ruddy complexions and the lines that come from too much time in the sun. The man to the left signaled the bartender for a refill, all around. "Another Dewar's, rocks, twist; take what you want for yourself." The bartender nodded and instantly produced their drinks before pouring a blast of vodka for himself. "Thanks," he murmured. "Only one more hour on my shift; may as well get an early start on tonight."

The blaring from the TV was interrupted by an explosion, sirens wailing, body parts, blood, screams, laments; a bus in Jerusalem has been vaporized by a suicide bomber. An excited announcer blurts,

"We're bringing this live from Jerusalem! It looks like twenty-five people, at least, have been killed – men, women children – a number more injured; however, we have no confirmation yet as to the actual numbers." The camera switches from the reporter and scans the tree-lined street showing bloody body parts strewn haphazardly around the blackened, smoking skeleton of what only minutes before had been a bus.

The FOX News announcer, calmer now, droned on in an all too familiar monotone describing the all too familiar scene. File footage came on showing Ariel Sharon lumbering variously into or out of a meeting room with his entourage ambling after him, while the voice of the announcer uttered the all too familiar words that the Israeli Prime Minister and his cabinet would be meeting to determine the Israeli response. This footage was followed by shots of Yasser Arafat shaking a palsied finger at a camera and warning of repercussions if Israel retaliated against the Palestinian people.

The man on the left poked a finger into the arm of his drinking companion and motioned to the TV screen in front of them. "Look at that shit; it never ends!" He shook his head lamentably. "I guess there's no hope. It's worse now than when we were working in the Middle East."

His drinking mate asked the bartender to turn the TV off. "We've seen enough of this crap." Turning to his imbibing partner he continued, "Jim, nothing changes in that zoo; it's the same old shit, over and over."

The bartender took a swig of his clear liquid and asked, "What were you guys doing there; working for the CIA? Or the U.S. Military?"

Jim smiled. "Nothing so dramatic, my friend; we were just a couple of oil field drillers trying to make a living. Tom and me spent about twenty years over there between us. Got out when 'Shit for Brains' went into Kuwait."

The bartender perked up when he heard that. "So, you were there when Iraq invaded Kuwait?"

"Not for very fucking long," said Tom. "Me and two other guys were at Mina Saud, only thirty miles from the Saudi border. We jumped in a company car and got the hell out of there, right into Khafji and drove across to Jeddah. Jim here was in Egypt drilling in the Gulf of Suez. The fucking Palestinians exploded when the latter-day Salah ah Din took Kuwait. They rioted in the streets of Cairo."

"Yeah," said Jim. "I decided to pack it in and get back to America. I had enough of those crazies; time to get out!"

"So you haven't been back? What do you do now;

like, are you retired?" asked the bartender.

"Mostly, but we take on small drilling jobs. With the price of oil where it is now, there's a lot of activity in bringing back some of the shut-in wells. We've got a job now working down in Kentucky. We figure it'll take five, six months to go back in and start it up. Tom and me will split the time, we'll pull seventy to eighty thousand. One thing about working over there, we learned a lot about bringing old wells back to life. Pays for a lot of golf balls," Tom said. "No, we've never been back and never will. It's really bad now; before, it was just terrible."

The barroom door swung open and a group of eight thirtysomething guys and girls strode in laughing and talking. They parked themselves at the end of the bar away from Jim and Tom, much to the relief of the two men. The bartender would now have to take care of the group, and maybe he would quit asking them questions. However, before the man could move away, Tom asked him to refill their glasses. "Looks like you're going to be busy, my friend, but check back occasionally to make sure we don't die of thirst."

Now that the bartender had left for more gainful employment and the blaring TV was silenced, the two old oil patch workers could engage in the favorite past time of drillers young and old: gossip. They had a lot of catching up to do; they hadn't seen each other since 1996. A lot goes down in eight years. Tom lived in Ventura now, and Jim stayed mostly in the Chicago area, but they did keep in touch by phone and e-mail. The Kentucky job would be the first for them together since the Permian basin in Texas. This job was right up their alley.

"You do know that old George Padgett left us two years ago, don't you?" said Tom.

"Sure, you old fart; you were the one who told me! Are you getting that disease: 'Old Timers?'" They both laughed good-naturedly and took a swig of their drinks before Jim continued. "You told me he died in Paris, in the arms of some young French babe. Old George was living in seventh heaven, I heard. Living in Paris and playing with those young French girls. George was eighty-three when he passed."

"Do you think we've got another eighteen years in us?"

Jim scowled at Tom before replying. "Who the fuck knows, but my guess is: if you're still having fun, you'll probably get the big call; if you're sitting around drooling, you'll probably hang around."

"Jesus, you're upbeat! But maybe you've got a point. Look at George Morris. When Texaco took over the company Morris got the golden handshake and walked away with millions; he retires to Lake Tahoe, and then gets killed in a skiing accident. What a bitch."

"Yeah, Morris was a pretty good head as far as company wheels are concerned. Tighter than a virgin with the bucks, gave all for the company. I worked for him for a while in Kuwait before he got promoted to London. He sort of kept his distance with us lowly peons, but he did actually smile once in a while. I never thought he was impressed with himself, pretty straight."

"That's when we crossed paths, in Kuwait, before I was sent to Egypt. Actually, it was Drew Cahill who asked that I be sent to Cairo to work for him. Must have impressed him when I worked in Wafra, Kuwait. What a dump that was! Cahill was Morris' number two; everyone thought he'd get Morris' job in Kuwait, but there were rumors about Cahill and some of the wives in the camp. His wife couldn't handle 'the big beach' and dumped him. So there was Cahill, single, good-looking, and, according to the gossip, pretty available. This got back to Los Angeles and the big shots didn't want Cahill in Egypt."

"I heard the same shit. Everyone was surprised when Morris pulled him out of Kuwait and put him in charge of the play in Egypt. Cahill was definitely Morris' guy. Word was that Morris acted first, then told the brass in L.A. Morris did have balls. If Texaco didn't buy Getty out Morris was heads-on favorite to be President of the company."

Tom took a big swig of the scotch and turned to face his drinking mate. "Cahill was a good head... for a boss. I was sent to Egypt early on; he had me recruit most of the Egyptian drilling people. I got there in early eighty, just a month after Drew; I was the first American on the job. Drew and me naturally got pretty close."

"I didn't know him in Egypt, but when I was in Kuwait everyone thought he was a real guy: smart, tough but fair. He did seem to have a good handle on all this Arab shit. He was the main guy in dealing with the Saudi and Kuwaiti bureaucrats. Rumor was that he was in deep with some Brit woman at London University – a Middle East expert."

"That was no rumor, my friend. He met her when he was in London getting ready for the Egypt deal. He would fly her down whenever he could. Had a funny French name but everyone called her 'Milly.' She was something else. Man, I would have given a year's pay to have been able to hump her; what a doll! She was half German and half Egyptian; what skin, and her eyes were like saucers and they sparkled like moonbeams! When she was in town old Drew and his Egyptian lawyer, Gamal Hashem, would throw some dinner parties, often at Hashem's Zamalek apartment. Servants, booze, great lamb, the works! I sat next to her at a couple of those deals. Like, I would swallow my tongue."

"You horny old fuck; I know where you'd like to put your tongue!"

Tom swiveled his chair and leaned in a conspiratorial manner to talk to Jim. "Well, you never met her so let me tell you: you would have sucked her toes if you had a chance – which you wouldn't have. But I'm sure Cahill did. They would moon over each other, man she was hot, and old Drew would, like, just melt away."

"No, I never did meet her, but I heard she was a number! Cahill had a real deal in Cairo, I heard. That Egyptian lawyer, Hashem, was a retired diplomat; heard he knew Nasser and was pretty tight with Sadat and Mubarak."

"And in with Sadat's wife, Jihan. Lot's of rumors about her. She was another beauty, half European and half Egyptian – like Cahill's woman; older, but a real number."

"So, what ever happened to Cahill, I heard he just dropped off the face of the earth."

"Don't know, lots of rumors but no one knows."

"How about the gal?"

"Not a clue. Like with Drew, lots of stories but no facts. No one knows."

***

[Not long after 6 October 1981]

Michael Ronne-Lotz was feeling elated as he hung up the phone on his desk. Kim David was one of only a handful of people who still called to just talk, and, occasionally, to even share a bit of gossip or news about some of the acquaintances their mutual professional interests dictated they had in common. *Kim understands that my heart is still theirs, even after all these years I've had to spend on the outside.*

Michael leaned back in his chair. This feeling of elation...and something else...had surprised him. *Is this pride I'm feeling?* The news about Yolande's daughter – her successful completion of her first assignment with the Mossad, and the plan to establish her in Brussels – had immediately lifted his spirits. He recalled the pride he'd often felt in his son's accomplishments, and he knew he missed being a father. He was startled and sat up straight in the chair. He now recognized this renewed feeling of parental pride. It had been Kim's conversation about Milledufleur's successful assignment that had generated it!

He sat motionless for a full minute staring down

at the letter he'd been reading when Kim's call had interrupted. It was an offer for a consulting position, one in which his experience with the Mossad would be a huge plus. He picked up the business card that had been enclosed with the letter and looked again at the address. Belgium...not very far from Brussels. He reached for the phone.